Bayou BRIDES

Four Generations of Couples
Are Bound by Love, Faith, and Land

JANET LEE BARTON ✺ KATHLEEN MILLER

LYNETTE SOWELL ✺ JANET SPAETH

BARBOUR
PUBLISHING

812485 718

© 2006 *Capucine: Home to My Heart* by Janet Spaeth
© 2006 *Joie de Vivre* by Lynette Sowell
© 2006 *Language of Love* by Janet Lee Barton
© 2006 *Dreams of Home* by Kathleen Miller

ISBN 1-59789-351-X

All scripture quotations are taken from the King James Version of the Bible.

This book is a work of fiction. Names, characters, places, and incidents are either products of the authors' imaginations or used fictitiously. Any similarity to actual people, organizations, and/or events is purely coincidental.

Cover image by Getty Images/National Geographic
Photographer: Eastcott Momatiuk
Illustrations: Mari Small

Published by Barbour Publishing, Inc., P.O. Box 719, Uhrichsville, Ohio 44683, www.barbourbooks.com

Our mission is to publish and distribute inspirational products offering exceptional value and biblical encouragement to the masses.

ecpa Member of the
Evangelical Christian
Publishers Association

Printed in the United States of America.
5 4 3 2 1

INTRODUCTION

Capucine: Home to My Heart by Janet Spaeth
Separated forever—from her mother, from her home, from her Acadia—Capucine Louet cannot forgive the British for tearing her family apart. Now in New Orleans, she has only one ambition: to get to Bayou Teche, where Acadian immigrants have settled and begun a new life. Can Michel LeBlanc, himself a relocated Acadian, help Capucine? Will she be able to overcome her hatred to accept love—and God?

Joie de Vivre by Lynette Sowell
Josée Broussard reluctantly weds the eldest LeBlanc brother, Edouard. Josée doesn't understand why God would have her marry a scarred former soldier who still visits memories of a lost love. The wife Edouard's parents chose for him disrupts his quiet world. But when a despair-filled Josée disappears on Bayou Teche during a storm, Edouard suddenly realizes the treasure he has. Is Edouard's chance for joy gone forever?

Language of Love by Janet Lee Barton
When Nicolas LeBlanc returns from World War I, longing to hear his beloved Cajun spoken once more, he finds it is in danger of being banned from the schools—and the new teacher is encouraging his siblings to speak English at *his* dinner table. While Suzette Devereux tries to convince him to help her for the children's sake, will the two learn to speak their own *Language of Love*?

Dreams of Home by Kathleen Miller
Lucy Webber has seen the world and all she wants now is to find a home she can call her own. At nearly 30, however, she wonders if these dreams are just that—merely dreams meant to be cast aside for the practicality of daily life. When a chance meeting with a college professor at a wedding she's shooting leads to an assignment photographing a centuries-old cabin for a college textbook, Lucy wonders if God has led her into a situation where she will see all three of her dreams come true.

Capucine: Home to My Heart

by Janet Spaeth

Dedication

For my family: You are my treasure and my heart.

"For where your treasure is, there will your heart be also."
MATTHEW 6:21

Prologue

*I am afraid, and yet I know I must go forward, not
just for my sake but also for Aliette and my mother. I am
a child and a woman. I am lost and I am found.*

One nun stood behind the others, her tall, thin body swathed in the black habit. Her dark eyes studied the two girls expressionlessly, and instinctively Aliette shrank against Capucine.

"That woman, she scares me," Aliette whispered into her sister's side.

Capucine didn't answer. She shoved her hands deeper into the pockets of her apron until her fingers closed protectively around the small rectangle—the leather-bound journal her mother had given her before they'd been separated. She stared at the gaunt nun and then whispered back. *"Non,"* she said. "She is strong, that one, but she is fair."

"She has the light of God in her eyes, eh?" Aliette looked up, her guileless blue gaze as innocent as a kitten's.

"Perhaps." Capucine's mouth straightened into a thin line. *The light of God?* Somewhere her mother cried for her lost children. Was the light of God shining on her? Or had it dimmed?

God seemed to have forgotten the Louet family. When the British had stormed in, they killed her father, took the two girls from their home in Acadia, and dropped them in this convent in New York.

Their mother—what had happened to Mama? Capucine had been literally torn from her mother's arms, and now she rubbed her wrists as if she could still feel Mama's fingers in their last futile grasp as they were wrenched apart. *"Moi, je prierai pour vous!"* she had called to her daughters in Acadian French. *I will pray for you.*

Capucine blinked back the tears. She would not cry. Tears would get them nowhere.

Once again she touched the beloved diary, as if the soft leather would somehow connect her with Mama. In it, her mother had written in her lovely flowing penmanship:

> *"Car là où est ton trésor, là aussi sera ton couer."* Matthieu 6:21.

Then, she hadn't realized how close her treasure was, let alone her heart.

Capucine made a promise. *I will find you.* And then, as ice began to wrap her heart, she added, *I will make sure the British pay for what they have done. I cannot forgive them. I will not forgive them.*

"Capucine?" Aliette tugged on her sleeve. "I am scared."

"I will take care of you," she answered softly.

The nun's face softened a bit and she swept toward them, not unlike a large raven, Capucine thought. From her great height, she bent her head slightly. *"Bonjour. Je m'appelle Soeur Marie-Agathe."* Then she added the words that sounded so wrong: "Hello. My name is Sister Marie-Agathe."

English, the hated language. There was no music in its words, only spread out vowels and sharp-edged consonants.

Aliette tugged fiercely at Capucine's sleeve. "She speaks to us!"

Capucine lifted her chin proudly and answered her in Acadian French. "My name is Capucine Louet, and I will never forget."

Chapter 1

Mama said that God does not forget His children, but
that His children forget Him. Does He remember me now?

Capucine's fingers ached. Aliette's grip was relentlessly tight, and every time Capucine tried to wiggle her hand free, her sister shook her head in a fury of blond curls.

"Aliette," she whispered furiously, "if you don't let go of my fingers, they'll fall off."

The young girl giggled nervously. "Why does she want to see us? Have you forgotten morning prayers again?"

"How could I? You've been with me every time, and she watches me to make sure I don't miss a single amen."

"Did you bow your head?" Aliette persisted. "Put your hands together? You know that—"

"*Sssh!* Here she comes."

Sister Marie-Agathe motioned them into a sparsely furnished room and sat in a heavy mahogany chair. She looked at them first, one at a time, quite seriously, but saying nothing. Then she held out her arms. "Come to me, children."

Hand in hand, the two girls approached the nun. Capucine's stomach twisted in dread as Sister Marie-Agathe wrapped them in her black-robed embrace. Capucine buried her face in the dark folds and breathed in the smell that she'd come to love, a mixture of lavender and soap. It was distinctly Sister Marie-Agathe's.

"I have something to tell you," she said to them, and from the way her voice broke, Capucine knew it was going to be bad news. "My uncle Claude has passed into our heavenly Father's hands."

Aliette breathed softly. "God rest him and save him."

"Bless you, child, for your prayers. Our kind Lord hears them all." The nun sighed. "My uncle and I were the only members of our family on this side of the ocean. The rest of my family still resides in France. The abbess, with her infinite good heart, has agreed with me that I can best serve by seeing to his estate on their behalf."

There was more coming. Capucine could sense the nun's tension.

"I will be leaving the convent to do this."

"You'll be back." Aliette patted the nun's arm.

Sister Marie-Agathe didn't answer. Capucine's heart froze in her chest, and her hands clenched into tight knots. Aliette would *not* be abandoned again. As the older sister, she'd manage somehow, but Aliette was different. She didn't have the independent heart that Capucine did. She needed an adult to guide her.

You're an adult. She heard the words as clearly as if they had been spoken, and she knew their truth. She would do whatever was necessary to make sure that Aliette was cared for.

But how?

She squeezed her eyes shut and tried to formulate a prayer. *Mon Dieu cher,* she began. *My dear God—*

"Take us," Aliette begged in her piping voice, and Capucine's eyes sprang open. God certainly was quick to answer! "Take us with you!"

The nun stroked their heads. "I am going to New Orleans."

New Orleans! The very name was mystery and intrigue and vivid color. Plus it was French, and in an instant, a longing for her own history washed over Capucine.

"It's very far away," the nun continued. She paused for a moment. "And I must speak honestly. There is unrest there. The Spanish—"

"Spanish?" Capucine laughed. "Don't you mean the French?"

"It is difficult to explain to young ears. You will find French and Spanish and British there, and sometimes they get along, but sometimes. . ." She shrugged and let the sentence finish itself.

"You must not go, then." Capucine clutched the nun's gnarled hands. "If it is not safe for us, then it is not safe for you.

"Oh, it's safe enough. I would not be in peril."

"Then take us." Aliette was more insistent. "You must."

"Aliette!" Sister Marie-Agathe reproved gently. "Such a way of speaking is impolite."

Capucine pulled out of the embrace and dropped to her

knees, still grasping the nun's gnarled hands. "Please, please, Sister, take us with you."

"I can't—"

"Please," she implored. "We can help. We will be your servants. We will cook and clean and say our prayers three times a day."

"Three!" A smile twitched around Sister Marie-Agathe's lips. "Well, that is an enticement."

Capucine held her breath as the nun smiled at them both. "Aliette is a blossoming cook, and Capucine, your needle skills are above compare. I suspect that I might find a use for you."

"So may we go?" Capucine asked.

Sister Marie-Agathe nodded. "Yes. We shall all go to New Orleans, to Claude Boncoeur's house."

Aliette stole a look at Capucine. "Boncoeur!" she whispered. "It means *good heart*. Surely it is a sign from God Himself!"

The nun rose to her feet. "Indeed. Claude Boncoeur was one of God's finest men, and I am proud to claim him as my uncle. Well," she finished briskly, "we leave tomorrow."

"Tomorrow?"

"There's no sense in waiting, is there?"

Capucine and Aliette shook their heads. "No, Sister Marie-Agathe," they chorused.

"Then start to ready yourselves." She touched their shoulders tenderly. "I am glad you're going with me, girls. Very glad."

Chapter 2

New Orleans, 1767

*I have determined to live my life as fully as I am able,
and to use my talents as I can to bring me forward. Who
knows what may happen to me now? But I am ready to meet
my future!*

The breeze off the bay ruffled the stray curls around Capucine's face. No matter how hard she tried, her hair simply would not stay bound in a sedate bun. Sister Marie-Agathe had sighed and poked more and more pins in, until even her patience had been tested to its limit, but to no avail.

Her hair had a mind of its own.

Like the head under it.

The wharf teemed with activity, and three languages melded into one that was uniquely New Orleans. Spanish and French and English. After four months here, Capucine was beginning to gather the Spanish words together into something she understood, but her French and English were flawless, thanks to the daily lessons at the convent, and she turned her head slightly as words floated her way.

". . .will change the order of things." The speaker's English was faintly tinged with a familiar inflection.

She tried to isolate his voice from the other sounds of the wharf. A very interesting conversation might be underway, one that she could find of value.

But the rest of his words were lost as a shout went up. A ship had come in, and from the way it sat low in the water, Capucine knew it was heavily loaded.

What could its cargo be? Perhaps bolts of fine satin and rich velvet from France, or silken embroidery threads from Italy, or perfumed oils from Spain, or tea scented with jasmine from China?

Her imagination soared, although she knew that with the limits of shipping, the contents were probably nothing more exciting than wine and flour.

The ship was quickly docked and almost immediately the crew leaped onto the wharf. A stout man with an air of authority shouted a few words at the men—words that the wind mercifully carried away, for she suspected they were quite rough—and the men turned back to the ship. Soon bale after bale began to pile up on the wharf.

They *could* be bolts of fabric.

One of the bales had broken open, and something was poking out of it, something silvery that caught the sun's gleam.

She moved in for a closer look.

Wham!

A white-wrapped packet crashed into her shoulder, throwing her off balance. She was knocked to the wooden planks, and very ungracefully somersaulted backwards, landing on the back of her head, with her heels on the top of the packet.

"Mademoiselle?" a solicitous voice inquired.

She opened her eyes cautiously. Stars and lights spun in front of her, and a pain that alternated dull thuds and sharp pangs began to gain momentum behind her ears. A man's face, his bright blue eyes soft with concern, blurred in and out of focus. She was vaguely aware that his light brown hair was being ruffled by the breeze off the water, and she wanted to smooth it back into place.

For some reason, she felt she had to explain to this incredibly handsome man why she was sprawled in such an unladylike position. "I fell." The words sounded garbled to her, and she winced as the mere act of talking sparked an entirely new set of fireworks.

Other faces joined his, those of the crew members who had been unloading the ship. One of them asked, "Is she injured, LeBlanc?" With a few words he dismissed them and turned his attention back to her.

"Mademoiselle? Miss? *Señorita?*"

She tried to laugh at his accent as he tried all three languages, but the sound came out as a dry croak.

"J'ai." Her voice came out as a dry croak, each word pronounced separately. *"Tombé."*

"So I see. You fell." He spoke in French as he rocked back on his heels and studied her, a tiny frown wrinkling his brow. "Would you like to see a doctor?"

She shook her head and winced. "Ow. No."

"Would you like me to help you to your feet?"

"That would be nice."

Soon she was standing, albeit a bit unsteadily.

"Can you walk? Do you want to walk? Would you rather stand here for a moment? Is anything broken?"

His words swam past her scrambled brain like tiny fish. She didn't attempt an answer.

"Let's take a few steps and see how we do."

His words struck her as very funny but laughing was out of the question. Not when her head felt as big as an apple basket.

With his arm around her waist, they took a few tentative steps. The ground seemed spongy, and Capucine felt buoyant, like a delicately bouncing bubble bobbing along the uneven wharf.

He frowned at her when they stopped. "I don't like your head."

This was too much, and despite the throbbing that threatened to explode her skull, she laughed. "Well," she answered, touching his elegant forehead, "I like yours."

And with those words, the world went dark.

❧

Michel walked along the tree-shadowed street. Evening was

coming with its relief from the heat of the day, and the air was heavily scented with the rich aroma of the white flowers that grew in the bushes beside him. He had no idea what they were called, which was silly, he realized, considering how long he had lived in New Orleans.

Perhaps the young woman at the wharf—Capucine Louet—knew their names. She had seemed like the kind that might. Her clothing was thick with her well-known embroidery, and her hair, which had shaken loose of its bun in her fall, flowed around her head like an ebony river. He could see a white flower tucked behind her ear.

He ran his hand across his eyes. His thoughts were as fanciful as if he had gotten hit in the head himself! The poor woman had gotten quite a wallop, and he was glad that he had been there to help her, and to take her to her home.

Nothing happens without a reason. God knows. God is in control.

The irony of what had happened struck him, and he had to smile. He, a mere boat builder, had come to the aid of Capucine Louet. He shook his head in amazement. He knew who she was, of course. Her beauty, so dazzling in the streets of New Orleans, had attracted as much attention as her embroidery had.

He'd known where to take her, to Boncoeur House. A nun, Claude Boncoeur's niece, he'd learned, had met him at the door, thanked him, and taken Capucine from his arms as easily as if she had been a bird.

Since then, he'd been walking, unable to go back to the close confines of his small cottage, preferring instead to roam the streets of New Orleans as the cooling night draped the village in darkness.

His stomach growled, reminding him that he hadn't eaten since noon, and he turned toward home.

He found himself unable to stop thinking about Capucine. He knew, even as he entered his own cottage, that he would be back to see her.

"Capucine?"

A disembodied hand touched her cheek, and automatically Capucine turned toward the welcome scent of lavender and soap.

"How is your head, dear?"

She lifted her head slightly from the cool pillow and stopped as the blood began to thump wildly against her skull. "It hurts, Sister."

"I'm sure it does. You took quite a tumble on the wharf."

"Is there some tea?" Her mouth was as dry as paper.

"Aliette has just brought you some. It should be cool enough to drink a few sips."

Capucine struggled to push herself up and winced as her shoulder flared into pain where the bale had struck her.

Sister Marie-Agathe shook her head as she helped Capucine sip some tea. "Move carefully at first."

Capucine sank back into the pillow. "I don't know if I will have a choice in it. I'm certainly not about to skip or twirl right now."

"True. You have enough bruises and scrapes to keep you in place for a while, but none of it seems too bad. Praise our dearest Lord that Michel LeBlanc was at the wharf today."

The name LeBlanc rang a faint bell. "Who is Michel LeBlanc?"

"He is the man who came to your aid. Do you not remember him?"

"Does he have kind blue eyes?" She smiled at the memory.

Sister Marie-Agathe moved uneasily in her seat. "I don't know that I looked at his eyes, but yes, I suppose they are blue."

"As blue as the delphiniums that grew at the convent?"

"Oh, those delphiniums!" The nun laughed. "How I struggled with them to make them grow."

"But they did," Capucine answered. She took Sister Marie-Agathe's hand in hers, and pressed it to her lips. "They were like me, struggling to die, yet you were there, struggling to keep me alive."

A flush stained the nun's cheeks bright red. "I was doing the Lord's bidding."

Disappointment sank into Capucine's heart. She and Aliette had come to love Sister Marie-Agathe as if she were family—in fact, she had become their family, since the chances that they'd ever be reunited with their mother were remote.

The nun had never said that she loved them. Perhaps it had been too much to ask, but growing up without parents had been painful for the girls, and Sister Marie-Agathe was the surrogate they'd found.

Sister Marie-Agathe must have seen her distress because she leaned closer. "And do you know what the Lord's bidding was?"

Capucine shook her head slightly, just enough for the pounding pain to start again.

"The Lord bid me to love you. I hadn't thought that would happen, my dear. I thought I would tend to your needs, both spiritual and physical. I would make sure you had food, clothes, a dry and warm place to sleep, and the knowledge of our gracious Lord and that you would come to be able to live with forgiveness. But He saw a need that I hadn't recognized."

Too many words. Her mind was still groggy, and the conversation was wrapped in a gauzy aura of unreality.

Speaking had tired her, and she couldn't quite follow what Sister Marie-Agathe was saying. Love. Something about love. And forgiveness?

Her head hurt too much to think about it now. Later, later she would, when the world wasn't filled with thundering drums and crashing cymbals and painful light.

Chapter 3

*I have met someone intriguing. He makes me laugh,
which may be the most wonderful thing on earth—or the
most dangerous. Only time may tell.*

"Capucine, would you mind going to the market for me?" Aliette's golden head peeked around the doorway. "I'd like to have the chicken done before the day gets too hot. It's already too warm for my comfort."

Every morning Aliette asked the same question, and every morning Capucine gave the same answer. *"Mais oui!"*

"And see if you can find some cabbage while you're there. If there's not cabbage, then look for a turnip. No, two turnips. Wait, a cabbage and two turnips."

Capucine nodded. "Yes. Cabbage and turnips."

"Now hurry!"

As wonderful as Boncoeur House was, she felt stifled inside its whitewashed walls. A walk in the fresh air was welcome.

Summer mornings in New Orleans were blessed with

only a touch of the blanketing heat that would follow in the afternoons. The city woke up with beauty. Flowers spread their petals, merchants opened their shops, and the streets were busy with people going about their daily business.

She paused outside the market and tried to remember what Aliette had asked her to purchase. She should have asked her sister to write it down, but Aliette had been in an unusual hurry to return to the kitchen and start the chicken stewing.

Capucine shrugged. Whatever she bought, Aliette would make it into a delicious dish. She had quite a talent for cooking.

What *had* Aliette wanted?

She reached for a cluster of onions, and at the same time, so did another hand.

"Oh, excuse me," she said, pulling back. "I didn't—"

"Mademoiselle Louet!" Michel LeBlanc tilted his head in greeting. Sunlight touched his honey-colored hair. "I see we have the same taste in onions."

"One onion, I suspect, tastes the same as another," she answered.

He grinned. "You are right."

His words had a familiar accent, and her heart raced.

"You are Acadian." She steadied her voice so that it would not quiver and give the secret of her heritage away.

"Yes, I am. I'm proud of it, although there are those here who are not as accepting." He tilted his head slightly toward the group of men who lounged against the wall.

The men stared back at them, their gaze challenging.

Probably British, she thought. It was hard to know how alliances were drawn, and that was the reason she was guarding herself so cautiously. So far, no one except a select few knew that she spoke English and Spanish as well as French, and even fewer knew that she had been born Acadian.

With each passing day, the chance that she would ever be reunited with her mother grew smaller. Mama could have been relocated anywhere, perhaps put in prison, or even—she swallowed hard—dead.

Capucine hated the British with a fiery anger that gnawed at her. The only appeasement was her dream that one day she would find other Acadians who had made their own community again, and she could rejoin with them.

"I understand that there are many Acadians in this area," she said, carefully nonchalant.

"Many of them have settled in this area."

"They've established new lives, I understand."

"Not at all." His words were clipped. "They are the same lives they had before, but they are living them here."

From the way he spoke, and the fervor behind his words, she knew she had found a compatriot who would be able to help her go there. But his hesitation was natural. She'd have to overcome his suspicions of her motives.

She changed the subject.

"I do feel that I am eternally indebted to you for saving my life." She laced her fingers over the edge of her basket to hide their trembling.

"Saving your life? You overstate my actions."

"If you hadn't been at the wharf and acted so quickly. . ." She let the sentence trail off.

He brushed away her gratitude. "Please, speak of it no more. A man who didn't come to your aid would have been no greater than a beast."

Her fingers twisted together. "Nevertheless, I thank you."

"I must admit, Mademoiselle Louet, that I find it a fortunate calamity."

"A fortunate calamity?"

"I was able to make your acquaintance."

She took a deep breath. Her plan had to work. If only he would stop watching her so intently with those brilliant-colored eyes, she could focus on the task at hand.

"And I, yours."

An awkward pause followed, until he picked up the bunch of onions and placed them in her basket. "I wish they were roses."

She couldn't help herself. She took the onions from the basket, held them to her nose, and inhaled deeply. "So do I."

He chuckled at her grimace. "Shall I select some daisies for you?" He gave her a cluster of carrots. "Some violets?" He dropped a handful of beans into her basket. "Or perhaps an orchid?" An oversized cabbage joined the other vegetables.

"Aliette will be delighted with such a bouquet," she said, totally charmed.

"Aliette?"

"She is my sister. As you know, we are staying at Boncoeur House. She cooks. I sew and do needlework." She held out the edge of her shawl, a delicate lace as fine as a spider's web.

"Your reputation as a needlewoman precedes you. I don't believe that anyone here doesn't recognize your work."

"Why, thank you!" she answered, a pleased smile lighting her eyes. "And you? What do you do in New Orleans?"

"I've been here only a few months. I am helping my cousin build boats at his shop."

"Ah. That's why you were at the wharf that dreadful day?"

He grinned. "That's right. But why were you there? What would an elegant woman like yourself be doing at such a place?"

She looked at him sharply. "I like watching the arrival of the ships and wondering what they carry as cargo."

"Inquisitive, eh?"

"Sadly, my downfall." She laughed at her own words. "Literally, my downfall that day!"

"You're as inquisitive as a cat," he said with amusement, "and as quick."

Capucine couldn't believe she was being so bold. She should simply thank him for his help and walk away, but before she could stop herself, she said, "Oh. And do you like cats?"

"Yes," he said. "Of all the animals, I admire them the most. It must be handy to have nine lives." He glanced past her shoulder. "And there is my cousin, looking stern. If I don't hurry, I'll wish I had nine lives."

He quickly paid for his onions, and as he left, he called over his shoulder, *"Au revoir,* Capucine Louet. *À demain!"*

Until tomorrow? What on earth did he mean?

❧

"Michel, are those stars I see in your eyes? Has the uncatchable been caught?" Pierre escaped his cousin's jab.

"She is a friend." He knew that his words wouldn't convince Pierre. They certainly didn't convince him.

"A friend? *Une amie?*" Pierre guffawed. "A certain kind of friend, I believe."

"She is an acquaintance. I barely know her," Michel protested.

"Ah. I see. First the young woman is a friend, and now she's been demoted to an acquaintance? Hardly the compliment, LeBlanc!"

"She is the one I helped at the wharf, the one who was hit by the packet and then struck her head on the planks. Whatever you care to call it, I know her to some extent. And that is all."

Pierre slapped Michel's back. "I'm teasing you. I must say that I'm glad to see you looking like a calf in love."

"A calf in love? What a terrible—"

"Don't be so serious about everything! Let me say one more thing, and then we will be through speaking of this. You've been alone too long. *Le bon Dieu* did not mean for us to spend our time on the earth alone. He gave Adam a helpmate, and He gives you one, too. Perhaps you are this woman's helpmate—as she is yours."

Michel opened his mouth to speak, but Pierre waved away his comments before he could speak. "We have work to do. No more talk about women, or *l'amour.* Go now, and see if you can sand the side of that boat more smoothly. Your mind hasn't been with your hands lately, and although I am your relative and forgiving, I do have a business to run."

"*Oui, oui.*"

Michel bent over the curved wooden slats, and with each stroke he repeated in his mind the prayer that had been his for months. *Thy will. Thy will. Thy will.*

For too long he had been living with a different prayer: *My will.* But age was seasoning his heart with wisdom. *Thy will.*

❦

Night fell upon the city like a blessing. The heat lingered, but it was bearable. Up in her room at the top of Boncoeur House, Capucine stared out the window, her embroidery forgotten on her lap. Lights glimmered, bobbing across the landscape like bright fireflies.

Somewhere out there were those from her homeland. They lived together, bonded by the past and by the terrible scourge that had thrown them into this terrain so unlike their own.

And, perhaps, somewhere was her mother. If, in fact, she was still alive. Not knowing was perhaps the worst state of being.

The tears rarely came any more. She'd learned quickly that tears changed nothing. They were simply a way of washing emotion out of the body.

She didn't want her emotion washed out. She wanted to hold it, to keep it near to her heart where it could boil and keep her resolve clear. Hatred was a strong, driving force. She intended to use its power.

With a sigh, she folded the fabric on her lap and laid it aside. It was a blouse for Madame Dubois, adorned with vibrant leaves and flowers, and it needed to be done soon, but now the light was gone, and her head was beginning to ache.

She wouldn't write in her journal tonight. Not the way she felt.

Once her mother had told her that hate festered and ate into the soul. Love, she had said, was redeeming and healing. Love seemed so far away, though, distant and small like a tiny star that faded in and out of her vision.

A small knock on her door was followed quickly by Aliette peeking inside. "Capucine? Are you asleep?"

"Non. Come in. I was just looking out the window."

Aliette crossed the room and knelt beside her. "This is an amazing place. I feel so free here, don't you? New Orleans is such a mixture of people."

Capucine stiffened. "No one is free," she said. "As long as there is war, there will be conquerors—and the conquered."

Her sister touched her hand. "We aren't conquered. Even when we were, we weren't. No one can take your heart from you." She laughed slightly. "Except, of course, when you fall in love."

"Even then," Capucine chided her, "no one should *take* your heart. It's your treasure."

" 'For where your treasure is, there will your heart be also,' " Aliette quoted. "Remember when Mama taught us that?"

"I couldn't understand why it wasn't the other way around, why it didn't read: Where your heart is, there will your treasure be also. That seemed to be more logical, but Mama assured me that some day it would make complete sense."

"Does it?" Aliette whispered.

Capucine paused. "It's beginning to," she said softly. "It's beginning to."

Chapter 4

Some people express themselves in music, or painting, or poetry. I record each moment in my embroidery, the green minutes, the blue hours, the black days. I see the rhythm in the flow of the thread and the dip of the needle as it weaves its way in and out.

I f only he could come up with some excuse to go to Boncoeur House, Michel thought, he would be able to stop this insane habit he'd developed of lingering by the market on his way to his cousin's shop.

But the residents of Boncoeur House—a nun and two young women—hadn't much use for a boat, and he spent way too much of his time mooning over anything that reminded him of Capucine. When he caught himself smiling at an onion, he knew that the time had come for him to act or forever abandon this fancy.

He tugged on his jacket and straightened his shoulders. Pierre would tease him endlessly about his side trip on his way to his job, but he'd understand that the course of true love sometimes took a detour.

The solid outline of Boncoeur House stood before him, and he paused at the foot of the stone pathway as he ran through possible scenarios to explain his presence.

"May I help you?"

He spun around as the voice spoke behind him and found himself face-to-face with a tall, black-garbed nun. He recognized Sister Marie-Agathe, whom he'd met when he'd brought Capucine home after her injury.

"Michel LeBlanc!" She beamed at him. "Please, come inside! I'm sure that Capucine would like to see you again."

He was swept into the house before he could object. "She's in the garden. Follow me, please."

Michel had only a hurried glance at the interior of the house as he trailed after the nun. Soon they were in the back garden.

Capucine sat in the morning sunshine, her head bent over a length of linen. A few ebony curls had escaped the loose bun that was knotted at the base of her neck, like black lace around an ivory cameo, he thought, surprising himself with the poetic image. A silver needle flashed in the light, dipping in and out of the fabric.

"Capucine, you have a visitor," Sister Marie-Agathe announced.

She looked up, squinting against the sun, and then sprang up, tucking the errant tresses into place. They promptly dropped down again.

"Michel! I mean, Monsieur LeBlanc!"

Sister Marie-Agathe looked at Capucine, at him, and then back at her. She smiled a little but only said, "Ah," before ducking back inside the house.

"She's watching from inside," Capucine said with a meaningful glance at one window where a drapery fluttered.

"She's making sure that you're safe."

Capucine tilted her head at him. "Are you saying that I might not be safe with you? Why, I thought you were quite a gentleman."

He knew he was blushing. It was one of the curses of being fair skinned. "I live my life as a God-fearing man should," he answered. "I would never do anything to hurt you."

"You're a Christian, then."

"I am."

She didn't respond right away. Instead, she took the fabric she was working on and shook it out and studied it critically. The snowy white linen was festooned with bright threads and ribbons in what seemed to be an abstract design.

"What are you sewing?" he asked. "It's quite pretty."

"I'm embroidering a tablecloth." She resettled the swath of cloth onto her lap and took the needle in her fingers again. "I prefer to work on it during the morning when it's a bit more comfortable, and when the light is good."

The needle dipped in and out of the material, leaving a trail of vivid green across the white fabric.

"Is it your own design?" The question was less from curiosity than the need to break the overwhelming silence.

She looked up at him, a half smile on her face. "I always

do my own designs."

"Interesting." He picked up a corner of the cloth, which was almost touching the ground, and examined the needlework. "I don't know much about embroidery—actually, I don't know anything about embroidery—but this is quite lovely."

"Thank you."

Neither of them spoke, and only a bird's song decorated the silence.

He swallowed. What was he doing here?

"You seem to be doing well. Are you recovered?"

"Completely."

"Well, then." He was completely out of things to say. He stood up abruptly. "It's been quite pleasant visiting with you."

She also rose to her feet, gathering the embroidered fabric to her. "I've enjoyed this, too."

Together they walked through the house, past a smiling Sister Marie-Agathe and to the entrance. Capucine opened the front door and called to a young woman coming up the stone path.

"Aliette, this is the fellow who saved my life that day at the wharf, Michel LeBlanc! Michel, this is my sister."

Aliette was as blond as Capucine was dark, and she cheerfully met him with an immediate and effusive greeting. "We all owe you quite a debt, *monsieur*. Would you do us the honor of joining us for dinner this evening?"

Capucine tapped his shoulder. "Aliette is a marvelous cook. You must come."

Was it her touch? Was it the invitation? Was it the chance to see her again?

Whatever the reason, Michel's spirits soared. "It would be my pleasure."

"We shall see you, then, at the close of the afternoon." Capucine's eyes twinkled as she leaned in and said in a stage whisper, "Be prepared to eat until you cannot stir. Aliette cooks enough for an army every evening."

Strands of her hair, softly scented with some floral aroma, curled around her face and brushed against his cheek as she moved away from him.

He bowed, unable to hide the smile that captured his face. "Au revoir—until this evening, mademoiselles."

His feet barely touched the paving stones as he returned to the street. Then, under the cover of the thick shrubbery that surrounded the house, he glanced back. The two women were turning to return to the house, and something flashed in the sunlight in front of Capucine.

It was the needle, hanging from the embroidery thread, and she quickly caught it up and returned it to the cloth, weaving it safely into the fabric.

From the far reaches of his mind came the uneasy feeling that he had missed something rather important, but the thought of spending more time with the fascinating Capucine drove back the thought.

Tonight would be more important than any bit of silver. Much more important.

❧

The sun was at its peak, driving Capucine from the garden.

Moist and intense, the damp heat was too much for her to work comfortably outside.

In the house was not much better. The rooms held the humid closeness, and eventually she was forced to put her head back on the settee in her bedroom, a wet cloth on her forehead to cool her, and close her eyes.

Sleeping was out of the question. Too much had happened today—all of it beginning and ending with Michel LeBlanc.

He was Acadian. The lilt in his words took her back to the precious years of her childhood, before she was separated from her mother and her friends. He would understand. He might even be able to help her.

She rubbed the bridge of her nose, trying to ease her headache that had begun to gather. There were times when her goal seemed so clear, and others when it was a garbled mess.

First, she had to find out what happened to her mother. Logic told her that she had probably died, either in those terrible days when the British had come sweeping in, or in the dark days afterwards.

But thinking what might have happened and knowing what really happened could be poles apart.

She owed it to her mother to try to find her. In her heart, she knew that Mama must have tried everything within her power to find her daughters, but her resources would have been limited. The realization that her mother missed her and Aliette as much as they missed their mother struck like a poisoned arrow. Was Mama, at this very moment, thinking of her daughters?

Capucine had heard murmurs that some Acadians had

been sent to this area. She heard the sounds of their voices on the streets, in the markets, at church. None had been even faintly familiar, though, and her careful questioning of the few whom she trusted hadn't indicated that her mother or friends were near.

One settlement in particular had her attention. *Bayou Teche*. The name was coming up in overheard conversations more and more.

The name took on a golden glow.

Bayou Teche.

She heard it in the stir of her skirts as she walked. *Bayou Teche*. It was whispered from tree to tree. *Bayou Teche*. The birds in the garden chirped it. *Bayou Teche*.

Somehow she had to get there. She had to see once again what had been taken from her. She was Acadian in her blood.

Of course, it might be, as rumors often were, untrue or only partially true. These days, with Spanish control of the city in the offing, the streets were abundant with rumor and speculation.

But as long as the slightest chance existed, she would continue in her pursuit, for her mother and for her people.

Michel LeBlanc might be just the person she had been looking for.

"Capucine!" Aliette spoke from the doorway. "I need to run a quick errand. Sister Marie-Agathe is out, so she can't help me. Can you come to the kitchen and watch the soup for me?"

"Me?" she asked, sitting up and letting the damp cloth slide from her face. "You trust me with your soup?"

"Silly goose!" Her sister laughed. "Everything's taken care of. All you have to do is stir it once in a while, and if you could peek in at the bread, that'd be wonderful, although I should be back before it's done."

Reluctantly, Capucine stood up and grumbled as she made her way into the stifling kitchen. She knew nothing about cooking, nothing except that the kitchen was her least favorite place in the house. How on earth Aliette could stand this heat was beyond her.

"There probably isn't any errand," she muttered as she moved the spoon slowly through the bubbling mixture. It smelled wonderful, but the cloud of steam rising from it just intensified the warmth of the room. *Aliette couldn't stand being in here one second longer—not that I blame her, not one bit—and she's gone in search of a breeze.*

The wisps of hair that refused to stay in place soon turned from spry curls to lank strings. Her dress stuck to her, and her face streamed with perspiration.

She muttered as she checked on the bread. "I can't believe Aliette left me here. How am I supposed to know if this bread is ready? The soup smells done, and—"

She wiped her hands on her skirt. She probably should have worn one of Aliette's aprons, but this dress would have to be washed anyway.

This dinner was so important. How could her sister abandon her like this? If anyone could ruin a dinner, she could. She'd have a stern older sister talk with Aliette before bed tonight about responsibility.

She turned gratefully at the sound of someone at the door. "Aliette, you may have your kitchen back. I am as thoroughly baked as one of your roasts."

Michel laughed.

Capucine gasped. She knew that she looked terrible, red and sweating and covered with splotches of soup. She wanted to grab one of the kitchen cloths and throw it over her face.

"Monsieur LeBlanc," she said, trying desperately to repair the damage as well as she could. She smoothed her hair back and wiped her cheeks with her fingers. "You've caught me by surprise. I'm afraid I'm not—I'm not at my best right now."

He shook his head. "On the contrary, mademoiselle. You are lovely, if I might say so."

"Lovely? I hardly think so, especially now."

"I disagree. Your cheeks are pink, your eyes are sparkling, and your skin is glowing."

Her dismay at being found in such condition evaporated into laughter. "In other words, I'm overheated, near tears, and perspiring."

He chuckled. "Aliette should be back soon. I passed her on the way here."

"Yes, she said she had some errand to run."

"Ah. Yes, she was just coming out of—"

"Michel LeBlanc!" Sister Marie-Agathe swept into the room. "It's so good to see you again." She frowned at Capucine, clearly noting her unkempt condition. "My dear, are you sure you should be receiving guests?"

"Sister, the blame is all mine. I'm afraid I was lured in here by the delicious aromas. My path had crossed with Aliette's, and she told me that you were out, so I was to let myself in."

Capucine growled softly. She was certainly going to have that talk with Aliette, but it was now going to include the folly of what she had done. Not only was it highly improper, she had created this awkward situation.

Sister Marie-Agathe murmured a few conciliatory words and led Michel from the kitchen. Moments later, Aliette arrived and within minutes had an apron on, the bread out, the soup off the fire, and her sister calmed down.

"*Sssh, sssh,*" she said, shooing Capucine out the door and waving away her complaints. "Later. Right now you need to put yourself to rights. Dinner will be served in a few moments."

Capucine scurried up the stairs and washed her face, rebrushed and pinned her hair, and changed her dress. Within minutes, she entered the main room of Boncoeur, where Michel and Sister Marie-Agathe sat.

He rose to his feet. "Mademoiselle!"

She dipped in a small curtsy. "We are delighted to have your company tonight, monsieur."

"My pleasure." He coughed. "I must apologize for intruding into your kitchen—"

"My kitchen? Hardly! I have no cooking skills. For food I rely upon my sister, Aliette. What I would do without her—"

Sister Marie-Agathe cleared her throat. "Capucine. . ."

Perhaps the heat had gone to her head, she thought, as she heard the words coming from her own mouth. "Well, it's true. When Aliette was born, the angels must have realized that they slighted me with culinary talent, so they gave mine to her."

The nun's lips twisted as she clearly fought an amused smile. "Capucine, that is not—"

Aliette appeared at the doorway. "I may cook, but my fingers turn to thumbs with a needle. The good Lord, le bon Dieu, has gifted us all differently."

"That is so," Michel agreed. "I'm afraid I would also be a catastrophe with an embroidery needle and thread, and in the kitchen I can prepare only the most basic foods, but give me a length of wood and I will happily build you a boat."

"A boat!" Aliette laughed. "I will remember it should the need for a boat arise, although I must honestly say that I cannot foresee such an occasion, right, Capucine?"

Capucine nodded, although the truth was that indeed there might be a call for a boat at some point. One never knew when the least bit of information might play a crucial role.

"Now, let us go eat, before the day's heat cooks the food even longer," she announced.

After they had seated themselves, Sister Marie-Agathe asked Michel if he would like to lead them in asking a blessing.

"Mais oui! Of course I will!"

Capucine peeked out of the corner of her eye as she bowed her head. He didn't seem to struggle to find the words, as she did when Sister Marie-Agathe occasionally asked her to pronounce the blessing.

His grace was short and direct. "Lord of all, we ask Thy blessing and Thy touch on all who are gathered here today."

Sister Marie-Agathe looked a bit taken aback, as if the brevity surprised her, but Capucine breathed a sigh of relief as the nun seemed to accept it.

The dinner was, as usual, splendid. Aliette had outdone herself, and how she managed to look cool and relaxed was incomprehensible to Capucine. She seemed to blossom with the extra attention, and Capucine looked quickly between her sister and their guest. Could it be Michel's presence that was causing Aliette's extra vitality?

But nothing passed between them. No shared glances, no coy smiles, no lingering touches as dishes were handed around the table.

"This is a lovely tablecloth," Michel said, touching the hem of the linen. "Is this your needlework, Capucine?"

"It is. I'm afraid it's an old one, but it's held up well."

"Wasn't this one of the first ones you made?" Sister Marie-Agathe asked as she took a piece of bread. "This is one of the convent designs, I believe."

"Yes, it is." Capucine picked up the corner of it and showed it to them. "This is the dove of peace."

"So I see," Michel said. "There are never enough doves, are there?"

She bit her lip to keep herself from responding as sharply as she wished.

Sister Marie-Agathe filled the uneasy silence. "Peace is something we all must work for." She laid her napkin across her plate and caught Capucine's gaze with hers. "Doves or no doves," she added sternly.

The sun was sinking into the horizon as Michel prepared to leave, and Capucine walked with him down the cobbled path to the street. Overhead, the weeping willows whispered to each other as a faint breeze ruffled the long strands. He couldn't think of a time when he had been happier, or more at ease.

"When Aliette first came here, she called these 'sweeping willows,'" Capucine said.

"That fits them better, I think," he answered. "They sweep, not weep."

They walked a few more steps, and he stopped. "May I ask you a question?"

"Yes."

"Will you answer it?"

"Perhaps."

He paused. This woman was at times so oblique that there seemed no chance of knowing her, and at other times so friendly that he felt he had known her since birth. "You speak French with your family and with me, but do you also speak English?"

Was he imagining it, or did her laugh have a tinny ring of nervousness? "Why on earth would you ask such a question?"

"The part about sweeping and weeping willows. That's English."

"Yes, I suppose it is."

"So you do speak English."

"Enough to know what the difference is between a sweeping willow and a weeping willow."

"And enough to tell me my answer, although you think you do not."

"I did not answer."

"Ah, but you did."

The repartee was frustrating.

He continued. "You must have learned languages other than French in the convent."

She shrugged. "These are no more than games, *mon ami*. Perhaps if you keep your eye on me, you may even catch me speaking Egyptian, or perhaps Chinese." She laughed. "Although my talents, I'm afraid, do not go quite that far."

"You are a fascinating woman, Capucine Louet." The last rays of the sun illuminated her rich ebony hair. "May I see you again?"

She tilted her head and studied him. "You do so at your own risk."

His breath caught in his throat. "It is a risk I am willing to take."

"Then yes, you may see me again." She leaned in closer to him. "But be aware, I am not one to fall in love with, for I am not one to fall in love."

And with those mysterious words, she turned and left him.

Chapter 5

Only in the silence do we hear.

Capucine sat on the stone bench at the edge of the courtyard, her embroidery spread out across her lap. Conversations flowed around her like water from a fountain, some in French, some in Spanish, and some in English. Months of experience had helped her sort through the barrage of words, to pick out exactly what was useful and what was not.

The government changeover was going well, but she knew that nothing was perfect. There would always be someone looking for a way to make his or her own nest a bit better feathered.

One cluster of three men in particular had her attention. They spoke in the flat broad tones of English, and when they talked of the Spanish and the French, the disdain in their voices was clear. They had something in mind, something that would disrupt the smooth flow of New Orleans.

With a quick tilt of his head, a short, stocky man in the group indicated her. "We need to be careful. She could—"

"*Pffft.*" The man with the oversized moustache waved away the other's concern. "She is French."

The third man hooted in derision. "Plus she is a woman. What danger can she be?"

What danger indeed?

Her fingers flew as her needle outlined an egret with fantastic plumage. Crimson, gold, and coral—the threads dipped in and out of the fabric, filling the bird's feathers with a rainbow of warm colors.

"I'll not leave here without what's due me," the barrel-shaped man declared. "I've come too far from my homeland to slink back like a beaten dog."

"I'm with you." The tall fellow rubbed his moustache thoughtfully. "And I have a plan, a smart plan, to make sure that this city pays me what I'm owed."

"You've got a plan?" The third man, nondescript in his work clothes, leaned in closer. "Let's hear it then, my good man. Time's wasting, and I'm not getting any younger."

The first man snorted. "That's the truth. Come on, Will, now let's hear it."

The three put their heads together and began to talk. Capucine couldn't make out the words clearly, just bits and pieces of sentences that didn't make much sense, but as the men grew cocky with their cleverness, they drew apart and their voices grew louder.

Her needle flashed in the sunlight, gaining in speed as she

glared at them under the cover of her eyelashes.

What danger indeed?

At last, with a great shout of laughter, the men slapped each other's backs and swaggered away. It took every ounce of will-power for her not to stand up and follow them, repeating their conversation in English—and translating into Spanish and then French.

Someday, she thought as she folded her sewing, they would get their comeuppance. Heaven wouldn't hold them, that was for sure.

She shot a dire glance at the retreating figures.

Sister Marie-Agathe would tell her to pray for them.

She couldn't. She just couldn't.

Michel stood at the side of the courtyard. Surely he wasn't mistaken. That was Capucine, sitting on the bench, her constant embroidery in her hands. Nearby her a trio of rough-dressed men, known in the town for their wild ways, carried on an animated conversation as they walked slowly out of the sunlit area.

Yet she seemed to be totally unaware of them. Or was she? Had she just raised her head a bit, to look at them with what was clearly contempt?

The men were British. Most of the British in New Orleans were gentlemen, but these three had come in on a vessel filled with rats and spoiled goods. He remembered it well.

The townspeople had taken the situation into their own hands. They'd towed the boat, a rickety thing called the *Gull*, well out into the water, far enough away that the rodents couldn't swim ashore, and sunk it. The owners had been furious and had vowed revenge. Fortunately—or not—they spent most of their time filling their mouths with ale, and their plans never progressed past idle threats.

He moved toward her, edging around the border of the courtyard. He didn't want to seem as if he were watching her, although of course he was. Somehow he knew that she would not accept his watchful attentions. She was too independent.

Yet these men were well known to him, and although they'd never caused any more real trouble, he knew that even an old powder keg could explode. He always acted with caution around them.

"Michel!" She called to him as she stood up. He apparently hadn't been as stealthy as he'd hoped. *"Comment t'allez vous?"*

"Bon."

His nightmare seemed to spring into reality. The three men turned around. "Bone, bone, bone, who's got the bone?"

"Take no notice of them," he said to Capucine in a low voice. "Their stupidity is exceeded only by their stench."

She tucked her embroidery into her apron pocket and looped her arm though his. "I'd noticed that."

"Bone, bone, bone!" The men continued their taunt.

"Why do they keep doing that?" she asked, frowning.

"They are ignorant. No more reason needed. Shall we go?" He held her arm tightly at his side.

"Mammy-zelle, show us your pretty stitches!" one of the men called.

"You fool," one of the others said, poking his companion in the side, "she can't speak English. You might as well be barking like a dog or snorting like a pig."

The third man took a bold step forward. "I'll go get that fancy needlework from her. I'd look pretty with a stitched-up cloth on my collar!"

Michel gripped her arm closer. "They are all bluster. Act as if they're not there."

"Michel, are you sure?"

Help me, dear Father in heaven. Help us. Show us the way out of this.

The mustachioed man shook his head. "Aw, that old cloth is probably just a rag she's making into a hanky. Let's go have us some refreshment, what do you say, men? This heat is causing me a mighty thirst."

With a show of laughing and shoving, the three confronters left the courtyard, apparently in search of more ale.

"Oh, Michel," Capucine said, sagging with clear relief against him, "I thought for sure they were going to come after us."

"Well, we were in the middle of this courtyard. I don't think you had much reason to be really afraid that they'd hurt you," he said.

"I wasn't afraid of that," she said. "But I—now, you're going to think I'm foolish for saying this—I was afraid they'd take my embroidery."

"You treasure it that much?" He couldn't keep the amazement out of his voice.

"It's my livelihood," she explained. "And I suppose, yes, it's my treasure. You know what the Bible says: 'For where your treasure is, there will your heart be also.' "

"I wonder if the gospel was referring to embroidery," he said lightly.

Capucine stared up at him, her eyes so dark brown they were nearly as black as the waters at night. "Why wouldn't it?"

He didn't have a good answer. Instead, he did what any good man would do—he changed the subject. "Were you returning home?"

"Yes, I was. Today is the day Sister Marie-Agathe is refreshing all the linens and draperies, and Aliette is furiously cleaning her precious kitchen and roasting what must be half a pig."

"Half a pig?" He tried to visualize that in the small kitchen, and failed.

"Maybe not half a pig, but it's a huge chunk of something pork, and between Sister Marie-Agathe's pounding of the drapes and Aliette's blazingly hot kitchen, I decided the best thing for me to do was leave them in peace."

"They don't expect you to help?" The question popped out before he could stop it.

"I did my part earlier. I'm taller than Aliette, so I emptied the cupboards for her, and I'll put them back to rights later. Sister Marie-Agathe and I took the linens down to the garden to air, and I'll have the distinct privilege of putting them in place again when she's finished. So no, I haven't been a sluggard, if that's what you're asking."

"I didn't mean to imply that at all!"

She shrugged. "I know what I do, and that's what matters."

He had the terrible feeling he was losing ground, and it mattered to him very much.

"Are you going home now? I would be glad to walk with you."

"Don't you have boats to build?" she asked, the humor returning to her voice.

"Possibly."

"Oh," she said, laughing, "you're being as circumspect as I! Actually, I'm not ready to go home at all. Would you mind showing me where you build your boats? I'd like to meet your cousin, too."

Michel's world shuddered to a stop. Taking her to the shop and introducing her to Pierre would set him up for a daily barrage of teasing. It was a terrible thing to do, just terrible, but worse would be to tell her no, that he wouldn't bring her there.

He pasted on a smile that he didn't really feel. "*Allons!* Let's go!"

The boat shop was only a few blocks away.

"Pierre, I've—" he began as he entered the doorway, but his words were cut short as his cousin exploded from the back room.

"Michel LeBlanc, you are a fool! I send you for a simple— oh, hello!" Pierre stopped in the middle of his angry spate of words. "What is this? Or should I say, *who* is this? Michel, please introduce me to your lovely companion."

"Capucine Louet, this is my horrible cousin Pierre LeBlanc. He is a slave driver, and a terrible flirt. You should always be careful around him."

"Mademoiselle Louet, it is a pleasure to meet you." Pierre delicately balanced Capucine's hand in his and bowed deeply, dropping a kiss on her fingertips as he rose. "You are always welcome in my humble shop, even when Michel, my bullish apprentice with two left hooves, has wandered off."

Capucine laughed. "The pleasure is mine."

Pierre winked openly at Michel. "She is charming, this one is. Take good care of her."

"He's already rescued me this morning," she said.

"Really?" Pierre glanced quizzically at his cousin. "What is this story?"

"Nothing. The crew from the *Gull* was a bit too interested in her embroidery."

"So you ran them off?"

"Not exactly. Their taste for ale got the better of them, and they left on their own. You know how they are."

Pierre rolled his eyes. "Mademoiselle, I regret that you had such an unlucky experience."

"Michel assures me that I was never in any danger, but this is the second time he has come to my assistance."

"Capucine—" Michel tried to protest, but she spoke over his objections.

"It's true. First by the water, and now this. I am indebted to you. I can never repay you."

Pierre's eyes twinkled. "Give him your heart, *cherè*."

She looked at Michel, a speculative gleam in her gaze. "My heart? Would you want it?"

Why not? he thought. *You already have mine.*

Instead, he shook his head. "I warned you. He is a romantic dreamer."

"Dreams are good," she said, "and romance is good, but I must agree they're not enough. They're not food, or a shelter over your head."

"She is practical," Michel said. "Practical enough to know that someone must buy the threads for her embroidery."

"Oh, yes," his cousin responded. "Her embroidery, which the men from the *Gull* found intriguing. I would be very interested in seeing it myself."

Capucine withdrew the folded cloth from her pocket.

"I won't spread the thing out. I don't want to get any sawdust in it, but you can see from this bit here what it's like. I'm just starting the pattern, making it as I go. Right now it just looks like a crazy rooster, but it's actually supposed to be an egret."

"An egret?" Pierre looked confused.

"It's a big bird that was in one of the books at the house. I must confess I've never seen one, so I've made up the colors myself."

"These spots of blue and green to the side?" he asked.

She put the cloth back in her pocket. "Those are the marks where the flowers will be."

Michel had the feeling that he'd just walked into the middle of a discussion that he didn't understand.

Capucine said to him, "I think I've stayed away long enough. I should get back and help Sister Marie-Agathe and Aliette."

"I'll walk with you—"

"No, no reason to. I'm perfectly safe. Thank you again for saving me once more. Monsieur Pierre LeBlanc, I'm glad to have met you. Au revoir."

With that, she turned quickly and walked out of the shop.

Michel frowned at his cousin. "Did I miss something?"

Pierre rubbed his beard thoughtfully. "Perhaps yes, perhaps no. I'm not sure, but I think our Capucine Louet might need a protector more than she realizes."

"What? Why?"

"I won't say, not yet, but we should pray for the young woman. Is she a Christian?"

"She grew up in a convent and lives with a nun."

"I grew up on a poultry farm and live behind a boat shop. That doesn't make me either a chicken or a sailing vessel."

The analogy wasn't quite sound, but Michel knew what his cousin meant. "I'm not sure," he acknowledged at last. "I do wish you'd tell me what this is all about."

A little line of worry etched its way into Pierre's forehead. "Not yet." He busied himself with some scraps of wood from the floor. "You do know she's Acadian. I can hear it in her voice."

"Are you sure?" Michel frowned. "I've thought it myself, but I couldn't be sure."

"I believe she is. She would have been very young when she left Acadia. There are, however, enough subtle nuances in her speech." Pierre met his eyes squarely. "I might be wrong. But promise me that you'll be careful. Very careful. All is not what it seems. Pray for wisdom, my cousin."

Chapter 6

*A small cottage in the country, away from others, just
my loved ones around me, and a dog and a cat to keep my
feet warm—my desires are simple.*

The Place d'Armes buzzed with rumor. Men huddled
together in animated conversation. Certain phrases
broke free of their conversations and floated in the air.

"—never allowed!"

"He would be wise to watch his—"

"—a stranger to us! What does he know?"

"He must be mad! Insane! *Dérangé!*"

Capucine bent over her embroidery, her fingers swiftly
guiding the needle as she eavesdropped.

She knew whom they were talking about. All of New
Orleans was talking about him.

Antonio de Ulloa. Spain had sent him to be the first Spanish
governor of New Orleans. Capucine was vague about what had
happened—it had all occurred before she had arrived—but

somehow New Orleans now belonged to the Spanish, not the French. Nothing had changed after the signatures had dried on the page, and the French, she'd been told, had lived as they always had. Now Spain was starting to flex its muscle, and de Ulloa was the fist.

She put her head closer to her embroidery as she put the last touches on a brilliant lily. The Place d'Armes was usually not this busy on a weekday. On Sundays, of course, people would stroll through it after services at the St. Louis Church, and Capuchins, the spiritual leaders after whom she had been named, were often there, too, trying to find some relief from the stifling heat.

Capucine kept the jail carefully out of her vision. She did not want to know what went on in there, nor what the men who were housed in it had done. There were some things best left unknown.

A shadow broke the sunlight across her fabric, and she looked up. It was Madame Dubois's maidservant, a charming young woman with skin the color of *café au lait*. Her voice contained the lilt of islands far away when she said in patois French, "My madame, she would care to know if the blouse, it is finished."

Capucine reached down for the carefully folded blouse that lay in a parcel at her feet. "Please tell her I hope that she wears it with health."

The servant's nod was barely visible. "Oui, ma'm'selle. *Merci. A'voir.*"

With a quick bob of a curtsy, the maid took the parcel and was gone.

The sun was nearing its zenith, and the shade Capucine had enjoyed was vanishing. Droplets of sweat were becoming rivulets, and she gathered her embroidery to leave.

"Capucine!"

With a quick intake of breath, she sprang to her feet, spilling her threads across the stones of the plaza. Then she slumped in relief.

"Michel LeBlanc, you nearly scared the life right out of me!"

She knelt to pick up the skeins of floss at the same time he did, and their heads bumped.

"I'm sorry. I saw you here and—"

A scuffle broke out near them.

"You cannot speak of what is right, not when you say that he—" one of the combatants growled.

"This is what must be—" another responded, but the rest of his sentence was interrupted when a blow struck his jaw.

Michel stuffed the last bits of thread back into her satchel. "Allons! We had better hurry to avoid getting knocked down ourselves. I don't look forward to an exchange with those fellows."

She allowed herself to be hustled out of the plaza, his arm protectively on her back.

"Do you often come to the plaza?" he asked.

"I like the vigor of it," she answered and then laughed. "Sometimes, like today, there was a bit too much vigor, though!"

"I agree." As they strolled back toward Boncoeur House, he commented, "I assume that you are firmly sided with the French on the issue."

She shrugged noncommittally.

With fury, he swatted at an insect that flew by his face, and the beetle barely escaped his hand. "It does seem right to side with the French, does it not, since this village has been French for so many years and is even named after a Frenchman, the Duke of Orleans, not a Spaniard."

She glanced at him covertly. He was quite serious about this.

"Plus," he continued, "I am dismayed, of course, that this exchange, if indeed it is an exchange, was done in secret, but more than that, once again we are being treated as if we are mere property to be handed back and forth."

She could see his teeth clench, and then he added, in a softer tone that was no less impassioned, "This happened to us once before, in Acadia, and now. . .now we are expected to bow and scrape and say, *Sí*? This is not going to go easily for de Ulloa, and I fear for the repercussions that he will suffer for his country."

"Your anger surprises me," she said when he had paused.

He smiled a bit. "I am sorry, Capucine. I suspect that we all have one part of our lives that are our—how to say it? The one thing that we cannot compromise on. For me, it is justice and fairness and truth. I do not tolerate lies. Not at all."

Her blood ran icy cold as he continued. "Those who live in the shadow of secrecy and untruths and even half-truths will have to explain their actions to their Maker one day. A lie is a detestable twisting of what is real, and I, for one, have had enough of that."

He rubbed his hand over his face. "I'm afraid the heat is getting to me. I usually don't pontificate like this to lovely young ladies."

Their footsteps had taken them to the walkway of Boncoeur House, and she paused. "You speak of what is important to you. I would not expect less of you, Michel LeBlanc, not at all."

Somehow she walked into the house, out of the oppressive midday warmth, and collapsed into a chair. What would he think of her when he found out what she was doing?

And why did it matter to her so much?

❧

Capucine put the fabric in the box beside her bed. Within a week, it would be done and she could deliver it to the woman who owned the shop where she bought her embroidery materials. In exchange for the tablecloth, she would receive several hanks of brilliant thread and a handful of coins.

She couldn't make her stitchery fast enough for the demand. More and more, she had visitors asking for garments and household linens. She needed more than two hands.

She couldn't do this forever. Her eyes burned, her fingers cracked, and her neck ached. Plus the stress of the deadlines was nearly unbearable.

And it wasn't safe. The other day she'd seen a flicker of knowledge in Pierre's face. What did he know? And how did he know it?

She shuddered as she thought that perhaps she wasn't as

skilled as she thought she was. Her designs might be growing too obvious.

An egret? What had she been thinking?

Things were changing too quickly for her comfort. In her grand plan for revenge, she'd never considered Michel LeBlanc. She'd told him that she couldn't fall in love.

But she'd forgotten to tell her heart.

Already he was moving into her mind. She'd never met anyone like him, a fellow who lived honestly, who respected his fellow human beings completely. And who seemed to find her appealing.

Could it be that at last she had found someone to love?

But her mission wasn't completed. She couldn't fall in love, not yet.

A gust of wind blew the curtains from her open window. A thunderstorm, bringing blessed relief from the heat, was moving in.

Capucine dropped into her bed. From her pillow, she could watch the rain fall on the trees. The long graceful branches of the weeping willow, caught by the storm's winds, stood at an unnatural angle to the earth.

Thunderstorms were wonderful. She'd always loved to watch the power they unleashed, to hear the rumble of the thunder, to see the mighty flash of lightning. When they'd been little girls, huddled in the convent, Aliette had told her that the thunder was God's voice. Capucine, always the practical older sister, had asked her to explain lightning.

The little girl had looked at her with wide eyes and

explained that the lightning was God's way of pointing at a wrongdoer, much the way Sister Marie-Agathe did when she was angry.

I have some suggestions for You, she thought, *starting with three men. You can point at them.*

Michel had explained about their boat, the *Gull,* being sunk, and she could almost feel a bit sorry for them. It wasn't fair, not really, that they lost what little they had, but on the other hand, the townspeople were right to stop the boat from docking there and releasing its pestilence on the area.

Maybe their anger was somewhat justified. Still, after a while, one needed to lay it aside and move on.

Something prickled at her heart.

Not everything needed to be laid aside, she qualified. Some things could not be forgiven. Nothing would be changed if someone forgave and forgave and forgave.

Nothing?

She picked up the small picture of Jesus that Sister Marie-Agathe had placed at her bedside.

You forgave and forgave and forgave, didn't You? And we're so slow that we still don't understand. I don't understand.

How could Jesus have done this? And how could He forgive even after His death?

He'd been hurt worse than she'd been. Yet still His arms were outstretched, welcoming, even loving those who had killed Him.

"I'm sorry," she said softly to the picture. "I'm sorry."

Deep inside her heart, a bit of ice melted.

Chapter 7

Forgiveness has a medicinal quality to it—and an equally medicinal taste. I struggle with this daily, keeping the hate close and not letting mercy temper my heart.

Days grew into weeks, and the weeks passed in a fast parade. The market burst with late summer bounty, and Michel found himself stopping on the way to the boat shop in the morning to pick up some fresh produce for his lunch.

Capucine was usually there, and the two of them chatted as they shopped together, occasionally stopping to share some bread and tea. The days that she wasn't there seemed to be covered with a gray pall, while the mornings that they were able to linger sparkled with joy.

It wasn't enough. He wanted to steal away from the shop in the afternoon and spend some time with her, but he and Pierre were busier than ever with a spate of orders for boats. Michel left the shop exhausted, but his footsteps often took him to the Boncoeur House. It was a circuitous route home but one he took at the close of business every day.

It was a busy road. He'd often see Aliette hurrying toward the house from one direction just as Capucine was returning from the other. Now that the weather was cooling somewhat, Capucine had explained, she was spending more time in the area by the marketplace. The bustle and colors of the wares being traded there were inspiration for her embroidery designs.

Her patterns were increasingly vivid. The last apron she wore over her dress had an abstract design of swirls and speckles in black and red and green on a snowy white background. He shook his head. God hadn't given him a creative eye like hers, one that could invent and concoct so freely. Instead, He'd gifted him with the ability to saw wood and nail it into the shape of a boat. It wasn't the same at all. He'd tried his hand once at painting a landscape, and when he had finished, it looked less like a tree-lined stream and more like a line of giraffes beside an oversized earthworm.

"You look as if you are thinking very hard." Capucine's voice had an amused lilt to it.

"I am. I was thinking about painting."

"Really?"

"Or not. Not painting. I am a terrible painter."

She grinned. "As am I. My skill is with my stitching, not with a brush. What scene were you thinking of painting?"

He looked at her, her dark eyes shining like black marbles, her hair, as always, struggling to escape the knot at her neck.

Her cheeks were highlighted with a sun-warmed bloom.

More than anything, at that moment he wanted to take her in his arms and hold her, to clasp to him her beauty.

"I'd paint you, just as you are now."

"Truly? You wouldn't put me in a grand chair, my hands primly folded in my lap, with perhaps a bird in a cage at my shoulder?"

"No. I like you the way you are." He felt like a schoolboy.

"You are too kind."

There were so many things he wanted to say, but the words wouldn't form. He wanted to see her more, spend hours with her instead of these "accidental" meetings, but he couldn't bring himself to say it. Instead he stood like a puppet, waiting for the heavens to open and supply the syllables he couldn't find.

"Aliette will be furious if I am late for dinner," she said at last. She started to walk toward Boncoeur House and stopped. "You could visit later tonight—if you wish. Aliette has made cake."

If he wished?

He knew he was grinning like a fool. "I like cake."

❧

"Michel might stop by after dinner," Capucine announced as she took a slice of pork from the serving platter.

Sister Marie-Agathe looked up sharply. "You've been seeing that young man quite a bit."

"Our paths cross regularly, but it's not as if we've been spending much time together," she protested.

"You might want to think about this," the nun cautioned. "He is a pleasant fellow, and I suspect that he would be very interested in pursuing something beyond a friendship."

Capucine knew that she was blushing, and she studied the beans on her plate, pushing them around intently.

"Are you equally as interested, my dear?"

"He hasn't said anything," she muttered, still rearranging the beans.

"And I suspect it might take him some time to do so. I do believe Michel is a bit shy." The nun leaned across the table and grasped Capucine's hand. "Don't toy with his heart."

"I—"

"And don't toy with your own." Sister Marie-Agathe pushed her chair back and stood up. "The heart is a sacred thing. Guard it carefully."

Oh, mine is guarded, Capucine thought. *It's encased in ice and metal. No one, absolutely no one, will ever intrude.*

❧

Michel stood outside the Boncoeur home. Perhaps this was a bad idea. He should turn around and leave, go back to his own small cottage, and think this through again. His hands clenched and unclenched in fists of indecisiveness.

Instead his feet marched forward, and his hand rose and knocked on the door.

Capucine herself opened the door.

"Might we go for a walk?" he asked immediately.

"I'd like that."

They walked slowly, commenting on anything and everything. The wall that needed repair. The flowers that bloomed in the moonlight. The dog that barked at everything that moved, including the leaves on the trees.

At last they were back at the house.

"I'm not ready to end this evening," he said, feeling extraordinarily bold.

"Shall we sit in the garden, then?" Capucine asked. "Let me get a shawl from inside."

They sat on the bench under the stars, neither saying a word until the silence was too heavy for Michel to bear. "Will you stay here forever, in New Orleans?"

She shook her head vehemently. "No. At some point—" Her words broke off, and then she started again. "At some point, I will find my mother, or at least my people."

"Your mother?"

Capucine stiffened, and she turned her face away from him. "I haven't told you, although I suspect you've already determined it, but I was born in Acadia. The British killed my father, and then they took Aliette and me and sent us to the convent in New York. I don't know what happened to my mother."

"Is she alive?"

"I—I don't know. I don't have any idea where anyone went, except for Aliette and myself."

He glanced at her. "Don't you know where they are? Your people, I mean?"

"No. I know that there are Acadians in this area. Have you heard of Bayou Teche?"

"Yes, of course."

"I often wonder if she is there." She bit her lip.

This was the chance for him to ask the question that had been eating at him. "You're an enigma, Capucine. You don't acknowledge in public that you are Acadian, yet your entire being is dedicated to your heritage. Why is that?"

"I can be who I want to be." Her voice was firm.

"That's true. But why deny being Acadian?"

She stood up suddenly. "I have never denied being Acadian. Never."

But you've never acknowledged it in public. In fact, she had never told him.

Still, there was pain here, pain and a deep unquenchable ache of questions left unanswered.

He touched her arm. "We are much alike, you and I. Acadians far away from our homes, but see how we've created our lives anew?"

For a moment she didn't speak. Then, in a voice so faint he couldn't be sure he'd heard it at first, she began to talk. "How do you do it? How do you go on with your life? Do you forget the lost ones? Do you forgive those who came in and ripped our families apart?"

"I pray. I pray and pray and pray. God has helped me heal. I can't imagine doing this without Him. Capucine, have you prayed?"

She made a small sound. "Pray. Oh, I've prayed, and do you see my mother? No. He listens to the prayers of the British, not the Acadians."

The desolation in her words gnawed into his soul. "He listens to all of us, no matter what our heritage."

"He hasn't listened to me."

"Perhaps you haven't listened to Him."

"Perhaps He needs to speak louder."

Michel laughed. "One day He might. One day He might."

"He will speak French, will he not?"

"Mais oui!"

She gripped his hand. "I do want to go Bayou Teche."

"What about Sister Marie-Agathe?"

"She is finding her calling here, tending to those who live in poverty and need. I am welcome to stay with her, yet she does not expect me to stay here forever."

"And Aliette? What about her?"

"She will come with me, of course."

"She wants to?"

Capucine shrugged. "She will come with me. I am her older sister. What else does she know? She cooks here; she goes to church. She barely knows the world."

Aliette's daily furtive rush to the Boncoeur House suddenly made sense. Capucine clearly didn't know that her sister was leaving the house every afternoon, and Aliette didn't seem as if she wanted her to know.

"Have you given any thought to the fact that she might want to live on her own, perhaps here in New Orleans?"

Capucine looked at him sharply. "No. She won't. Aliette doesn't leave the house if she can avoid it. Why would she want to be independent? She even has me run her errands for her."

"What would you do if she, oh, fell in love?"

Capucine hooted. "With whom? She doesn't even see the poultry man!"

Be careful, he warned himself. He had no proof, only the vaguest suggestion that something was happening with Aliette.

He quickly changed the subject. "Aliette is a cook, and you are a needlewoman. How did you start on that?"

Her eager smile told him that she was grateful for the switch in topics. "My mother started me, of course, but I owe my growth to Sister Marie-Agathe, who encouraged me to master the basics and then explore the possibilities."

"You've been very fortunate to have her."

"I know. When I needed her, she was there for me. You know, I have a vague memory after I was struck with the bale at the wharf. I was in my bed, and she was at my side, and she said the oddest thing. Or at least I think she did." Capucine frowned.

"What was it?"

"She said that she was doing what God wanted her to do, not just to feed and clothe and shelter me, but to love me. I find that unusual, don't you?"

He thought about it. "We are instructed to love one another."

"But it was what I needed. I wonder if we can force ourselves to love someone."

"What do you mean by that?" He leaned forward.

"The Bible tells us to love each other, but it doesn't tell us how to do that. We are human, after all. How do we make ourselves feel that way? I can't order you to love me."

The cover of darkness hid his flush. "If I were a lovable person, it would certainly be easier. You know, that may be why the Bible doesn't tell us to love *everybody*. It tells us to love *each other* so that there's a flow of emotion among all involved."

"The village of New Orleans could use less emotion right now," she said.

"It is all coming to a head, *ça, c'est vrai*," he answered, reverting to Acadian French.

She stood up. "No politics tonight, please. I want to have only the most pleasant of dreams."

"Yes. Politics does not make for a restful sleep, nor does sitting in the moonlight, no matter how lovely the companion."

He didn't want the evening to end, but if he was not going to fall asleep over his work at the boat shop in the morning, he'd have to get home.

They returned to the house, where Sister Marie-Agathe and Aliette sat reading by a lamp.

"May I see you again?" he asked as he opened the door.

"Yes," she said softly. "Yes."

Chapter 8

My treasure, my treasure. Have I lost my treasure?
And in doing so, have I lost my heart?

The plaza was filled with even more people. Madame Frenier, who held the tablecloth that Capucine had embroidered for her, looked around in growing apprehension.

"Capucine, are you not concerned?"

Capucine settled herself in her usual spot and took out her embroidery. "I am quite fine, I believe."

The older woman sat beside her. "Capucine, listen to me!" She scooted closer. "It's getting increasingly dangerous. I know that you think you are perfectly safe, but you are not. I hear murmurs of suspicion. 'What is she doing in the plaza every day?' 'Michel LeBlanc is a well-known oppositionist to the Spanish—why is she spending so much time with him?' 'What is her sister doing near the Corps de Garde?' "

"My sister? What is this about Aliette?"

"Aliette is seen every afternoon in that area. I do not know if that's her destination, just that she is—"

"Aliette? How can it be? She spends every afternoon in the kitchen. Why, she doesn't even leave to go to the market. . . ."

Her voice faded out as the blood froze in her veins. She had been so focused on her own mission that she had not been paying much attention to her younger sister. What had she been up to?

"Capucine, these are dangerous days," Madame Frenier said, tucking the tablecloth into her bag. "Be careful."

As she walked away, voices came from behind the shrubbery.

"The sixth. It is the sixth."

This was the fourth of September. She knew what this meant.

Capucine didn't even fold the fabric. She wadded it up, shoved it into her apron pocket, and quickly fled the Place d'Armes.

God, if You are still with me, I need You now. She hadn't prayed for so long that the words were wooden at first but then began to flow with intensity as she rushed to Boncoeur House. *This is beyond my control. Please, let it not be beyond Your control.*

She remembered how indignant Michel had been about the political situation, and she knew that he would be involved. He could be hurt, even killed!

I know what will happen. It is all told in my embroideries, and I have sewn my fate into each stitch. But I never, ever meant to hurt Michel. And I don't know what Aliette is doing, but please, please, spread Your protection over her.

She took a deep breath. *I cannot do this alone.*

She ran all the way to Boncoeur House, only to find Aliette happily singing in the kitchen. There was no way that she could have been all the way to the Corps de Garde and back and still have dinner well underway.

"Capucine, why are you so flushed? Come and sit in the garden where it's cooler." Sister Marie-Agathe led her to the back of the house. "Sit now, and tell me what is going on."

The entire story poured out of Capucine, like water from a jug, and soon she was wrapped in a lavender and soap scented embrace. "There, there," the nun soothed her. "We will put this in the Lord's hands. His reach far exceeds our own."

And then, as Sister Marie-Agathe rocked Capucine, she whispered in her ear, "But I will see to Aliette myself."

❦

Michel hummed to himself as he made sure his shirt was presentable. Tonight he intended to declare himself to Capucine.

Perhaps, if she was receptive, he might even ask her to marry him.

The thought elated him—and terrified him. A lifetime with Capucine would be one filled with laughter and excitement and energy. She would be a wonderful mother, involved with her children and encouraging them to strive to greater heights.

If only he knew how close her relationship was with the Lord. Her doubt was understandable—he certainly had known those reservations himself. He had a vague feeling that she really was a Christian, but an unwilling one.

That made him smile. Only Capucine would be in that position!

There was one unanswered question—did she love him?

On that matter, he could not be as sure.

He straightened his shirt one last time, ran his hand over his hair in case some strands had decided to go astray, and left the house to proclaim his heart.

❧

Aliette's *fricot* was magnificent, Capucine knew, but she could barely taste the Acadian stew, lush with chicken and vegetables and dumplings. Too much was on her mind tonight.

"Are you all right?" Sister Marie-Agathe asked Michel who, like Capucine, was only picking at his food.

Aliette's delicate forehead creased with worry. "Does it not taste good? Is something wrong with it?"

"No, no," Michel and Capucine chorused together.

Sister Marie-Agathe poked Aliette and nodded at them meaningfully. "This is not a time to worry about food, I think."

Aliette nodded knowingly and smiled.

Capucine could feel her neck reddening and pushed her chair back suddenly to hide her embarrassment. "Michel, let's go into the garden."

He wiped his mouth. "Yes, let's."

As soon as they were seated, he faced her. "I have something to discuss with you."

"And I with you." She was about to explode with nervousness.

"I must say this, Capucine." He took a deep breath and exhaled. "I love you."

She couldn't speak. This was what she had wanted to hear—and what she had dreaded to hear.

"Did you hear me?" he asked. "I said I love you."

"I heard." If her heart didn't stop beating so loudly, it would fly right out of her chest. "But I'm not what you think I am."

He shook his head. "Are you sure of that? Perhaps I know exactly who you are."

Tears stung at her eyes. "If you knew, you could not love me."

"There cannot be something so terrible that it would stop me from loving you."

"There is."

"Let me ask you one thing. Do you love me?"

If she lied, it would be easy to move on. Once again, the truth was the hardest. "Yes," she whispered.

"Then perhaps you should marry me."

"Marry you! Michel, I—" She leaned over and grasped his hand. "Michel, take me to Bayou Teche. Tonight. Or tomorrow."

"Bayou Teche? Whatever are you talking about? Is this about marrying?"

"I want to go there, as soon as possible," she said.

The intensity of her voice worried him. "What is wrong?"

"Take me, take all of us, out of New Orleans. Let's go to Bayou Teche, where we can be among people who are like us."

"Sister Marie-Agathe and Aliette?" he asked stupidly. "They want to go, too?"

"They will go. I can ensure that. Please, please, *je, je plaide*, I am pleading!"

He shook his hand free. "You are talking like a madwoman. If you truly want to leave New Orleans and go to Bayou Teche, then let's plan it by the daylight sun, not in the shadows of the night."

She didn't answer. A small sound in the darkness startled him. "Capucine, are you crying?"

She still did not respond, and a heavy sadness came over his heart, as if it were suddenly weighted down with stones. "Capucine," he whispered, "if you truly want to go to Bayou Teche, let's go in two weeks. Then it will be nearly the end of September, and Pierre will not need my help as much."

"I will find someone else, then, to take me."

"You don't have to. I will take you, but I can't leave—"

Her whispered response as she rose to leave was swallowed by the rustle of the weeping willow, but he thought she said, "Too late."

He sat in the garden of Boncoeur House alone and watched as she entered through the doorway and stood there, silhouetted against the golden glow of a lamp.

He loved her. With all his heart and soul, he loved her, and he'd heard in her voice the raw need to leave New Orleans.

If he did not take her, he would lose her. And that he could not bear.

❧

A young man, barely whiskered, ran into the boat shop. "Pierre

LeBlanc!" he called. "The day of infamy is at hand!"

Michel poked his head out from the back of the shop. "My cousin is not here. May I help you?"

The fellow leaned against a half-built boat as he struggled to catch his breath. "The sixth. The seventh. *Je ne sais quoi.* But the plan is for the Spanish to make a great show of power. They will march through the streets of New Orleans and make a proclamation."

"About what?"

"Trade. Antonio de Ulloa says it is for the good of the people, so that we are not charged so much for that which comes from France, but in the market, the anger grows. All I know is that the message is for all of us to be at the Place d'Armes, to show who we are!"

His stomach twisted, but even as it did, he knew that he would be there. He also understood why Capucine wanted to leave New Orleans so desperately.

He returned to the back of the shop. There was much work to be done.

Chapter 9

Often what we've been waiting for has simply been waiting for us.

The September day was clear and warm early on. Pierre hung a sign on the boat shop door, announcing that it was closed. Then he and Michel walked to the Place d'Armes.

A crowd had already gathered. The sound of a drum, its steady beat like the thud of men's pulses in their ears, broke through the morning. The crowd grew silent as a line of soldiers, bayonets in their hands, followed the drummer. On they walked, through the streets of the village, many of the townspeople following them.

Voices rose again. Protests and arguments filled every inch of the plaza.

Michel saw a familiar face beside the church.

"Go," Pierre said, motioning to her. "Your heart is over there."

He crossed the plaza to where she stood. "Capucine, this is what you feared, am I right?" he asked her straight out.

"Yes. I knew—"

He put a finger across her lips. "There are ears everywhere. But I don't think we are in such danger after all. There will not be an open revolt, not today."

She sagged in relief.

"Do you still want to go to Bayou Teche?"

"Yes, of course. I love New Orleans, but I want to be with Acadians again. I've lived this duplicitous life too long. And perhaps I can find my mother."

"I will be bold here. You said you loved me. Is that true?"

"It is."

"I have arranged for us to go to Bayou Teche in four days. Capucine, we—we are in front of a church. Inside is a priest. We could be married, now, today, here."

She stepped into his arms. Her voice, muffled against his neck, said only, "Yes."

❧

Capucine stood outside the church. She had gone inside as Capucine Louet and had come out as Capucine LeBlanc. This man at her side was her husband, and soon she would be on her way to live, once again, in an Acadian settlement.

How quickly life could change!

Soon they were in his cottage. "Look," he said, "I've set this up for us. A chair for you by the fireplace, and one for me. We won't be here long, but we will be comfortable."

The sweet gesture took her heart by surprise.

Then he gripped both of her hands in his.

"I will tell you again," he said, his voice cracking with emotion, "as I did before God in the chapel, that I love you with all of my being, and if I cannot have your love, I will accept your happiness."

"We are so different," she whispered, blinking back the tears that stung her eyes. "You are so noble, so kind, so honest, and I am. . .not."

"Dearest Capucine, you slight yourself."

"No, I am a deceiver. You don't know." Shame washed over her in a hot flood. She did not deserve this wonderful man.

"You deceive yourself."

She shook her head furiously. "I have been lying to so many people. The embroideries are—"

"Maps. Yes, I know this."

"You do? How?"

"Pierre noticed it first. The curve of the egret was the same as the river, and the green and blue stitches were encampments of British discontents. Am I right?"

She sank to the small chair by the fireplace. "You're right."

"It's time to stop." His words were gentle.

"I see that." She could barely speak. "My work is over. It's no longer as concealed as it was, and that's dangerous. I don't want to hurt. . .anyone."

"It's also time to stop hating." He pulled his chair up beside hers. "Let the wounds heal."

"The only thing that can heal me is Bayou Teche."

"No. The only thing that can heal you is in yourself. Capucine, let God help. Allow His healing touch—"

"I can't. When the British killed my father, when they tore Aliette and me away from our mother, God wasn't there."

"He was."

Tears streamed down her face. "How would you know?" she lashed at him. "It's not like—"

He put one finger over her lips. "I was there. Remember, I'm Acadian, too. That's how I ended up with Pierre."

"You were—" In all this time she'd known him, she'd never asked how he'd come to live in New Orleans, questioned why he hadn't mentioned parents or brothers or sisters, had no stories about where he'd lived before.

"Yes, my family was ripped apart, too."

"And you don't hate them?"

He shook his head. "I can't. I did for a while, but I can't any longer. I hate what they did, but I can't hold onto that hate for them. It's like a vicious animal that snaps and eats at your soul until nothing is left but shreds."

She thought again of the picture of Jesus, His arms open and inviting. "It's not that easy."

He wrapped her in his arms and murmured into her hair, which had once again escaped its moorings, "It is that easy. It is just that easy."

❧

"Thank you for everything," Michel told his cousin. "Are you sure you don't want to join us?"

Pierre shook his head. "No. My place is here, in New Orleans, building boats. But I will come visit you, once I find someone who will be as strong a partner as you were."

They clapped each other on the back and then embraced. "Au revoir." The words stuck in Michel's throat.

He walked slowly back to the cottage. He would miss his cousin. Pierre had been his entire family for a long time.

His little cottage had been emptied. The packets were in the yard, ready to be loaded, and words, strident and furious, echoed from the open windows.

"Traitor! You are no better than the men who killed our father!" Capucine's voice was strained and angry.

"Don't say that!" Aliette's teary response was faint. "Please don't say that."

"It's true. How can you call yourself Acadian? How can you expect me to take this monster into my home? Will he be welcome in Bayou Teche? Think about it, Aliette! Think!"

A man spoke, but his voice was too low for Michel to make out his words.

Capucine burst from the house, her hair sprung free from the bun. It stood out in a wide black spray, and she looked like a madwoman. "Get away from me!"

Aliette, followed, begging, "Please listen to me! You know what it's like to be in love."

"Love? Don't talk to me about love! You don't know what it means."

"I do, too. Capucine, listen!"

Michel felt like he was watching the scene from a distance.

What on earth could have caused such a rift between the sisters?

The answer walked out the door of his house. A man strode to stand beside Aliette, his arm around her shoulders.

"Get him out of here!" Capucine's voice had dropped from a scream to an even deadlier stage whisper.

"Capucine!" The venom in her voice terrified him, and he ran to her side. "Capucine, what is the meaning of this?"

"This man, this beast, has married my sister! This is what she was doing each afternoon, sneaking out to see this man! Not only that, she is his wife!"

"Aliette?" He turned to her in confusion.

"This is John Powers, Michel. We were married three days ago." She smiled at her new husband and then back at Michel. "It's all right. He speaks French, too."

The realization of what had happened dawned on him. "He's British. That's what it is. Am I right? He's British."

Capucine stood beside him, hands on her hips, glaring at the newcomer. "Not only that, he's the son of an officer!"

If Aliette had married the king of England himself, it couldn't have been worse.

He put his hand on Capucine's elbow. "Aliette, Mr. Powers, I think Capucine and I need some time alone."

"Good," Capucine said. "Get him out of here."

There was one table left inside the cottage, and he drew their chairs up to it.

"Capucine, if you refuse to see your sister because of him, then you have lost."

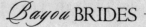

"Lost?"

"You will have lost her to the British, too."

"Then she must have the marriage annulled." She sat back in the chair, her lips in a tight line.

"No. When you were a child, the troops came in and tore your family apart. You had no choice in the matter. You were a scared little girl who did the best she could, am I right?"

She nodded as a single tear traced its way down her cheek.

"Now, if you make Aliette decide between Mr. Powers and yourself, you will lose again. Either way, you lose her. If she chooses him, she is gone. If she chooses you, that will be a stake in your closeness that might never heal."

"He's *British*, Michel."

"He's British, but he could just as easily have been Spanish. Or German. Or Chinese. I think they love each other." He touched her hand. "And she loves you. Walk in the way of the angels, Capucine. Choose love."

"They want to come with us," she said.

"Then they shall. And we will welcome them, will we not?" She managed a faint, watery smile. "We will try."

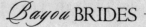

The sun set with a glorious radiance. "Our last night here," Capucine said, cradling a cup of tea in her hands. "Are you sad?"

"I must admit that I am, a bit," Michel answered reflectively. "I'll miss Pierre, of course."

They sat in front of the small cottage, watching the colors

shift across the sky from luminous pink to glowing orange to vibrant scarlet.

She reached across and covered his hand with her own. "I know. Sister Marie-Agathe has been with me for many years, and I can't imagine life without her. But she's going back to the life she knows, in the convent. I know it's for the best, but still, I will miss her dreadfully."

"She leaves, though, knowing that her girls are happily married and returning to their heritage." He looked at her. "You are happy, aren't you? Or you will be when you get to Bayou Teche."

Capucine sat the tea down on the ground beside her and faced her husband. "Michel, I love you. With all my heart, and with all my soul, I belong with you. I love you."

The final slants of light caught the tears in his eyes. "Capucine, dearest Capucine, my own Capucine. . ."

The wagon creaked over trails and through soggy areas that Capucine was sure teemed with wildlife that she didn't want to see. Some she did see: snakes that slithered past with silent intent, frogs that jumped out of nowhere and disappeared as quickly, birds that cawed overhead.

John Powers was, amazingly, a nice fellow. He gladly spoke French with them and had quite a store of tales to share with them of life in Florida, where he'd grown up. As they traveled together, she came to realize that once a nameless hate has an identity, it will either explode or it will die out. In this case, it changed into an appreciation of the man who was sharing her sister's life.

Love, she discovered, was indeed stronger than hate. Her love for her sister far outweighed any hatred she might retain for the British. And, even more oddly, once she let that go, the remainder dissolved.

"You're writing in your journal again," Michel said to her as he looked over her shoulder. "More patterns?"

She laughed. "Any new patterns that go in there will truly be just that—patterns. There'll be nothing secretive or furtive about them at all."

"Will you miss it?"

"I'll have other things to keep myself busy," she answered. "Starting our new life together, for one thing."

He planted a kiss on the back of her neck. "Are you ready to meet your new home? Bayou Teche is just ahead."

Bayou Teche. After all this time, she was going to Bayou Teche!

She moved to the front of the wagon and leaned as far forward as possible to watch for her new home.

Suddenly, she was there. The wagon was surrounded by people. The distinctive Acadian accents filled her ears, and welcoming hands offered to help her down.

Capucine stood on the lush green expanse, her fingers laced with Michel's. Behind her, Aliette stood with her husband. "We're home," she whispered.

A woman broke through the crowd and dropped to the ground at their feet. Her face was familiar—Capucine had seen it a million times in her dreams.

"Mama!"

"Capucine! Aliette!"

The tears of the reunited women joined together. "It's been so long," Capucine murmured through the tears.

"I was almost afraid to hope," her mother said as she hugged her daughters to her, "but I never quit. God was watching over us, all of us."

Capucine touched the small cross around her mother's neck as a wave of memories swept over her.

"Do you remember it?" Mama asked gently. "I was wearing it that terrible day we were separated, and I've never taken it off since."

She kissed the forehead of each daughter and sighed. "I thought I'd lost everything—my husband, my daughters, my home—but I knew I could not lose God. He would be with me, no matter where I went, and He would be with you, no matter where you went."

The ice surrounding Capucine's heart fell away. All these years, God had been with her. She'd known that, and no matter how she'd pushed Him away, He'd never left.

The arms of His Son were open, as they'd always been, and she walked into them, into the peace of trust and certain faith.

"I never gave up on God," Mama whispered.

"And He never gave up on us," Capucine added. "Never."

She held out her hand to Michel and breathed a wordless prayer of thanks. Love was triumphant, and she was home.

Epilogue

I have found my treasure, my heart. And all along, God has not only been watching over me, He has been leading me by the hand. I am so happy!

The cabin seemed to burst with life. Laughter and song filled every corner. But the baby slept on.

"She's beautiful," Michel said. "As beautiful as her mother."

A tall figure swooped toward them. "May I hold her?"

"Sister Marie-Agathe," Capucine said, laughing as she handed her daughter to the nun, "you're going to spoil her."

"This is a special day for a baby," Sister Marie-Agathe said as she nuzzled the baby. "Her christening day! Comforte Acadie LeBlanc, we are delighted to have you with us."

"I'm so glad Sister Marie-Agathe was able to come and be with us for Comforte's christening," Capucine said as the nun carried Comforte into the sunlight where Aliette and her husband, John, and Mama were sitting. "It makes the day complete.

I'm going to write this all in my diary, so that even when I am old and Comforte is grown, I can relive these moments." She leaned against Michel's shoulder. "I would never have thought that it would be possible to be this happy."

"God has blessed us, indeed," he said, kissing the top of her head.

" 'For where your treasure is, there will your heart be also,' " she said softly. "I have found my treasure, and my heart."

JANET SPAETH

For as long as she can remember, Janet Spaeth has loved to read, and romances were always a favorite. Today she is delighted to be able to write romances based upon the greatest Love Story of all, that of our Lord for us. Janet has published three books—*Candy Cane Calaboose*, *Angel's Roost*, and *Rose Kelly*—with Heartsong Presents. She has also written numerous novellas—"Only Believe" in *Harvest Home*; "Christmas Cake" in *Christmas Threads*; "Marry for Love" in *Scraps of Love*; "This Prairie" in *Attic Treasures*; "Joyful Noise" in *The Bachelor Club*; "Dreamlight" in *Mackinac Island*; and "Capucine: Home to My Heart" in *Bayou Brides*—all Barbour anthologies. When she isn't writing, Janet spends her time reading a romance or a cozy mystery, baking chocolate chip cookies, or spending precious hours with her family.

Joie de Vivre

by Lynette Sowell

Chapter 1

La Manque, Louisiana—July 1819

H
urry!" Jacques LeBlanc shouted over his shoulder. "We'll be late!"

"If Papa LeBlanc is angry, it'll be your fault." Josée Broussard held her skirt high enough with one hand to keep from tripping on the hem. "You're the one. . .who let Philippe. . .fall into the bayou."

She gasped for breath. Little Philippe bounced on her hip while she trotted along the path through the tall grass. The boy was too small to keep up with their hurried pace, yet heavier than a sack of flour. Josée tried not to think he might not settle down to sleep tonight after Jacques telling him the legend of the great snake of Bayou Teche.

Jacques paused and faced her. He grabbed her hand, and the touch made her stomach turn like the curving dark waters behind them. *Jacques has been my friend for so long, why should his hand make me feel. . . ?* Josée's skirt swirled down around her ankles.

He smiled and his black eyes sparkled with a secret. "Ma'amselle Josée, it's your birthday, and Papa will be in a good mood. *Bon temps* tonight!"

She tried to smile but bit her lip instead. Couldn't Jacques carry his younger brother?

Prickly heat surrounded them like a heavy blanket. Josée longed for the cool bayou, thick with moist air, but cooler than where the larger LeBlanc house stood, farther away from the banks of Bayou Teche. Papa had turned from the bayou to farming.

Philippe wriggled from her hip and ran. *Not through the garden!* Jeanne and Marie scolded him where they stood by the house, their arms reminding Josée of flapping hens' wings. She waved at them.

"Happy birthday, Josée!" they called.

"Merci. I'm sorry Philippe ran through your garden."

Jeanne, six months older than Josée, ruffled her littlest brother's hair. "Why so wet, then?"

"He thought he was a fish," Jacques said. The sisters both laughed, then fell silent and stared at Josée's and Jacques's hands clasped together.

Josée pulled free and wiped her palm on her skirt. "It's hot today."

"Oui, and you're brown already, just from being down by the water." Jeanne linked arms with Josée. "We must get you ready for the party tonight. I think Mama has a surprise for you."

"Wait for me." Marie followed behind.

"How does it feel, being eighteen?" Jeanne leaned closer. "Now you've caught up with me."

"Eighteen's not much differen' from seventeen."

"Ah, t'is different. When you're eighteen, you're a woman. As soon as I turned eighteen, Josef Landry asked Papa for permission to marry me." Jeanne sighed. "He already has a small farm next to his papa's. Then once his house is built. . ." She sighed again.

Josée laughed. "I can guarantee you that no one will be asking your papa's permission to marry me."

They entered the LeBlanc farmhouse, and the three girls climbed the ladder to the loft where they shared half of the space with the boys. A curtain divided the long loft in two.

Mama LeBlanc, the only mother Josée had ever known, had hung a new dress where they could see it. Mama turned as the girls entered the loft. "Beautiful, *n'est-ce pas?*"

"Yes, it's very beautiful." Josée wanted to cry. She held scant memories of her own parents. The fact that the LeBlancs accepted her as one of their own comforted her, yet the same fact reminded her that they had taken her in when she had no one.

"Merci, Mama." She hugged the short, stout woman who stood beside the dress.

Mama LeBlanc returned the hug, then held Josée at arm's length. "Your papa LeBlanc has another su'prise for you tonight."

"I wonder if he's found a man for you, Josée!" Jeanne started brushing her own black tresses. Marie, sixteen, giggled and flopped onto the mattress so hard that a tuft of Spanish moss stuck out the side.

Josée touched the soft cotton frock and almost shuddered. Marriage? A man? Yet if she were to marry anyone, it would probably be Jacques. At least he would make her laugh and listen to the songs she made up. But she, Josée Broussard, orphan, had nothing to offer a man. "I couldn't imagine."

❧

All afternoon, Edouard LeBlanc had endured the squeals and laughter that disrupted the tranquility of his secluded LeBlanc bayou cabin. If he hadn't caught enough fish for the day already, he'd have sent the brood back to the big house. To him, violating the quiet of the bayou was sacrilege.

Edouard stared up at the canopy of cypress trees that blocked most of the late afternoon heat. He had time to shave before the party. No sense in hurrying. If it wasn't that Papa had requested—no, demanded—his presence, Edouard would be content to lie in his hammock and watch the fish jump from the bayou tonight. Or maybe not. A wayward mosquito found Edouard's arm, and the sting spurred him to leave the hammock and enter the cabin.

Today Josée Broussard turned eighteen years old. All grown up and always with a song on her lips and spring in her step, Josée's ways needled him like pesky mosquitoes. Not that he'd been close enough to feel any bites. Listening and watching her from a distance was enough.

Edouard prepared his shaving mixture and propped up the chunk of mirror, a remnant from an old looking glass. Careful of the long scar running from under his ear to the end of his chin, he used the long shaving blade to remove his scruff of beard.

The scar made its appearance on his face. He would dare anyone to stare at him tonight, like Celine had done on his return from the war. Believing in a cause and following its course had made him follow Jean Lafitte to New Orleans five years before. If he had known his actions would cost him his only true love, he would have planted himself along the Bayou Teche and never have departed from La Manque.

Satisfied he'd removed enough of the beard, Edouard put the glass away. After sunset, maybe the light of the bonfire and lanterns would give enough shadows to cover most of the scar. He found his comb and pulled it through his wet hair, then secured the length in the back with a leather thong.

Edouard limped to the bureau at the other end of the cabin and took out a clean but rumpled shirt. He could endure the fiddle music and the songs, so long as he didn't have to dance. Storms approached. His bad leg told him so.

Out of respect for Papa and because of Josée's birthday, Edouard resolved to go to the party and stay no longer than necessary. Then he could retreat to the cabin and try to forget the life that swirled around him persistently and tried to draw him in.

❧

Josée's sides ached from laughter. She smoothed the skirt of

her new dress and gave Mama LeBlanc another smile of gratitude. Jeanne had helped her put her hair up on her head, and
she felt as fancy as any lady over in Lafayette. Merry fiddle
music matched the bonfire's roar, and Josée tapped her bare
feet to the beat of the drum played by one of the village boys.

Then she saw *him* at the edges of the crowd. A tall man with
eyes as black as the murky bayou water at midnight. Jacques's
brother, Edouard, the eldest of the LeBlanc clan.

"Looks like my brother made it to the party," Jacques murmured into her ear.

"I. . .I'm glad." Although, Josée wasn't sure how she felt.
Dark. Brooding. His eyes spoke of a soul deeper than the waters
that flowed through La Manque. She wondered if he ever
laughed. The only time she ever saw him was when she and the
other LeBlanc children would go to the bayou to fish and play
by the water. If the children grew loud, Edouard would hop into
his pirogue and drift away.

Whenever Josée would ask Jeanne or Marie if they should
be quieter, one of them might say, "Ah, pah. It's just Edouard
sticking his head from his shell like a *tortue*."

Tonight she could feel his gaze on her when Jacques gave
her a bottle of ink as a gift, and when Jeanne and Marie gave
her their present, a writing pen. Where had they found such
treasures?

Josée was, as they called her, "the smart one" and could read
and write. Perhaps the LeBlanc children admired her, even if
they did not grasp the use of such activities. Tonight when
she met Edouard's gaze, she couldn't tell how he regarded her.

A'bien, she wouldn't let his opinion bother her. She stuck her chin out and tried to stand like a lady.

❧

"My son, my eldest." Papa clapped him on the back. His voice boomed loud enough to be heard over the crowd's chatter. "You honored your papa and your family by comin' tonight."

"I could do no less." Edouard knew he should have left after the dances began. Yet the sight of Josée, her hair up, and flitting like a bird around the bonfire, her arms linked with his sisters', had made him stay. Several times he caught her stare at him. Did she see the scar, or was she watching his limp? He dared her to say something.

Here she was now, arm and arm with Mama LeBlanc, so close he could see the skin peeling from her sunburned nose. Her hair glowed almost blue black in the firelight. He wondered if she looked like her *mère* who had borne her. She gave him an uncertain smile.

Then Papa bellowed again, "*Mes amis* de La Manque, tonight we celebrate! Josée Broussard, raised as my daughter since she was but six, is now eighteen years old!" He gave a great laugh. His belly shook and the buttons on his vest threatened to pop. A few whoops and hollers and cheers rose up from the merry group.

Josée's already bronze skin glowed with a deeper blush that crept to her neck, which curved gracefully to her shoulders. Edouard's throat felt like he'd put on a tie tonight, except he had not.

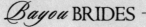

After the cheers gave way to silence, Papa continued. "Tonight, I have a special su'prise for Josée an' another member of my family."

Edouard saw Josée dart a glance at Jacques, who jerked his head in their direction. Then he watched Josée's gaze shift to him, and he saw her eyes dawn with a sudden, horrible recognition.

"As is the custom of our people," Papa shouted gleefully, "I announce the betrothal of Josée Monique Broussard to my eldest son—Edouard Philippe LeBlanc!"

Chapter 2

Like the tears coming from Josée's eyes, rain fell on the LeBlanc's farmhouse roof. The crowd had celebrated until late, but Josée found it hard to sleep after the family settled to bed for the night. Snores from various areas of the attic told her the LeBlanc siblings rested with as much vigor as they'd rejoiced at her betrothal to Edouard.

In two weeks, the priest would meet them at the village common house. He would marry and bury, then move on and leave them until his next passage through.

Mon Père, I do not understand Your plan. Josée rolled onto her back and looked up into the darkness, as if to see through the ceiling above her and up to heaven. *My mama—my real mère— always said You work Your will in our lives. How can this be Your will, if I'm not happy? Edouard is moody and dark. Jacques is—*

Everything Edouard was not. Josée sighed. She should accept what Mama and Papa LeBlanc had decided for her— for *them*, she corrected herself. After all, her world wasn't the only world that had been disrupted. Edouard looked as if

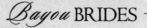

he'd been sentenced to hang.

She couldn't picture any other unmarried man in the village being happy at the prospect of marrying an orphan without a dowry. She had nothing except herself to bring to the marriage. Josée shivered and pictured lonely years ahead.

Forgive me, Mon Père. I should be thankful You are providing for me for the rest of my life. Yet like a snake from the dark waters not far away, fear slithered around her heart. What if Edouard was a cruel man?

Josée flung back the quilt and tried not to disturb Jeanne who slept next to her. *She* was destined to marry someone she cared for, and he for her. Tonight the soft mattress that smelled of moss did not comfort Josée. Her feet found the cool plank floor. Perhaps a cup of coffee, reheated on the coals, might do her good. She descended the loft's ladder and entered the kitchen.

Mama LeBlanc stood at the table in the warm glow of lamplight.

"Mama?"

A wooden trunk lay open before Mama LeBlanc. "I thought you might be down, chere."

"I couldn't sleep." She hoped Mama did not see the traces of tears on her face. "What's this?"

"Some things from your family. Look." Mama patted a yellowed paper wrapper.

Josée pulled the paper away to find an old dress that pricked at the edges of her memory and hurt a little. Her real mère's dress. A lump swelled in her throat. "Oh. It's beautiful. I'd almost forgotten."

"We'll have jus' enough time for you to try it on and see if I need to sew the hem." Mama's rough fingers smoothed the lace. "Your mère would be proud to see you wear her dress. There's more in here for you. You may take this trunk when you move to your new home."

Josée's heart beat faster, and she nodded. A new home. With Edouard.

"The coffee should be ready. Would you like a cup?" Though her surroundings remained the same, for the first time Josée felt as if she'd changed merely by reaching her eighteenth birthday.

"Of course." Josée settled onto one of the wooden benches, as if she were one of the local village women, visiting Mama for a cup of coffee and a talk.

Mama LeBlanc placed two mugs of coffee between them and rested her ample form on the bench across from Josée. "Marriage brings lots of changes."

One sip of the dark brew made Josée sit up straighter. "Oui, I am sure." She clutched the mug with both hands.

"Edouard is a good man. A hurt man, a disappointed man, but a good man." The older woman exhaled deeply, as if unburdening herself. "I know, deep down in his heart, Edouard understands le bon Dieu carries his troubles and cares for him. But—"

"Then why couldn't I marry. . ." Josée made herself stop. She had no right to question the LeBlancs' choice of husband for her. She had grown up with the knowledge that one day she'd likely marry one of the older LeBlanc brothers.

"Why not Jacques?" Mama patted Josée's hand. "Jacques is

too young. He is impulsive. He would keep you laughing, oui. However, he cares more for himself than anyone else. He is a *pourri*, a spoiled young man. I am to blame, and his papa."

"I care for Jacques, and I think he cares for me, too." Josée's dismay at the words she spoke aloud caused her to touch her hot cheek.

"Ah, but is his affection the kind of carin' that would last? *Chéri*, I love my son, but Jacques is too young to marry and shoulder such responsibility. For when marriage comes, then come *bébés*."

Bébés. Josée's mind spun like a top. She could scarcely breathe. If only she could have stayed seventeen forever.

Edouard let the July sun soak into his bare shoulders. He spread more pitch on the cabin's roof. In spite of his anger at his father's decision, he wouldn't dream of causing his family—or the innocent Josée—any dishonor. So he must prepare the cabin and make it fit for a young bride. A woman around would be like having a hen loose in the cabin all the time.

"You don't want to marry her, do you?" Jacques scuttled across the roof like a crab and squatted next to him. "Wish I was older."

"Not her, not anyone." Edouard spoke the words truthfully enough. Heat radiated from the tar paper and roofing. Jacques was delaying their job by his talk. Edouard wanted nothing more than to be done.

"Not even Celine Hebert?"

"Celine Hebert forgot me and married another four years ago." Edouard clenched his jaw. Jacques's words irritated him more than the sweat trickling a path down his back.

The anguish over his lost love that had once torn his heart had dulled to a dismal memory, but Edouard still hadn't the inclination to seek anyone else as a wife.

"You haven't forgotten her."

"I don't love Celine, if that's what you mean. What's done is done." Marrying Josée without any thoughts of love would be best.

"Yet you'll marry someone you don't care for to please Papa." Jacques shook his head and picked up a hammer.

"For honor's sake I marry Josée Broussard. She has no feelings for me, so we begin the marriage even." Edouard recalled her dark-eyed expression the other evening at the party, as if she were trying to see inside him. He wasn't sure he welcomed her curiosity. But at least she didn't flinch from the sight of his scar. Aloud, he continued, "And perhaps over time she will forget what feelings she *thinks* she has for you."

Jacques shrugged. "I should have never told you what I heard her say the other night, the night of Papa's announcement and the big storm. Like I said, if I were older—"

Edouard's gut twisted and he glared at Jacques. "Once Josée and I are wed, you'll not come around and cause trouble. I'm marryin' her. You are not. And I noticed you speakin' with several young ladies at the party. I will be faithful to Josée—Mon Dieu requires no less."

"As you try to forget your lost love Celine!"

Enough! Edouard shoved Jacques and sent him hurtling over the edge of the cabin's roof. The young man whimpered like a pup on the ground. Edouard sprang from the roof. He managed to land on his feet, his hands curled into fists. How dare Jacques accuse him of harboring love for Celine?

Jacques leaped to his feet and doubled over. He used his shoulder to ram into Edouard's midsection. Edouard let the motion carry him backwards and onto the grass. He flipped Jacques over his head, then whirled to pin his brother down.

"I. . .don't. . .love her. Now you see why I wish to be left alone!" Edouard ground out the words. He held Jacques by the shoulders.

A sudden shadow blocked the light. Edouard glanced up to see Josée standing over them. The summer wind teased her hair, and she clutched a basket over one hip. A tendril of blue black hair, glossy as ink, wafted across her full lips.

Josée's capable hand moved the offending wisp out of the way. "I. . .Mama sent me with lunch. You both must be hungry and thirsty." A blush swept down her neck. She averted her gaze from their shirtless figures and looked at the cabin instead.

Edouard remembered where he was and released Jacques. He grabbed his nearby shirt and gestured for Jacques to do the same. "Jacques and I are done workin' on the roof for today. I can finish the rest on my own. Thank you—and thank Mama—for lunch."

Jacques, who took longer putting on his shirt than usual, busied himself with the contents of the basket. Josée ambled around to the entrance of the cabin that faced the bayou.

Edouard wanted to stop her. He hadn't finished making the place habitable for a lady.

Which is exactly how Josée carried herself. He tucked his shirt into his trousers and caught up with Josée. "The cabin ain't very big. Two rooms. I have a good fireplace that is easy to cook over and makes good fires. I keep some things cool in the bayou water." He found himself in a struggle for words. He did not understand the effect this young woman had on his speech. She could see this for herself.

Yet she paused on the tiny porch and turned to face him and the bayou. "I—I wanted to see the view. If it's not ready, I won't go inside. Not yet." Then came another blush.

Edouard felt unspeakable relief. "Mornings are best here. Early, you can see the sun risin' up over the cypress trees and hear the birds calling. The pelicans feed and you fight 'em for a catch of fish."

"It's very peaceful here," Josée said. She looked as though she was being fitted for the hangman's noose.

He knew she could read and write. Maybe Josée would be better off in a place like Lafayette, where she could be a nanny or a governess or work for a rich Creole family. If the prospect of marriage seemed as undesirable to her as to him, now would be a good time for them to talk. Maybe it would be better if they didn't marry after all.

"Josée, I didn't know my papa had planned this for us."

"I know. You looked as surprised as I imagine I did." Josée leaned on the porch railing. "Remember, like Papa said, it's the custom of our people."

"We don't have to follow the custom, not if both of us don't wish to." Edouard felt a pang at the clouded expression that crossed Josée's face at his words. "It wouldn't be the first time I went agin'st my papa's wishes."

"What about the plans of our bon Dieu? Could He be plannin' this for us?" Josée faced him again, her arms crossed across her body. "And when you went to war, it cost you greatly to go against Papa LeBlanc's wishes."

"Our bon Dieu." Edouard ground out the words. "He let me be scarred. He let my one love marry another. He left me with a bad leg. What is good about such things?"

Before Edouard could undo his hasty speech, another voice intruded. "Bonjour, young Edouard! We bring a gift from the Landrys, a new bed for you and your bride!"

Jean Landry and two of his sons came around the edge of the cabin. They carried a bed frame wrought from cypress wood, sturdy enough to last generations.

Edouard saw Josée glance at the bed before she fled toward the main house. First the fight with Jacques, then his words with Josée, and now a marriage bed, paraded down the path to his cabin.

Chapter 3

For the next week, Josée purposed in her heart not to speak of the conversation she had shared with Edouard on the cabin's porch. He didn't want her. Worse, he seemed angry at God, his anger like a festering wound that would not heal.

The families of La Manque had sent gifts along with gentle teasing, and others teased not-so-gently about the upcoming union. Josée tried to smile and give her thanks. Already she had several bolts of cloth as well as pots and pans. Edouard had already cleared a small patch of land by the cabin so she could plant a late-summer garden. The tilled land waited for her after it had lain dormant for years.

Now, Josée perched on a footstool in the center of the kitchen while Mama altered the hem of her mother's old dress.

"You will soon call the LeBlanc family cabin home, chere." Mama LeBlanc took up another section of the hem. "The first LeBlanc settler, Michel, came here after Le Grand Dérangement and built the cabin for his young bride, Capucine.

Oui, the LeBlancs have much more now than then. But my Nicolas keeps the cabin to remind us of how good our God has been to us. And now our joy spills over, knowing that you and Edouard will start your lives together there."

The heat was unbearable, the prickly kind that made Josée want to run for the cool bayou, shed her garments to her pantaloons, and dive in. Marriage. In seven days, the priest would pass through La Manque and change their lives forever.

Anger that rivaled the summer heat rose within Josée. "Mama, I do not think Edouard wants to marry me. He. . ." She struggled to find the words. On that day when the Landrys brought the bed, at first Edouard seemed proud of his cabin, as if he wanted her to like it. Then he changed, as if he believed she didn't belong there and wanted to convince her of that, too.

"Edouard has spoken to his papa." Mama seemed to consider her words carefully. "He somehow thinks that you are too good for this place, and for him."

"Why? La Manque has always been my home." Josée sighed.

"You can read. You can write. You speak like one who has been to school."

"I know that my mère would want me to study. So I have, borrowing books and helping Jeanne, Marie and the others. Books aren't much use to them, though."

"Edouard is searching for reasons which do not exist. His papa has persuaded him that marriage is for the best." Mama LeBlanc patted Josée's shoulder. "There. You can put your other dress on. This one will be fine for the wedding. Perhaps

110

you can find Edouard and bring him a piece of that pie you made for supper last night."

Josée's pulse thudded in her ears. "I don't think pie will convince Edouard."

"Go. Speak to him. I have been married many years and I know this: Good conversation and a slice of pie cure many things."

Minutes later, Josée headed toward the bayou cabin. She clutched a plate of pie covered with a cloth napkin. She felt as if the *teche* waited, coiled and ready to strike, as she approached the cabin. When she rounded the corner, she saw Edouard stretched out in his hammock, his eyes closed. *So the teche sleeps.*

Josée cleared her throat. "*Pardon*, I brought you some pie."

Edouard opened his eyes and sat bolt upright, as if embarrassed to be caught lounging. "Merci."

She could not gauge his expression. He took the plate from her hands, and Josée watched him taste the pie. She tried not to grip the edges of her apron. She wanted him to say something. Why wouldn't he? Should she speak first? An inner nudge suggested she sit on the porch step. And so she did, though keeping silent about the pie and the more urgent matter of the wedding nearly smothered her.

"The pie's good. You made it?" came Edouard's voice. He settled onto the step next to her and took another bite.

"Oui. Mama said I should share it with you, and she said that you talked to your papa." Josée watched the bayou drift silently by. She took a deep breath and let the dark green canopy of trees calm her.

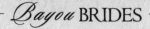

Mon Père, help me. I want whatever You have for us, Edouard and me. Help him see it, too. She heard a bird's call far away through the trees.

He finished the pie, acted as if he were going to lick the plate, and then stopped. Josée would have chuckled if Edouard's silence hadn't made her want to drag conversation out of the man.

"I. . .my papa says I am much like his papa, who built this cabin." Edouard gazed out at the dark water. "He lost many things. His home in Acadia. My papa's mama, Capucine—she, too, knew loss."

Josée watched his hands. He placed the plate on the top step behind them, then rested his chin on folded fingers.

"Jacques, he is like Papa, so full of *joie de vivre*." Edouard turned to face Josée, and she could scarcely breathe. She had never been within arm's length of the man, and now he seemed to loom over her, although he was sitting on the top step. "I think more than I speak. But you would not miss such liveliness here? My life is simple."

"It's—it's peaceful here." Josée realized she was studying the scar on Edouard's face, dulled by stubble. "And I would not miss Jacques's liveliness so much. When we marry, I will not think of him again." She shifted her gaze to his eyes. Their brown depths almost begged her to explore the secrets inside.

❦

I haven't wanted to kiss anyone since—

Edouard wished that he no longer thought of Celine but

of the young woman who had willingly come and offered him part of herself with a simple piece of pie. He had sensed Josée's urgency to speak and gave her credit for her silence. Her mouth opened and closed like a fish several times while he ate the pie.

Now while she waited, her mouth, well, it practically begged for a kiss. Thoughts of fish left his mind.

He stood and tried to keep his wits about him. This was Josée Broussard, who tutored his younger siblings and had somehow grown up when he wasn't looking. And soon she would become his wife.

"Josée." Edouard bent, took one of her hands in his, and pulled her to her feet. "My papa has arranged for us to marry. I doubted his choice at first, but then I do not trust easily. I cannot promise you much. I have little. But"—he gestured to the cabin behind them—"the cabin is snug and the bayou is good to me. I will provide for you and you will lack nothing."

Her fingers tightened around his hand. "Edouard, I know you will. While you may not, as you say, have the joie de vivre of your papa, you work hard. And I promise you I shall be true to the vows we make before *notre* Dieu. I can do no less. I will be a good wife to you."

At that, Edouard raised the hand he held to his lips and sealed their agreement with a kiss.

❧

Josée carried the memory of Edouard's chaste kiss for the next several days. Sometimes she found herself rubbing the spot his lips had touched with the thumb of the other hand. No longer did she want to cry when considering the idea of the upcoming marriage. It was also too late for her to make plans to escape to Lafayette or another large town.

Jacques even kept away, which was also a relief to her. She didn't understand how the dizzying sensations Jacques used to cause inside her by his very presence instead occurred at the mere thought of Edouard. She wanted to find a reason to visit the bayou cabin, yet didn't want to overstay her welcome. And perhaps Edouard was only making the best of the situation he'd found himself in. She reminded herself he didn't promise to love her.

She did cry, though, when she slipped her mère's dress over her head and Mama LeBlanc fastened the buttons at the back. The afternoon sun made long shadows through the windows.

"No, no tears today! This is a day of joy for our families." Mama dabbed at Josée's full eyes with a handkerchief. "Plus, your Edouard would be worried to see you with red eyes."

My Edouard. Evidently Mama LeBlanc carried the notion that love would grow between them. Josée tried not to think of love.

Mon Dieu, I submit to Papa and Mama LeBlanc. For the rest of our lives, Edouard and I will be together.

"I wish it was my turn." Jeanne's wistful voice summoned Josée from her thoughts. "Papa and Josef have agreed to wait until spring. And Mama and I have yet to sew my new dress."

"You'll be happy to move into a new home, too." Josée resisted the urge to suggest to Jeanne that she and Josef take her and Edouard's place in front of the priest.

All too soon, the LeBlancs set out by wagon and across Breaux's Bridge to the common house where the villagers gathered. Josée did not see Edouard; perhaps he had traveled alone. Her throat hurt. She wondered if she would find her voice once it was time to say her vows.

Two other young couples of La Manque also waited to be married, and Josée didn't mind sharing the day with them.

She saw Edouard standing by himself outside the common house as they approached. She felt herself smile. He stood tall and broad in his suit coat, his ink-dark hair pulled back from his face and shoulders, his face clean shaven. He hadn't seen them yet, and Josée's throat constricted when she saw what had caught his attention.

Celine Hebert—no, Celine *Dupuis*—had arrived, her features evident even from a distance. Her husband's back was to them as he helped Celine from their farm wagon.

And the closer Josée got to the common house, she wondered if she saw regret in Edouard's eyes.

Chapter 4

The pounding drums matched the beat of Edouard's heart. He and Josée led the *promenade* of newly married couples as the entire party performed the traditional wedding march around the edge of the grounds. The well-wishers' cheering grew louder than the blare of horns and the wail of fiddles.

Edouard clutched Josée's hand, whether to hold himself up or keep her from toppling over, he didn't know. One thing he did know was they were now officially married.

He did not look at Celine, though he knew her to be there with her husband. He had glimpsed signs of a life growing inside her, and tonight as he whirled Josée into his arms at the dance, whatever he felt for Celine died inside him.

Surprise entered his wife's eyes. Maybe he held her too tightly. *His wife.* Perhaps they would learn to love each other.

At that, he found himself stepping on her feet. "I'm sorry."

Josée drew in a sharp breath but stayed in the circle of his arms. "I don't dance so well, either."

"Oh yes, you do. I've seen you." He should have kept his mouth closed. Now she would know he sometimes used to watch her play with the others on the banks of the bayou. "Here. We'll sit down to give your feet and my bad leg a rest."

Edouard kept an arm around her as they headed to the edge of the crowd where the LeBlancs had spread blankets on the ground along with the other families of La Manque. The other two married couples continued to dance, and the villagers rejoiced with them.

He looked at Josée's slippered feet. Where she'd found dancing slippers was a mystery to him. "Do your toes hurt?"

She smiled a slow smile at him and blushed. "The cow has done worse to them on milkin' days." Looking as delicate as a blossom as she took a place on the blanket, Josée had opened a door inside him he thought had been shut forever. With one smile. But he could ask nothing of her that a husband had a right to demand, not without having her heart first. He would not crush the sun-kissed flower that sat at his feet.

Edouard's throat felt like the time he'd been out fishing for two days and his water jug ran dry. "I—I'll get us somethin' to drink." He stalked off toward the family's wagon to find the water cask and a cup.

Someone clapped him on the back along the way, and Edouard tried to make out the face in the shadows cast by firelight. Josef Landry.

"Edouard, mon ami, you are undone. No more eating what you will, no more sleeping and working when you want. *Quel dommage!*" Josef's grin took the bite out of his words.

"Oui, it's a pity." Edouard shook his head.

"So where do you go with the long face?"

"To get water for us."

"Ah, the hen is already pecking at the rooster!" Josef let out a whoop and slapped his knee. His gaze darted over to Jeanne. "Dance, ma'amselle?" With that, Edouard's sister gave a toss of her black hair and entered the crowd with Josef.

Edouard reached the family wagon, found the cask, and fumbled for a tin cup. Papa waved at him from where he sat with Mama. They should have chosen a better husband for Josée. He did agree that Jacques was unsuitable—the boy would probably have broken her heart—but marry *him*? In truth, Edouard had not thought much beyond the actual idea of being married—past the ceremony—and on to life with a woman underfoot.

A pecking hen. Someone to tell him not to track dirt in the cabin, to work, to not sleep when he wanted. He had not shared a bed since he was a child and piled in with Jacques. Marriage was a different matter altogether. The hangman's noose settled around Edouard's neck once again. *Mon Dieu, why are You doing this to me?*

The contents of the cup nearly sloshed over the sides. Edouard looked down to steady his hand and nearly collided with a figure in his path. Celine, with her husband looming beside her.

"Bon temps *ce soir*, non?" Jean-Luc Dupuis shook hands with Edouard.

Edouard shrugged. "Je ne sais pas." He did not know if

tonight was a good time, nor if the days to follow would be either. Celine looked like a startled *grosbek* about to flap its long wings and soar away over the bayou, instead of ending up as someone's supper. Edouard hoped his expression read that she had nothing to fear from him.

"A'bien, Edouard, I wish you and your bride long life, happy years, and many children together." With a nod, Jean-Luc whisked his wife away from Edouard and toward their wagon.

Many of La Manque stopped to speak with Edouard on his way back to Josée. He did not regret so much his decision to keep to himself and stay at the bayou.

He wondered if any of them whispered, "That's the one who left our village to join with Lafitte. He should have left well enough alone." Did they laugh at the hermit, saddled with a lively wife? Or was she the object of their pity?

No matter how many well-wishers greeted him, cheered him, punched him good-naturedly in the arm, Edouard knew that their sincere efforts could not ensure him and Josée much of anything.

❧

Josée let her feet tap to the sound of the merry dance. She longed to have someone whisk her out into the happy group of villagers. But she remained seated on the blanket and clapped along with a few of the others. Where was Edouard?

"He's left you alone, has he?" Jacques's lanky form blocked her view of the firelight.

"Edouard is getting us a drink." Josée would not rise to her feet. Jacques, she knew, wanted to pull her to the dance. The band now played a mournful ballad of a lost love.

Jacques reached down for her hand.

"Non. I'm waiting for Edouard."

"One dance?" Jacques's voice took on a wheedling tone.

Josée shook her head. "I promised. . . ." She did not think it would be difficult to refuse Jacques's request.

"Find someone else to dance with." Edouard stood next to Jacques. Josée had never seen such a look on her husband's face. Like a gator prepared to attack, Edouard's expression should have been enough to make Jacques leave them alone.

"Josée looked like she was not havin' fun."

"She is my responsibility, not yours." Edouard used his free hand to point a finger at himself, then at Jacques's chest.

Josée stood and took the cup from Edouard. She had to tug a little to get him to release it. Perhaps a distraction would sooth his irritation.

"I was resting, Jacques. Good night!" She sipped from the cup and returned it to Edouard. "Merci."

"Yes, good night," Edouard echoed. He slung the cup to the ground. It scudded across the grass. He grabbed Josée's hand so hard that tears pricked her eyes. "Josée, we'll go home."

"But—"

He swung away from the party. Josée's shoulder jolted and she gasped.

"Edouard—" She flung a glance back at Jacques, who stood staring after them.

"I have had enough of people for one night, perhaps for a good many nights." Even in the moonlight Josée could see the pulsation of Edouard's jaw. She trotted to keep up with him. Words seldom failed her except for now. Crickets clamored in the summer evening.

Edouard slowed his pace and grimaced. "I'm sorry I pulled your arm like that. I wasn't tryin' to hurt you. I did not think. Mon Dieu reminds me of my bad leg."

"I do not think your pain was God's doing. I think if you had remembered and walked more slowly—" Josée stopped and bit her lip. "Anyway, my arm is fine, no worse than a cow pulling on its rope, trying to get away. Jacques—"

"Jacques is an *idiote*. He does not listen, and it was not your fault."

"Thank you. I did not speak to him first." Josée squeezed his hand, but he did not return the gesture, and she blinked back tears. "Do you mean for us to walk all the way home?"

"Oui. Last I knew, I had no grosbek wings."

Humor on the heels of his outburst spun in Josée's head. "True." The trees shadowed them along the road, and Josée shivered. She let go of Edouard's hand and rubbed her gooseflesh-covered arms.

They approached Breaux's Bridge, a recent boon to La Manque and the surrounding farms. A half-moon showed them the way to cross. One of Josée's slippers skidded on the new planks.

Edouard took her hand. "Careful. I don't want you to slip." Josée wondered what had happened to his earlier tones, when they had danced. The only depth of feeling his touch held was protection. Bayou Teche drifted below them.

Once back on hard ground, Josée's feet began to throb. She should have never accepted Jeanne's loan of slippers a size too small. "You'll wear them only for a few hours," Jeanne had assured her.

Edouard stopped and looked at her slippers. "You can take those silly shoes off." He shook his head. "Women!"

Josée straightened her shoulders after she found she could not wiggle her toes inside the slippers. "I'll be fine."

He fell silent the rest of the walk home. Josée never wanted to walk that far again. Between her feet and the thick silence, Josée was ready to explode. The bayou cabin waited in sight. Josée wished she had listened to Edouard and taken off the slippers, but she did not want to bend.

They moved around the side of the cabin and saw the bayou. A lump the size of an apple lodged in Josée's throat. Her new home. A breeze tugged on the moss draped on the cypress trees, and their branches moved as if to wave her inside.

Edouard climbed the steps and flung open the door. "Er. . . I will rebuild the fire."

Josée followed him. "No, I can." At least she hoped she could. Around the LeBlanc family, most of them took turns. And most of the other females would end up helping Josée coax the smoldering embers to life.

Feeling Edouard's gaze on her, Josée kicked off the slippers by the door and crossed the room. She fell to her knees and glanced at Edouard, who lit the lantern.

"Do you have moss?"

"There's a box by the hearth." Edouard sat on one of two stools at the table and took up a knife and a piece of wood.

Josée found the moss and placed it on the glowing embers. She wanted to beg the moss to catch fire, but did not dare ask aloud.

"Burning a hole in the moss with your eyes won't start the fire."

Her face flamed. "I always had help with the fire. I thought I could do it."

Edouard swung around and set his whittling down. "I'll take care of it. You, you, just. . ."

Josée realized he did not know what to do with her. She was not a new cow or a chicken that could be fenced in or cooped up.

Her throat hurt. "Are you hungry?"

"No, no." While she watched, Edouard soon had the moss aglow and piled some kindling on top of the flames. "I am fine."

She stood back, feeling useless as a leaky cup. They were not the first couple wed because of a family's wishes. No one was guaranteed love.

I want to be happy again.

"There." Edouard stood and brushed dirt from his trousers. "A fire. In case it rains, we will not be cold tonight."

The distance between them might have been miles, but Edouard made no move to get closer. He tossed his hat onto the table and gestured to the doorway leading to the back room.

"If you are tired, you can. . ."

A'bien, so that was it. Josée's gaze glimpsed her quilt, spread over the bed tucked in the corner of the back room. The bed, handcrafted for them. New, never used. The remembrance of the Landrys' pride when they toted the bed to the cabin as a gift flickered in her mind.

"Thank you." Josée rubbed her arms. The gooseflesh would not go away, and she dared not draw closer to the fire. . .and Edouard.

"I. . .I. . ." Edouard shifted from one foot to the other, and he looked at the door as he spoke. "I'm going to check the pirogue. I must go fishin' soon." With that, he clomped to the door and left the cabin.

Josée burst into tears. Her feet felt like she had walked on glass for three miles, her head pounded, and she realized she was hungry because she failed to eat any of the lavish dishes brought by the villagers to celebrate the weddings. She satisfied her hunger pangs with generous gulps from the water bucket.

She found the trunk Mama LeBlanc had sent down to the cabin earlier that day, and took out a soft chemise for sleeping in. She washed her dusty feet before climbing onto the soft mattress.

Josée said her prayers, missing the whispers of Jeanne, Marie and the other girls alongside her as they prayed. *Notre Père—*

Our Father. She had never felt so alone in her life. Josée finished praying and tasted more tears before sleep overcame her.

Chapter 5

Edouard jerked awake on the hammock and nearly rolled over and hit the ground. Shouts rang in the air, and his gun remained inside the cabin. Was a group of bandits descending on them? No, it was Papa, Mama, and the rest of the clan racing toward the cabin. Edouard squinted at the morning light shining through the trees.

"Bonjour, my son! And where is our daughter-in-law?" Papa reached him first, clasping Edouard to his chest and then planting a kiss on both cheeks.

"Ah, she still sleeps." Edouard could not bring himself to say he had slept on the steps the night before. He could face a gator on the bayou, but not a woman alone in a cabin.

"No matter. We are here for breakfast!" Papa's voice thundered across the water.

"Edouard, we are hungry. Ask your bride to feed us!" one of the family shouted.

"Oui!" They called to him like a flock of gulls. Did he ever act so when he was a child?

Edouard retreated to the cabin and headed for the bedroom. Josée lay sleeping, her breaths even. A blistered foot peeked out from under the blanket. Hair dark as midnight streamed across the pillow and begged for him to touch it.

"Josée, wake up."

She stirred, a flush blooming on her cheeks. "Edouard?" She propped herself up on an elbow and snatched the blanket to her chin with her free hand.

"Don't worry, nothing's wrong. The family is here for breakfast."

"Breakfast?" A furrow appeared between her brows.

Edouard licked his lips. "*Oui*, you know the tradition. The new, uh, bride always makes breakfast the morning after the weddin'." It was his turn to feel color blazing into his neck. Worse, he realized if he remained in the cabin too long. . .

"I'll be up and dressed." Josée reached for a simple dressing gown on her small trunk. She held the garment in her hand and stared at him.

"Oh, yes. *Pardon*." Edouard turned and faced the fireplace and the table. "You will find cornmeal on the shelf. I have salted fish. Mama left dried herbs for you to use as well. She knew I did not have much to make a suitable meal."

"Ed–dee! Why take you so long waking your wife?"

"I had to tell her where the food was!" he shouted toward the door.

"Then tell her faster!"

Mon Dieu, I prayed to be left alone. I prayed for peace, and this is how You answer me? Edouard didn't dare turn around until he knew Josée was finished dressing. He couldn't let himself see her, although he knew he had the right by marriage.

"I'm ready." Josée had also made the bed and stored her clothes in the trunk. Edouard reminded himself to take his shirts down from the rope he had stretched across the cabin.

"*Bien*, 'cause I'm hungry, too." He tried to smile, but at his words her eyes grew round as a fish's. "I'll draw us more fresh water from the cistern." He grabbed the bucket on his way out the door before the family really started to tease them.

Josée's head ached as if someone had danced a jig on her forehead all night. Cook? Breakfast? She wanted to climb through a window and run up the familiar path, back to Mama's table and the warm, snug, happy kitchen. This place? It held nothing to comfort her.

She ducked under two hanging shirts she'd missed the night before in her struggle to light a fire. They had plates, cups, and bowls, thanks to Mama and Papa LeBlanc. But food? For everyone?

Nestled in a nook in the fireplace, Josée found her new pots and pans. She did not have the heart to tell Edouard all she could make without burning it was pie.

"Mama, if only I could have written the recipes down." Josée shook her head. She couldn't remember how much lard to add to the cornmeal to start biscuits. Worse, no biscuit cutter. She fingered the edge of a cup. A'bien, that would have to do.

Where to make the dough? Josée took one of the two bowls and placed it on the table. She guessed at how much cornmeal and lard to use, and started mushing them together. Biscuits weren't much different than piecrust. Ah, wait. She needed leaven for the biscuits to rise like Mama's.

Josée slapped her forehead before she remembered her hands were covered with cornmeal. Oh, she was failing miserably in the kitchen. Or cabin, rather. She did not know if she wanted to be outside, hearing the family tease them both.

Tease them? Josée shook her head. For all she knew, Edouard had slept outside on his trusty hammock. Poor man. He had gained a wife, but lost his bed and privacy.

A soft rap on the door made Josée look up. "Who is it?"

"Bonjour, may I come in?"

"Oui, Mama." The door opened, and Mama entered. She placed a round covered pan on the table. The sight of her brown rotund figure made Josée wipe her hands on her skirt and embrace her.

"So, how goes it?" Mama asked.

Josée shrugged. "I have no breakfast cooking. I have no coffee to offer my guests." She gestured to the table.

Mama made a soft hissing noise. " 'Tis my fault. I did not pay attention enough when you helped in the kitchen."

"Truthfully I was wanting to read, so it's partly my fault as well." Josée wanted to toss the lump of meal and lard into a refuse bucket.

Mama gave her a pointed look. "Yet when I asked, 'how goes it,' I was not asking about your cooking this morning."

"I. . ." She could not tell Mama she did not want to be there.

Mama smiled. "Ah, l'amour. There is more to love than an embrace, a touch. Much more. Just as there is more to joy than feelin' happy."

Josée found a rolling pin and tumbled the dough onto the wooden table. "I don't know what to do."

"Do?" Mama patted the hand that rolled out the dough. "Make cornbread. Learn to make gumbo. Know Edouard. And speak to notre Père. He will show you the way and bring you the joie de vivre you seek."

Josée nodded. For now, making biscuits was enough for her.

"I'll leave you be, unless—"

"Breakfast?"

Mama patted the pot she had placed on the table when she came in. "See to the biscuits, and place this pot to warm until the biscuits are done."

"Oh, Mama, merci—"

"*D'rien.* You can tell Edouard about my help with the meal after we have gone." After a kiss on the cheek, Mama left the cabin.

Josée placed the pan of dough in the oven. They would bake and not rise but would be better than nothing. While crouched down, Josée saw a thin spine of a book nestled between the fireplace bricks and the wood box.

A book? As best Josée knew, Edouard could not read.

Josée pulled out the volume, parchment bound in leather. A book handmade with much care, left in a hiding place. The pages crackled when she opened the cover and read the first page.

> *In the year of our Lord, 1769*
> *I, Capucine LeBlanc, write this with my own hand. These are my thoughts in this new land. After much sorrow, much joy. My dear Michel has built me a home. My long-lost mère is nearby. Comforte sleeps on my shoulder as I hold the pen. Life is full.*

She closed the book and ran her hands over the cover. Capucine, the mère of Edouard's papa. This treasure was different than the usual stories passed down through the family. Why had this been placed in the nook? The books in the LeBlanc home had been Josée's, secured away in the trunk that rested next to the bed, and were only taken out by her.

"You will no longer be hidden, little book." Josée's face grew warm. What if one of the others heard her? She stood, crossed the cabin, and placed the book in her trunk. As she went to check on the biscuits, she cast a glance over her shoulder.

Did Capucine burn her food, or was she a fine cook? Did she have songs springing forth, unbidden, from her heart? Perhaps instead of songs, she wrote from her heart. Josée would have to find out. It warmed her to think that another woman cooked at this hearth and bounced bébés on her knee in this very room.

"Josée! We're hungry!" chorused the voices outside.

"*Un momente!*" she called back. *Mon Père, merci for the book.*
But she would appreciate help in learning to make gumbo. As
for Mama's suggestion to know Edouard, that would wait. . .
for another time.

Chapter 6

As if in answer to Edouard's prayers for help, rain poured from the heavens upon La Manque. He stood on the tiny porch he had built overlooking the bayou, which swelled with fresh water. After three days of rain, the tiny garden which Josée had lovingly tilled now looked like stripes of mud and water. He did not understand le bon Dieu's joke. Since the wedding two weeks ago, he had spoken to God more than he had in a long time. And he did not remember asking Him for rain.

This morning the melody that Josée sang lilted above the drumming on the roof. Edouard's stomach growled. He had thought *his* cooking was bad. After two bites of her gumbo last night—the first to be polite and the second out of hunger—breakfast arrived after a long night. He had not meant to cause her tears. He ended up listening to her sniffle as they fell asleep. The rain would not allow him to sleep in his hammock or on the porch, so he had claimed one side of the bed. An invisible line seemed carved between them. Edouard did not mind that so much. He did mind waking up cold in the hours before first light, with no quilt. Josée slept, wrapped like a moth in its cocoon.

"Edouard, this journal, it's so beautiful. Her words, after going through so much. . ." Josée's voice rang out inside the cabin. He heard her feet grow louder on the wooden floor.

Ever since Josée had found that journal, she trotted behind Edouard, reading parts of it. He did not mind stories so much, but the fact that Josée understood the writing—he shook his head. After three days of rain and her chatter about the journal, he didn't know which noise grated more to his ears.

"What is that?" Edouard turned to face her where she stood in the doorway. She looked like a spot of brightness in the gray day. Of course, she had slept well the night before. In other circumstances, he might want to steal a kiss. That is, if she would keep quiet long enough. What had happened to her demure attitude on that hot day she brought him a slice of pie?

"Listen. Capucine writes, 'As I look back upon the years of sadness in my darkest days, I see how my heavenly Father watched and worked on my behalf. Even though I did not believe for a time, my questioning did not banish the truth, that my God is still there. I wish I knew then that joy is not based on people, places, and things. Those change. My God does not.'"

In spite of his growling stomach, Edouard almost believed the words. Then his bad knee twinged. "But my knee, my heart." He touched his chest.

Josée placed her warm hand over his, and his heartbeat

kept pace with a woodpecker. "I am sorry, so sorry, that these things happened to you. Will you let your heart heal?"

"I don't know how." Edouard moved from her touch and looked out at the bayou. Where had his quiet life gone? "I was fine here by myself. I did not have you askin' me questions and reading from that—that book!"

Edouard glanced back to see Josée whirl on grubby feet and enter the cabin. He turned again to face the water. Joie de vivre, oui, Josée had plenty of that. He had not intended his words to hurt, but there it was. So he was not used to having someone around all the time. He had himself and the water's inhabitants for company.

Her approaching footsteps made him turn yet another time. Josée blazed through the open doorway and came so close he could see dark flames in her eyes.

"You are not the only one who has suffered loss." Josée's face reminded him of a storm on the gulf, with its clouds rolling in before the full fury broke.

"You are not the center of the world! That family"—Josée pointed toward the LeBlanc home—"loves you. They wept and prayed and begged for God to return you to them. But *nooo*! No one has suffered like the great Edouard Philippe LeBlanc. You act as if you have had no one to help you. You act as if no one's love is enough. Not your family's, not God's, not—" Josée clamped her hand over her mouth and hiccupped. Tears streamed down her face. She ran inside the cabin.

Edouard curled his fists. His eyes stung and his breath came in short gasps. This was a new pain, to be sure. Josée had no right to come at him with the vengeance of a mama gator. She did not know him or his pain at all.

❧

Josée paced the floor. *That man* was right outside, and if she wanted to race to Mama LeBlanc's home she would have to pass by him on the way. She had never thought one person could cause her so much fury. And she had almost admitted that she loved him. A one-sided love that would surely crush her heart. That man had to have been one of the most selfish creatures le bon Dieu had ever created. *My knee, my heart, indeed.* Yet here she was the one crying like a bébé.

She dashed the tears from her cheeks, then stoked the fire. After tossing more moss on the embers, she coaxed the flames back to life and added a fresh log. A cold spell with the rains brought a damp chill into the cabin, unexpected in this summer season.

A smile tugged at her mouth. Poor, poor Edouard. He had eaten two bites of supper and no doubt had a long hungry night. She had also stolen the blanket, and by the time she realized it, Edouard had already risen and built the fire and made coffee. She did not admit she was as hungry as he after she tasted her gumbo. The burnt roux did not a savory gumbo base make. Edouard had pitched the mess into the rubbish pile outside, then fished to no avail.

"No rules here," he'd assured her in their first few days together. "I get up when I want, eat when I want, sleep when I want."

Life must be very different than when there was only one person under the roof. *Très différent* for both of them. At the large LeBlanc house, Josée knew her place. Here, she did not know when to cook, or try to. She did not know when it was time to sleep, other than Edouard turning off the lamp on the table. He did not wake her most mornings. How could she learn her place when Edouard treated her as if she were not there?

Enough! Josée snatched her shawl, wrapped it around her shoulders, and pulled a corner over her head. She *would* pass him and go up to the house, whether Edouard liked it or not.

She moved for the doorway and was relieved to see Edouard leaning on the porch railing. He faced away from her.

"I'm goin' to see your mère." Josée did not ask permission to go. Nor was he a child who could not be left alone. He could fend for himself quite well without her. She pushed past him and pounded down the wooden steps. She did not look his way but trotted through the rain and along the muddy path to the big house.

By the time she reached the kitchen, her feet and ankles were covered with mud, her shawl soaked, the hem of her dress soiled. She knocked on the door.

Mama LeBlanc answered. "*Ma chéri*, what brings you here?"

"I needed to see you. May I come in?"

"Of course. Let me bring you some water to cleanse your feet."

After Josée washed the dirt from her feet, she entered the warm home. By then her hands had stopped trembling, and she no longer felt as angry. She'd also just made extra work for herself come washday.

Mama placed a steaming cup of coffee on the table. "I have not seen you for days."

"It's the rain. I tried to start the garden, and now that is flooded and I am stuck indoors. Edouard can't fish right at the moment either, so. . ."

"I see. Well, Papa LeBlanc has remained inside, as well. I send him out to tend the animals and he's welcome to stay out there a while, also." Mama stirred a bubbling pot over the fire.

"I know Edouard is your son, and you love him, but now he's worse than a mosquito bite on my back that I can't scratch." Josée frowned. "I do not know what he expects of me. I burned the gumbo last night. The roux smelled strange, and I should have known. And did you know? Edouard does what he pleases, when he pleases."

The thoughts tumbled out. Josée did not know how to tell Mama about the extent of Edouard's bitterness. She did not know how to admit that she loved the man, as well. How could you love someone you'd like to throw in the bayou?

"You two have been like a hen and rooster cooped up with nowhere to go. The cabin is Edouard's. But it is yours to run." Mama pointed at Josée. "You decide when breakfast is served. You clean the floor. You tell him to clean his boots and not track mud, although, after twenty-five years Papa LeBlanc will leave a trail on the floor."

"Papa LeBlanc, still?"

"Oui, even after I made him scrub his tracks."

Josée grinned at the thought and blinked back the rest of her tears. "I thought—"

"You thought we never argued?" Mama shook her head. "I must forgive Nicolas daily, and he must forgive me. Would you like a bowl of gumbo?"

"I *am* hungry," Josée admitted. "Is Papa LeBlanc in the barn?"

Mama simply nodded, a twinkle in her eye. "And I have good news. The Landrys sent word that they are having a *fai do do* tomorrow night at the common house. We will dine together, play music, and dance, if there is room enough. You must ask Edouard to bring you."

Oh, a fai do do! Time to spend with the LeBlancs, the Landrys, and other families who decided to venture out. Josée's heart leaped in anticipation.

"Mama, please help me make a roux. Then I shall go home and try again." Home. She realized she'd called the cabin *home.*

"That I can do. You must feed well the man you love."

Josée touched her hot cheeks. "You can see that?"

"I saw the moment I opened the door."

"I'm afraid he does not love me." It hurt to speak the words.

"Time, chéri, it will take time. Pray to le bon Dieu, and He will answer you and show you what to do."

Josée hoped so. Both her heart and her stomach were hungry.

❧

Edouard took the path up to the big house, passed it, and went to the barn instead. He saw the trail of Josée's footprints to the kitchen door. Better he not go there. Instead he sought out Papa, who had probably gone to check the animals.

He entered the barn, and the scent of straw and horse pricked his nostrils. "Papa?"

"Up here." Papa's voice came from above.

Edouard looked to the hayloft and climbed the ladder. His Papa was lying on his side, whittling a lump of cypress wood.

"Ah, so she drives you from your home, eh?" Papa chuckled.

"She does not. I. . .I needed to get out. After three days of rain, I needed. . ." Edouard shrugged, then found a comfortable spot to stretch out.

"Remember, son, Josée is very young. She does not know how to run a house. My sweet Clothilde was a good mère to her after Josée's parents died, but I'm afraid with all these children, she did not see to Josée's trainin' as well as she should." Papa shook his head. "That, and Josée always wanted to read the books left by her own mère."

"Oui, I know. Josée found a journal written by your grand-mère, Capucine. She is always reading to me." Edouard waved his arms. "It's 'Edouard, listen to this,' and 'Edouard, listen to that.' The only time she ceases talking is when she sleeps."

Papa leaned back and laughed, his belly heaving up and down, his face red. "*Bienvenue* to marriage, Edouard. Women must talk. It's their nature. Let her."

Edouard did not find this advice helpful or humorous. No one seemed to understand the quiet he craved had been denied him and would never come again.

"And you, you treat her well. Teach her what you know of

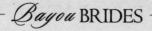

cooking, if you must. And let her do her job." Papa shook his head. "I should have dragged you back to the house years ago instead of letting you take the cabin by yourself. It was not good for you—"

"Papa, I was injured and broken—"

"Listen to me. You have built strong walls that you no longer need. I see what Celine Dupuis did to you. I was sorry for your pain, but a faithless young woman was not fit for my son. You must go on, with Josée. She is full of faith and joie de vivre. She will share with you, willingly, I believe."

Edouard nodded. He had to agree with Papa. Wasn't that what Josée had been trying to do? "I have not been so smart."

Papa chuckled again—Edouard had forgotten how much Papa loved to laugh. "My son, that is the first thing you've said in years that makes sense."

An hour or so later, Edouard left the barn and headed back to the cabin. It had felt good to talk to Papa, man-to-man. No longer was he an unmarried man but had to consider someone else in his home. He had no doubts that he and Josée would clash heads again, except he knew he must learn to build bridges between them.

The rain had slowed to a gentle patter on the trees. As Edouard rounded the corner of the cabin, he heard a voice praying. "Notre Père *qui est aux cieux! Que ton nom soit sanctifié. . .*"

He paused and whispered the words. "Our Father in heaven, Holy is Your name. . ." Oui, he wanted to do God's will, provide for Josée, and he needed to learn to forgive. One step at a time, he would.

Chapter 7

"The fai do do, Edouard, it's tomorrow night." Josée served up steaming gumbo and freshly baked cornbread (a bit flat) for supper. Thanks to Mama LeBlanc, Josée had realized she needed to count to three hundred when stirring the roux. Stop stirring too soon, and the roux would not thicken. Stir too long, and the mess would burn. The thick soup smelled heavenly tonight. Josée determined she would write down how to make roux so she would not forget. She watched Edouard inhale the aroma.

"My mama helped you."

"She did. I am going to try to do better."

He surprised her by clasping her hand. "I know." His thumb rubbed her palm. "Me, too."

Josée's head swam, and she pulled her hand away to cut the cornbread. "Like I was saying, your mère told me the Landrys are having a fai do do, and we must go. Oh, I mean, I would really like to. I think it would be good to get out of the cabin." She sat down across from him.

Edouard nodded. He said the blessing, and Josée waited for him to continue talking about the fai do do. She ate, although she was not too hungry after two bowls of Mama's gumbo.

"I suppose we can ride in the wagon with Papa and Mama and the others." Edouard sounded reluctant.

"It's been so long since we've spent time with anyone besides your family, and—" Josée heard herself starting to talk up a stream and fell silent. She took another bite. Edouard had managed to net enough fine sweet shrimp that blended with the broth.

"You should wear the dress from when we married." Was that a smile she saw tugging at the corners of his mouth?

"I think I will." She didn't mention she would change dresses because what she wore had mud caked at the hem. Even if she washed the dress tonight, it might not dry come tomorrow. Worse, what if the stains were permanent?

Edouard apparently did not see the need for further conversation, so Josée figured now was as good a time as any to follow Mama's suggestions.

"I will be sure to make breakfast in the morning." Her voice sounded unnaturally high to her ears. "I'm your wife, and I have responsibilities, too. I will cook for you. Mama's been helping me, and I will keep improving, I'm sure."

Josée did not miss the expression on his face.

She continued in spite of it. "If you are going to fish and will be away, I will send something with you to eat. I don't know what you have that you can trade, but I want to buy more seed and replant the garden. I will sew and hang curtains, too.

Also, I will be moving the line where you hang the wash to another place where the shirts don't get in my way. Washday will be Mondays." She hoped he would remember everything. The clunk of a spoon in a bowl surprised her.

"You're goin' to make me scrape my boots before I come in, too, I suppose?"

"It will save scrubbing the floor so much." She smiled at him, thinking of the way he'd touched her hand earlier. He did look handsome by firelight, now that her anger had burned off. She prayed his heart would soften.

Edouard tugged at his suspenders and pushed back from the table. "I left one mère to gain yet *un autre*." He had spoken as if she were a thorn in his foot. A mosquito on his neck. Josée kept eating and did not break his gaze.

Josée thought her anger had burned off, but a few embers reignited. "I am not your mère. I am your *wife*."

"And I am finished." Edouard stood up and left the table and tromped to the porch. She heard nothing except the dripping trees and the crickets singing their nightly songs. Josée did not touch the rest of her gumbo. She poured it back in the pot over the fire. Her appetite had left her. She scrubbed their bowls and spoons and heard the sound of Edouard whittling outside.

※

The rain had stopped, though clouds hung in the sky. Edouard looked westward down the bayou. The sun was trying to peek at them on its descent into night. Josée hummed again inside

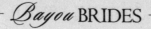

the cabin. After their words the night before, Edouard had apologized. He had not acted as if he were trying to build a bridge. Change did not happen quickly, either, and he asked if Josée could make one change at a time. She responded with a breakfast of *couche-couche* that almost rivaled his mama's. But then a body couldn't easily ruin fried cornmeal drizzled with cane syrup. She must have gotten the milk from Mama, besides the recipe.

Now Josée bustled from pantry to table as she packed a basket to take to the fai do do tonight. Her capable hands folded a cloth to cover the bread. Her hands. Edouard wanted to touch them again, as he had when he woke up that morning to find one of them clasped to his chest in both of his. They were small, yet very strong, and one finger of the right hand had a spot of ink from writing in the book she had found. He remembered touching the ink stain. She had a burn on another finger, which he also caressed. It must have hurt, for she murmured in her sleep. He had not known what it felt like to protect someone, to have someone so close. . .

He swallowed hard and called out, "Are you almost ready?" His neck hurt from the freshly pressed shirt buttoned to the top.

"Here I am." Josée emerged from the cabin, her shoulders wrapped with a shawl and the basket hung over one arm. She had somehow braided her hair and wrapped it around her head like a black crown. Her cheeks flushed, she smiled at him.

"You look très *jolie*," he whispered. Where had his voice gone?

"Merci." It sounded as if she had lost her voice, as well.

Edouard tucked her free hand over his arm, and they set out together for Mama and Papa's house, where they would ride with the family on the wagon. He would have preferred to walk with her so they could be alone, but he knew she would not want to soil her dress on the muddy roads. Even with hard scrubbing, Josée had not been able to remove the mud from the dress she had worn yesterday.

"Don't worry, we will get you another dress," he assured her.

"Edouard! Josée! We are ready to go!" someone called from the wagon. He waved to them and walked faster. Already he could smell the good foods wafting from Mama's baskets.

The wagon seemed more crowded than usual, and Edouard ended up pulling Josée onto his lap for the ride. Nearly cheek to cheek with her the entire trip, Edouard could scarcely breathe. He sensed Josée's heart galloping away with her, and the pretty blush colored her neck.

Jacques stared at them from across the wagon until someone asked about a girl he planned to see at the fai do do. *Patience, little brother,* Edouard wanted to tell him. He would not wed his first love, but le bon Dieu would take care of him. It felt as if salve had been rubbed on the painful spots of Edouard's own heart. He wanted to hold Josée closer, if that were possible. *Merci, mon Père.*

When they reached the common house, Edouard regretted having to release Josée. He did not notice his knee hurting so badly, either. Perhaps he would work enough to buy or trade for a wagon and an animal to pull it.

Josée hopped from the wagon and received the basket

Edouard gave her. "I'll put this with the rest of the food and meet you inside." Her eyes twinkled at him. Mama gave him a knowing smile.

The fiddles called them indoors, where the benches had been cleared away for the dance floor and a table for the food had been set up at one end of the room. Edouard found Josée right away.

"Edouard, I'm glad we came." She clutched his arm, and his stomach turned over. "Merci."

"I'm glad we did, too." Although he wanted to whisk her away from the crowd, he would not because of the others' teasing. The two couples who had also been married at the same time were present, and soon it seemed like all of La Manque and those who lived on outlying farms had come. Night fell and still the music played on.

Edouard managed two fast dances with Josée, who was extremely light on her feet. A familiar face flashed by him. *Celine.* He was surprised to find he felt the barest twinge instead of feeling like a scab had been opened on his heart.

The dance ended, and Josée stepped back. "I'm going to speak with a few of the other ladies. They are in a sewing group and meet together sometimes, and I should like to go and learn how to sew better."

"Of course, go on. Are you hungry?"

She shook her head. "Not yet." Then off she went, Edouard following with his gaze. He wanted to have her at his side, but he would definitely be teased if he tried to enter the circle of women.

He tugged at his collar. The room swelled with people, and Edouard wanted air. He decided to go outside, where some of the men gathered, talking about the farms and feed and the bayou. And the rain.

Once Edouard left the crowded building, he inhaled the night air as he stood on the steps. Laughter filtered outside. He went out toward the wagons and the side of the building.

"Edouard LeBlanc, so how goes marriage?" Josef Landry tugged on his sleeve as Edouard passed a trio of men who stood and talked by torchlight.

He stopped. "It has been. . .très different. I'm not used to having someone around."

Josef sighed. "I count the days until your sister and I marry. I expect to have the house finished by spring and a new pirogue. Lucky for you, you had your family's old home."

"I was glad they let me keep it." Edouard shifted his weight from one foot to the other. "You have a good night."

Josef nodded, and Edouard went on his way to the outhouse. A figure stood under a cypress tree, shadowed by a canopy of moss. He could hear sniffles from where he stood.

"Qu'est-ce que c'est?" Edouard walked in the direction of the tree. What was it? Were they hurt? The hazy moon slid out from behind a cloud, though thunder rolled in the distance and humidity hung in the air. Another storm was brewing. His knee could feel it. Edouard stopped short when the figure looked up at him.

Celine. She wiped her eyes.

"It's you," she said. "Please, I don't know what to do."

"Is there something wrong? Shall I fetch one of the women?"

She flung herself at him and clamped her arms around his waist. "I was so *stupide*! I was so blind. I should have waited for you."

Edouard tried to get himself out of her gator's grasp before someone saw them. "I think you should speak with someone else, my mère perhaps?"

Her arms tightened. "Jean-Luc, he does not understand me. You always did."

He pushed harder but did not want to hurt someone in her condition. "Celine, this is wrong. You should not be doing this."

"*Je t'aime*, Edouard." Her big eyes, dark as the bayou water, pleaded with him. "I need your comfort."

He managed to get free and held her by the shoulders. "I don't love you. Not anymore. We can never go back. Our lives are different. And I love Josée." The whispered words rang through his mind at the realization.

"Edouard—" She came at him again, her lips parted. Light footsteps on the grass sounded behind them.

"Edouard, are you there?" an all-too-familiar voice called.

Josée. Edouard whirled to face her, knowing he had done nothing wrong. The look she gave him spoke more than any words she could say.

She ran off toward the front of the building.

"Josée. . ." Edouard left Celine without worrying about her troubles. He needed to explain to Josée. Quickly.

He started to run, not caring about the pain in his leg. "Josée!"

She stopped and turned to face him. "How could you?" They stood in a triangle of lamplight shining through the window.

"Let me explain."

"I saw nothing that needed explainin'." Josée's words felt like darts. "I saw clearly."

"Things are not like they seem."

"What am I supposed to think, my husband hidden under a tree with a woman?" Lamplight reflected from her flashing eyes. "I am young, but I am not stupid."

"Josée—" He reached for her.

"Don't touch me." Josée waved his arms from her shoulders. "And to think I looked forward to having you hold me in your arms tonight, thinking that *I* was the one you wanted to be with."

She *wanted* him to hold her close? Edouard rubbed his forehead. "I did not break my vows to you, even in thought." Celine marched past them and around the corner of the building. Another clap of thunder rolled.

"I'm goin' inside." Josée shrugged him off again, though he walked by her side. "We will talk when we get home. Do not think I will forget this."

At that, Edouard dropped the matter for the time being. Later tonight, he would try to explain. *Mon Père, please, do not disappoint me again.*

Chapter 8

Josée cut her loaves of bread at the serving table and felt like her heart had been cut into slices as well. She closed her eyes, trying to forget the sight of Edouard with Celine under the tree. Josée was the one who had hoped to find her husband outside for a moment.

If Mama LeBlanc or Jeanne had noticed her expression, she could not tell. She managed her brightest smile while the women served the meal. She could not bear to look at Edouard. Nor could she stop glancing at Celine. Josée wanted to cross the distance between them and rip the woman's hair out. However, such an act would displease le bon Dieu. Celine would pay the price in her own way, and Josée would not pay with her own bitterness.

She had not known loving someone would cause her to want to behave in such a way. Her heart swelled as she at last let herself look at Edouard, already seated between Josef and Simon Landry. One of them said something, and Edouard appeared to chuckle.

Josée clamped her lips together. He was having fun, and she was here only taking up space. Her stomach complained, but she did not think she could eat. Neither could she breathe after the room had filled with villagers. The air felt thick after the many dances throughout the evening.

She leaned over and whispered to Jeanne. "I'm going outside."

"Why? The rain comes."

Josée reached for her shawl and put it around her shoulders. "I do not feel well, and the fresh air should help me." She reached for a nearby lantern.

"I'll get Edouard if you want."

"No!" Josée touched Jeanne's arm with her free hand. "I do not want to speak with him right now." She did not want to continue the conversation they'd had earlier. Not until they were back in the cabin, anyway.

"Are you sure?" Jeanne's forehead wrinkled.

Josée nodded. "I. . .I'm not very happy with him tonight." She slipped through the crowd and paused at the doorway. Edouard looked toward the serving tables. When he turned back to face Josef, he wore a frown. Josée stepped into the night. If anyone saw her, maybe they would think she was headed for the outhouse. She covered her hair with the shawl and inhaled, the air thick with the promise of rain. The falling rain would mask her tears très bien.

When Josée crossed the yard where the animals stood hitched, a clap of thunder made her jump, but she continued walking. The teams of horses and mules pulled on their leads and one nearly trampled Josée's foot.

"Whoa." She patted the mule's neck and quickened her steps.

Raindrops hit the muddy road that wound to the edge of La Manque and eventually crossed Breaux's Bridge. Josée pictured the LeBlanc cabin, waiting for her. When she made it to the cabin, she would build a fire and start the coffee and wrap herself up in their big blanket. She would have her cry, write down more recipes in Capucine's journal, and wait for Edouard.

Another boom shook the ground, and Josée started to run. The lantern in her hand made wild arcs of light in the darkness. Yet she was not going back to the common house. She could not. She would make it home, even though the rain would soak her through.

Breaux's Bridge lay ahead of her, outside the circle of lantern light. The cold wet surface, slick with mud from the crossing wagons, would be hard to tread. Josée leaned into a fresh gust of wind and winced at the stinging rain. She took a few hesitant steps onto the bridge, her feet slipping on the mud. The overflowing bayou roared below her.

A rumble from behind made Josée stop and grab the thin railing. Hoofbeats on mud and the rattle of a wagon. Josée skittered like one of the LeBlanc's young foals trying to stand. She hit her knees, and the lantern rolled away from her reach.

Josée squinted back in the dark. "*Arret*—wait, I'm on the bridge!"

The wagon did not slow. It hugged the bridge's rail. Josée knew she could not make it to the other side of the bridge without being struck. She scrambled to the edge and squatted near the railing. Rain soaked her hair and ran down her neck. Somehow her shawl had slipped from her shoulders.

Lightning flashed. The team of horses barreled onto the bridge. Their reins dangled, without a driver on the wagon seat. Josée reached up to grip the railing. The wooden planks shook as if a giant hand jerked the bridge. Her feet slid out from under her. Her fingers lost their hold.

She fell into empty space, and the roaring water rushed up at her.

A crack of thunder shook the common house. Edouard glanced to the serving table, where the women were packing up the food. Where was Josée?

He should have turned and left the moment he had seen Celine under that tree. Now he was faced with waiting until his wife's anger cooled enough for her to listen to him. He knew a tirade would come, one that he did not deserve completely.

Like a thunderclap, the realization that she loved him jolted him to the core.

"Ed–dee, we are leaving." Papa put on his hat. "The storm is going to be bad—Simon Breaux's team already ran out of here like their tails were on fire."

"Oui, I must find Josée." Edouard began to search the room. No one had seen her.

Then Jeanne offered, "She told me she was goin' outside. She was unwell."

Edouard moved through the crowd leaving the building. He didn't ask why she did not come to him. He would have taken her home had she not felt well. Women, as mysterious as the dark bayou. And he knew the bayou much better.

Wind yanked at his shirt and the pelting rain stung his freshly-shaven cheeks. He borrowed a lantern and searched the grounds. After most of the families of La Manque had left the common house, he could see Josée was not among any of the wagons nor under any of the cypress. He also found the outhouse empty. Papa, Jacques, and Josef Landry joined the search.

Simon Breaux returned with his team. "I caught these rascals on the other side of the Teche and found this on the bridge. Whose are these?"

He held up a lantern and a muddy shawl.

Edouard felt his stomach drop into his feet.

❧

Josée surfaced, flailing her arms in the darkness. The cold of the bayou water, fed by fresh rain, sucked the breath from her lungs. As the current dragged her along, Josée felt as if an unseen force had her in its grip. She could not see the banks, the trees, or worse, anything in the water with her. Closing her eyes made no difference. The darkness remained unchanged. She tried to find the bottom with her feet, but her skirt twisted around her legs like a funeral shroud. Her efforts at kicking were futile. She fought down panic, yet screamed.

A flicker of light from the bridge gave her hope. "Help me! Please!"

The light grew smaller as the bayou pulled on her, along with the shrinking hope that she might be heard as she fought against the current. The beating rain numbed her head and shoulders above the water. Her teeth chattered.

Wind howled through the trees and carried a hint of an old song. *"Watch, petite enfants, for the teche of the bayou. He will come to find you if you don't watch out."*

The stories told around the fire when she was a child hissed in Josée's ears. *Please let the gators stay in their warm hideaways deep underwater, and let the teche sleep through the rains.* The natives considered the teche sacred, but Josée shuddered at the slithering way they moved and their narrow eyes.

Something hard bumped against her, and Josée screamed again. She reached out, unsure if it was friend or foe. The something turned out to be a chunk of wood not much larger than the top of her footstool. She clung to it and leaned her cheek on its solid surface and floated to give her legs and arms a rest.

The glow from a cabin's window pierced the inky night. Josée let go of the wood so she could kick through the water toward the light. An undercurrent tugged at her dress again, and she ended up farther away from the light, probably back in the center of the bayou. She shouted for help again. No one came to the window. If she could get close enough to grab one of the knobby knees of the cypress, or a hanging frond of moss, she might be able to pull herself out.

After she passed the lighted cabin, the darkness swallowed her up once more.

Mon Père, please help me!

With the twists and turns of the bayou, she hoped to find a place to get her footing, but in the shallows, she did not know if she would disturb a sleeping gator. If she were attacked, no one would know where she was.

Just like no one knew where she was now.

Then Josée slammed into something so large and solid it rattled the teeth in her head. She screamed.

❧

Edouard hugged the shawl to his chest and a deep moan came from his throat. He thought he was beyond such pain, but this was worse than coming home and learning of Celine's betrayal, and of feeling like an outcast for leaving the seclusion of their bayou world.

"We must find her." He looked at Papa, who was helping Mama into the wagon. "She should not have left on her own."

After a thorough search of the grounds, he guessed that Josée had begun to walk home. He helped Papa get the family loaded onto the wagon.

Jeanne shed many tears. "I should have come to find you when she did not come back."

Edouard hugged his sister. "You did not know. Do not worry yourself."

Papa urged the horses as fast as they could safely move on such muddy roads. Edouard wanted to beg him to drive faster. Papa slowed the horses to a halt on the bridge and lifted the lantern to show where Simon had found the shawl.

Edouard inhaled so fast his chest hurt. "It looks like—"

"Someone might have slipped from the bridge." Papa shook his head.

He could hear Mama praying, "Notre Père qui est aux cieux! Be with our Josée. Deliver her from evil."

Papa turned to face him. "Your Josée is a smart girl and strong. We will go home and start searching for her by foot along the bayou. We will stop at every cabin and tell them to listen for someone and search for her."

"Or," Jeanne spoke up, "maybe she made it home."

Edouard did not tell his sister he knew she was wrong. The one time he had walked Josée home after the wedding, she had not liked it, and it would have been worse for her in the dark. He would not rest until he found her and spent the rest of his life telling her how much she meant to him.

They reached the LeBlanc house at last, and Edouard leaped from the wagon before it stopped moving. Yet even from here, he could see no light in the cabin window.

"My son." Mama touched his shoulder. "We will find her. We must believe."

"I do not know why I should. Le bon Dieu has taken from me once again my joy."

"You cannot make Josée your joy. Ah, she is joyful, but she is just a woman." Mama ran her hand on his hair, a gesture which used to comfort him when he was a bébé. "Even if you have her safely in your home, you know she will disappoint you at times, and you her."

Edouard nodded at that. Mama had probably been talking

to Papa. Fresh memories of Edouard and Josée's silly fight from the day before swam through his head.

"Trying to make her your joy is like trying to catch a fish with your hands. The harder you grasp, the more it struggles to get away."

"I must find her." Edouard grabbed a lantern. He did not have time to stand talking. Why did women try to talk everything into the grave, when a man could be *doing* something?

"You will." Mama nodded. "And I will wait up with warm blankets and hot coffee."

Edouard set out with Papa and Jacques to the bayou's edge. *Oh, my sweet Josée, I am so sorry to have caused you pain. Please, bon Dieu, do not take her away from me.*

Chapter 9

A pirogue. The boat smelled of fish, but at the moment Josée could not think of a better thing to find. She did not know whose boat it was, or how it had come to be in her path in the water. She tore the encumbering skirt from the bodice and leaned onto the side of the pirogue. With a heave, she swung her legs in their waterlogged pantaloons onto the floor of the boat.

She was out of the water, no longer feeling at its mercy as the rain drummed down. In the dark, she reached around to see if she could find an oar, or even a pole she could use to maneuver to the shore. Nothing.

Battered by rain, Josée hunkered in the bottom of the pirogue and cried.

A wild thought struck her. *You could float away to the next town. Start over. . . .* She could go far away and teach in a school. *Stop it.*

Acadians, with their language, were not welcome everywhere. If she stayed among her people, Edouard would find her. Did she want to be found? *Oui, except. . .*

Le bon Dieu had let her marry Edouard. If He was all-wise and all-knowing, He knew this would happen, this fiasco with Celine. Josée found no joy in that knowledge. Despite their troubles and childish disagreements, she had begun to look forward to her future with Edouard. Until now.

What had happened with Edouard and Celine? She could remember seeing Celine about to kiss him. She closed her eyes and turned on her side to keep the pelting rain from hitting her eyelids. *Think harder.* Edouard. He'd had his hands on Celine's shoulders, his arms straight out in front of him.

He'd been trying to hold her away.

Josée sat up straight at the realization, then screamed when a drape of Spanish moss touched her neck. She slapped at the air around her head and yanked the end of some moss from whatever tree she had passed under. The coarse fuzzy moss made a shawl to block out the chill. Wind moaned in the trees as the storm roared on. She did not know how long she lay there in the dark, begging le bon Dieu to let the storm end.

Bone-jarring shivers set in as Josée recalled her anger at Edouard. Tonight she had not let him explain himself, but when had she ever let him speak? She always wanted him to listen. She realized she needed to apologize. She huddled down in the pirogue to find relief from the storm's chill.

The wind and rain lessened, and Josée sat up again and squinted through the darkness. She would never tell a scary tale to the younger LeBlancs again, should she ever get the chance to tell them another story.

A rustling, close at the edge of the bayou, made her freeze, yet her pulse hammered in her throat.

❧

Edouard held the lantern aloft and his rifle over his shoulder. Papa and even Jacques tromped along farther down the bayou and called out for Josée. But the rushing water and occasional clap of thunder covered up the sound of their voices.

He would find her. Not Papa, and especially not Jacques.

Josée was probably frightened, cold, and unsure of where she was. Edouard refused to think of the water claiming her like it had claimed a child one spring. He would not imagine a gator dragging her under in the dark. That had happened to him before, and even with daylight shining into the muddy waters, Edouard had felt like he was dying. He had been strong enough to fight the animal off and get away. Josée was not.

Le bon Dieu would take care of her. Edouard refused to believe that God would turn his life upside down with a wife only to rip her away from him when he learned to love her. The darkness did not scare him, because he knew this bayou well.

Then Edouard stopped a dozen paces or so from the bayou's edge. Shallow water from the brimming bayou swirled over his boot tops. He thought he heard a scream.

"Josée!" He ran, spraying up water that sparkled in the lantern's light.

Edouard saw her inside a pirogue tilted against the stump of a cypress. A gator growled, mere footsteps away from her, likely disturbed by the water and a pirogue drifting into his shallows.

"Edouard!" She squinted at him where she hunched in the pirogue, just beyond the circle of the yellow light. Then she glanced into the shadows. He saw her reaching for a broken-off cypress branch, thick as a man's leg and just as long.

"Don't move!"

She grasped the branch with both hands, not taking her gaze off the gator. The animal's tail started to curl. Edouard took a step toward them.

"*Ooo-eee!* Brother Gator!" He moved the lantern in an arc, hoping the gator would turn this way. "I am here! Come, fight me! It will be more to your liking."

"No, Edouard!" Josée crept from the pirogue as the gator turned to face him. The gator's head cocked to one side, as if it were unsure of whom to approach first.

Edouard set the lantern down on the nearest patch of grass that peeked over the water. "Josée, don't move." He readied his rifle. When he moved his foot, he kicked something solid. He glanced down. The lantern had fallen onto its side.

In a flash, the gator came for him. Josée screamed like a wild woman. Edouard fell onto the mud. The gator whipped its tail around and clubbed him with it. Gasping for breath, Edouard reached for his gun. He glimpsed Josée, hitting the gator with her cypress branch as if she were beating a rug.

The gator whipped its tail again, knocking Josée to the ground, before the beast fled to the water and disappeared.

Edouard crawled to Josée, who had rolled onto her side.

"We were more than he wanted to fight with tonight."

She nodded, her normally sun-browned skin pale by lantern light. She sat up and wrapped her arms around her waist. Tears streamed down her cheeks along with the rain.

"*Mon amour*, I am so sorry." He reached for Josée, pulled her onto his lap, and held her while she cried. Even with her matted hair and torn clothing, he thought her beautiful.

"I'm sorry, too." She leaned back and caressed his face. "I didn't mean to fall in and worry everyone. I was going home, and then this wagon came, and—"

"*Shh.*" He placed his hand over her mouth, a mouth he very much wanted to kiss. But he would wait until they were back inside the cabin and warm once again. "Let us thank le bon Dieu for saving us and go home." After signaling to Papa and Jacques with a shot from his rifle, Edouard picked up the lantern, and they started on their way.

Josée never wanted to let him go. She did not know how far they walked through the night to get to the cabin. She waved at Papa LeBlanc and Jacques, who headed to the big house. Edouard told them to tell Mama LeBlanc that *he* would take care of Josée.

He whisked her into the cabin and lit the fire while Josée slipped out of her wet clothes and into her chemise. Her breath caught in her throat. When they had left for the fai do do, she knew they had grown closer, in spite of their bickering like rooster and hen. Tonight, safe at home, her stomach quivered at the thought.

"Warmer?" Edouard approached with a blanket.

"I'm better now." She tried not to let him see her shiver.

Edouard took her hand. "I am sorry about what happened earlier. I did not realize it was Celine under that tree. . . ." He glanced at the fire, and Josée made herself wait for him to continue.

"Then she kept comin' towards me. I had to hold her off like a gator. I was trying to get Mama or someone else to help her, and then you appeared." He pulled the blanket around her shoulders.

"I am sorry that I did not let you explain. I only knew how bitter it must taste for one's heart to break—"

He fairly crushed her in an embrace and gave her a kiss that she never wanted to end. *This* was what she had longed for while out in the darkened waters. The shelter of her husband's arms and knowing he loved her with his whole heart. Edouard kissed her again, something she knew she'd never tire of now that she knew what a kiss was like.

They sat before the fire and shared the blanket. Edouard poured coffee for them, and Josée sipped hers at first. Then she hurried and burnt her tongue, so she waited until the brew cooled.

"Edouard, I must ask you something. What did you mean earlier, when you said le bon Dieu saved you?"

"When you were missing, I was angry at the thought of losing you. I do not always understand you, but you are my world now." His eyes glittered in the firelight. "Then I realized

I had been wrong ag'in, as I had been about Celine. When I lost her, I thought I had lost my world, and had no reason for joie de vivre. Not that I love you less than I once loved her, but I hope to love you better, my sweet Josée, and love our bon Dieu most of all."

"He is good to us, isn't He?" Josée ventured another sip. "Even with the bad that has happened, we can trust Him to watch over us."

"That is true."

Josée set the cup on the hearth. She stroked the scar on Edouard's cheek with one finger and shook her head. "I also meant to say, when I had time to think on that bayou, I realized you were doing nothing except trying to keep her away from you. I grew so angry because I knew how you had loved her a long time ago. I should have known how you truly felt now, though, because of how you held me on your lap on the way to the fai do do."

Then she stopped talking, because Edouard covered her lips with his. After the kiss, which ended too soon, she sat there, saying nothing.

"Well, that's one way to quiet you." His dark eyes twinkled.

She smiled at him. "In that case, mon amour, I'll make sure I always have something to say."

Epilogue

Josée sat back on her heels after pulling a handful of weeds from her garden and watched her *enfants* playing in the sun. Francois and Mathilde giggled and clapped. Francois, happy and singing; Mathilde, quieter like her papa. They kept their mama busy.

Edouard had been gone for three days on a gator hunt. Josée touched her growing stomach. Another bébé to feed soon, but le bon Dieu would take care of everything. That, and help Edouard get a good gator to trade for more lumber. The bayou cabin seemed to be shrinking.

She hoisted herself to her feet, not as easily as a few weeks ago. "Children, let's eat dinner, and then I will tell you stories."

They clapped again, then grabbed each other's hands and ran ahead of her to the cabin.

Josée made them wash their hands before they ate. A familiar journal lay on the table. She would teach her children to read and write and love the language of their people. For now, her time of writing in this book was over. Josée no longer needed the recipes to help her remember. Edouard was starting to get a bit round like Papa from her cooking.

She touched the book's cover. One day, another LeBlanc might read these pages and learn from her as well as Capucine.

"Bon soir, *journale*," she whispered. Josée rose and placed the journal with the other books in the trunk, to keep until her children were old enough.

The sound of a pirogue moving over the waters made Josée look toward the doorway. The children scrambled to their feet and ran.

"Papa, it's Papa! He's home!"

Josée moved as quickly as her feet would let her. The familiar face and form she knew and loved so well came into view. "Oui, he's home."

LYNETTE SOWELL

Lynette Sowell works as a medical transcriptionist for a large HMO. But that's her day job. In her "spare" time she loves to spin adventures for the characters that emerge from story ideas in her head. She desires to take readers on an entertaining journey and hopes they catch a glimpse of God's truth along the way. Lynette is a Massachusetts transplant who makes her home in central Texas with her husband, two kids by love and marriage (what's a stepkid?), and five cats who have their humans well trained. Lynette loves to read, travel, spend time with her family, and she tries not to kill her houseplants. You can visit her Web site at www.lynettesowell.com.

Language of

Love

by Janet Lee Barton

Dedication

To my Lord and Savior for showing me the way,
to my family for all the precious memories we share,
and to "The Aunts."
I love you all.

Chapter 1

Breaux Bridge, Early December 1918

After days of travel, and wondering if he'd ever get home, Nicolas LeBlanc finally stepped off the train that brought him back to his beloved Breaux Bridge. One arm still in a sling, he took a deep breath and, with his good arm, picked up his duffel bag. He slung it over his good shoulder and headed for home.

There was a crispness to the air that could only be felt in the late fall and early winter in this part of Louisiana, and he knew his mother would be feeling the chill of the morning. But, after being in Europe for the past year and experiencing a different kind of cold, he felt quite comfortable.

Hungry for the sight of home, he couldn't get enough of the scenery as he walked away from the railway station. Just past dawn, the mist rising up from Bayou Teche spread up over the bank, while tall live oaks, dripping moss from their branches, grew beside the bayou. Bald cypress trees that had lost their leaves for the winter rose out of the water, and here and there grew magnolia trees, their glossy green leaves wet with dew. He could almost smell the sweet, huge white blossoms that would bloom, come spring.

Although he'd let his family know he was coming home, he hadn't told them what train he'd be taking. No need to worry *Maman* if the train wasn't on time. She'd been through enough, worrying about him overseas and suffering through the death of his papa from the influenza that had swept the country this past year.

Nicolas sighed deeply as he neared the cemetery. His heart felt as if it were in a vise, being squeezed tighter and tighter at the thought that his dear papa had died while he was gone. His father had been a good man, loving his family, and teaching them to love God, to have strong faith. But now, as Nicolas walked toward the LeBlanc family plots, he acknowledged that, unlike Papa, he'd been questioning God more than he'd been praying.

He'd seen so much. Lost so much. When he'd been wounded, his best friend had taken his place in the foxhole and lost his life that same night. Nicolas had been sent to a hospital in England, and it was there that he'd received the letter telling him about the death of his father. Even here in this place, beside his father's grave, he couldn't seem to find the words to pray, and the sorrow of it all had his throat so full of unshed tears he could barely breathe.

The crackle of leaves sounded behind him, and with the

instinct of a soldier, he quickly whirled around. Nicolas let out a relieved sigh as his brother-in-law came walking out of the mist.

"Nicolas! It's about time you returned. I've been meeting the train for a week. You would pick the one morning I was late getting there!"

"Adam! It's good to see you." Nicolas patted his brother-in-law on the back with his free hand while the other man enveloped him in a bear hug. "How did you know I was here?"

Adam took Nicolas's bag and headed for the 1916 Model T parked outside the cemetery while Nicolas followed close behind. "The stationmaster told me you'd headed home. As I hadn't met you on the road, it didn't take much to realize where you were."

"Maman? How is she doing?" Nicolas asked as he settled himself in the passenger seat, while Adam started the car.

"She'll be better once she sees you." Adam shook his head. "I won't lie to you. Maman has aged this past year. She misses your papa. It's helped having Suzette around to help with the children."

"Suzette? Who is this person?"

"You don't remember my little sister?"

Nicolas vaguely recalled a young blond girl at the wedding of Adam and his sister, Felicia. But she was several years younger than Adam. "Oui. I do—"

"Well, she's grown-up now. . .and she's a new teacher here. Your parents were kind enough to offer her a place to live. You didn't know?"

"No. Oh, I think there was mention of a new teacher, but I didn't know she was living with Papa and Maman." He wondered why no one had written him about it.

❧

Suzette hurriedly washed the last of the breakfast dishes as the children prepared for school. She brought the coffeepot over to the table. Lucia LeBlanc was not her mother, but she'd opened her home to Suzette and made her feel one of her own. She loved the older woman, and it hurt her to see her so sad. Would Nicolas never get home? "Would you like more coffee before we leave for school, Maman LeBlanc?"

"Yes, thank you, dear. Is there anything particular you'd like for supper?"

"Anything you decide on is fine with me." Suzette prayed that Lucia would get her appetite back soon. . .she'd lost too much weight. "The children love your gumbo."

Lucia nodded and smiled. "They do. And should Nicolas return today, he'll be very happy. It's one of his favorites."

Suzette hoped that this Nicolas, whom she only vaguely remembered from her brother's wedding but had heard so very much about since moving here, would indeed return today. His mother needed him, and the children needed him. She glanced at the clock and called to the children, *"Dépêchez vois autre!"*

"We're hurrying," Amy, the fourteen-year-old, and the oldest still at home, answered as she rushed into the room and kissed her mother. "Have a good day, Maman."

Lucia's other children—twelve-year-old Julien, ten-year-old

Jacques, and seven-year-old Rose—followed behind, each kissing her on the cheek before heading out the door.

Lucia followed them outside and leaned against the porch railing, to see them off to school. "Amy, make sure Rose stays up with you. And the rest of you, behave yourself for Suzette, you hear?"

"We will, Maman!" Amy called back as the children waved to their mother and headed down the path.

Down the road a bit, Suzette and the children drew close to the house of her brother Adam and his wife, Lucia's daughter, Felicia. Felicia came outside to greet them, a cup of coffee in her hand. "How is Maman this morning?"

"Hoping your brother makes it home today."

"Oui. Adam has been gone longer than usual. I am hoping he brings Nicolas back with him."

"I'll pray he does," Suzette assured her as the group continued on.

"Thank you. I'll walk over to Maman's to be there either way."

"That's a good idea!" Suzette called as she waved and hurried to catch up with her students.

❧

"What is that?" Nicolas asked as a new building came into sight when they rounded a bend in the road.

"That's the new schoolhouse," Adam said. "The one your brothers and sisters attend and the one Suzette teaches at."

Nicolas nodded. "It's good that it's so close."

"Yes. It's very modern on the inside. You'll have to take a look one day."

"How did your sister become a teacher out here, so far from New Orleans?"

"Oh, I'd been telling her how badly we needed good teachers here and how hard it was to find one willing to live away from the cities. I've also been telling her, for several years now, how beautiful it is here on the bayou. She came to visit and decided to stay."

Nicolas wanted to ask how she came to live in his home, with his mother and siblings, but he didn't have to as Adam continued.

"As teachers are hard to come by down here and the community can't afford to pay much, your maman and papa offered her a place to live. We've all been glad she was there, especially after your papa died. She's been good company for Maman and the children."

And now she will either have to move back to the cabin—or I will. "I'm sure Maman has been glad of the company. It was hard for her?"

"Oui. It's been very hard. I think the only thing that may pull her out of it is seeing you, *beau-frère*. Your papa was very ill. So many were sick. . . ."

"I wish I'd been here."

"You were doing what you had to do. You were one of the first from Breaux Bridge to be drafted. . . . Papa was very proud of you. It was. . .bad over there?"

Nicolas sighed deeply. "It was bad."

"I am glad you are home. Your arm will heal. Things will be better after a while."

Would they? Nicolas knew they would never be the same. Could they ever be better? "I thank you for working both your farm and ours, Adam."

"No thanks are needed, you know that. Your papa and I shared the work when he was well, and you would have done the same. And everyone helps out at harvest so we can all get it done. But I'm glad you are back to take your place at the head of your family." He turned to grin at Nicolas. "Your sister and I are starting our own."

New life! Nicolas could honestly be happy about that! "Now that is some good news to hear, mon ami! That is good news for sure!"

They rounded another bend, and Nicolas caught his breath at the sight of home. It looked the same as when he'd left—the long porch along the front of the house, the chinaberry tree in the front yard, and the garden out back. He could make out the roof of the cabin down closer to the bayou. Home.

"You go on in and see Maman. I'll bring your bag," Adam said.

Nicolas needed no encouragement as his mother opened the screened door to see who'd driven up in her yard. The look on her face was enough to send Nicolas hurrying out of the car and up the steps to envelop her in a hug. She did indeed look older, sadder, and very tired.

"My son, oh, my son! You are finally home!" Her arms wrapped around him.

"I am, Maman!" Nicolas couldn't keep his own tears from forming as his mother began to cry. He bent and kissed the wetness of her soft cheek. "I'm so sorry I wasn't here for you—"

"You are here now. And your papa was so proud of you. . . ." She nodded. "He was proud. So was I, my son. But I'm glad you are home."

"So am I, Maman." More than he'd even realized he would be.

"I knew God would take care of you. He wouldn't give me more than I could bear. It was a hard time over there?"

Nicolas couldn't speak for a moment. Instead, he rocked his mother back and forth, his chin resting on the top of her head, until he found his voice again. "It was. But it's over now. And I'm home to stay."

"And we're all so glad of that, brother! We've missed you!"

Nicolas turned to see his sister Felicia slowly climbing the steps with Adam. Obviously, she was indeed expecting a baby. He grinned at her. "I'm to be an uncle, am I?" He turned to wrap his arms around her, being careful not to hug too hard.

"You are. . .after the first of the year—but it can't be too soon for me!" She rested her head on his shoulder, and Nicolas could tell she was stifling a sob. "It's good to have you home."

Nicolas nodded as he held her. "It's good to be home. . . . I just wish—"

"Maman," Adam interrupted, "Nicolas was on the early train. I think he must be hungry. . .do you have any breakfast left for him?"

"No leftovers for my son. I will make him anything he

wants," Lucia said, leading the way into the house. "And tonight for supper we'll be having the gumbo for Nicolas's homecoming. You both must join us!"

"As if we don't take most meals together, anyway, Maman," Felicia said. "Oh, Nicolas, just wait until you meet Suzette!"

"Oh yes, Nicolas. . .Suzette has your room. You won't mind taking over the cabin as your own, will you?"

"Of course not, Maman." The cabin had been the original home of the LeBlanc family, until this larger home had been built. Several of the male members had lived there through the years. Now it seemed it was his turn. "I'll get settled after breakfast."

The rest of the morning was spent trying to catch up on all that had been going on in his absence and answering the many questions they had about the war and all the places he'd seen. After breakfast, Adam walked with him down to the cabin to settle in, while Felicia helped his mother clean up.

He was surprised to find the cabin so clean and inviting. There were curtains on the windows and fresh linens on the bed, now covered with a homemade quilt. All he really had to do was unpack his duffel bag and buy the few groceries he'd want to have on hand. "Maman must have been cleaning for weeks to get this in shape for me."

"Actually, Suzette cleaned it up. She lived here up until your papa died. Then we all decided that Maman could use the company, and so she moved in the big house. It's worked out well. And we've been expecting you for several weeks. I'm sure she's tried to keep it clean."

Nicolas was having a difficult time picturing Adam's sister as an adult, but the more he heard about her, the more anxious he was to meet this woman who'd been such a help in his absence. "I'll have to thank her for all she's done."

"She's come to love Maman and the children. And she's grateful for a place to live. Felicia and I offered, but our home is still very small, and with the baby coming, Suzette felt more comfortable accepting your parents' offer of a place to live. Now she feels that at least she's giving back something by being there for Maman."

"Still, I will thank her." Nicolas was getting more curious about this sister of Adam's with each passing moment. . . . She sounded too good to be true.

Nicolas spent the rest of the day with Adam driving him around both farms so that he could see how things were doing. It was nearing suppertime when they returned home, and Nicolas looked forward to a supper of the gumbo he'd dreamed about while he was away.

❧

Suzette and the children came home to a different Lucia. The look on her face, one of sadness mixed with joy, was one Suzette knew she would remember forever. Nicolas had indeed returned, and Lucia and Felicia were busy making a celebration meal. Suzette said a silent prayer of thankfulness as she donned an apron and lent her two hands to the task.

The children helped with setting the table and filling glasses with water, practicing their English as had become the custom ever since Suzette had come to live with them. In their excitement, their words seemed to tumble over each other as they waited for Nicolas and Adam to return.

Suzette found herself looking out the open window in anticipation of meeting this son and brother that she'd heard so much about. She'd never say a word to any of them, but he sounded a bit too good to be true.

Chapter 2

The smells wafting out of the house as he and Adam walked up to the porch had Nicolas's mouth watering in expectation. He couldn't wait to see his siblings and share a meal with them, speaking once more in the familiar language of his ancestors rather than the English he'd adopted during the war.

He walked into the house and was quickly overtaken by the hugs and laughter from his siblings. . .they all seemed to have grown at least a foot in his absence. He hugged each one before turning to find Adam pulling a petite young woman forward.

"Nicolas, this is my sister—"

"Suzette. I'm pleased to meet you—again. I've heard much about you today, but Adam did not tell me I would not recognize you," Nicolas said, taking her small hand in his.

"Ah, my brother has been talking, has he?" Suzette smiled up at him.

"A little." Nicolas was surprised at the way his heart seemed to skip a beat as he looked down into her blue eyes. He could see no resemblance at all to the awkward adolescent he remembered. Adam's sister had grown into a beauty. An enchanting one at that, he thought, as he watched her blush when he held her hand for a moment too long.

She gently slipped her fingers out of his grasp and took her seat at the table. The ongoing chatter hadn't stopped, but it wasn't until Nicolas took his place at the table that he realized they weren't speaking in Cajun. They were all speaking English—and being corrected by the vision sitting across the table from him.

"What is this? When did this family start speaking the English at home?" he asked.

"Since Suzette moved here and became our teacher. It's a game we play that she thought would help us to learn faster," Amy said.

Nicolas was a little confused. What had changed since he'd been gone? "Why do they need to be in a hurry? The language spoken here in bayou country is Cajun."

"Yes. But it won't be many years before *only* English is spoken at school," Suzette said.

"Then they can speak it at school—at home they will speak the Cajun."

"But if they speak English more at home, the easier it will be—"

"Not in this house. They can learn at school." The conversation was over as far as he was concerned. She was the teacher. She could teach them at school. He watched as Suzette took a deep breath and exhaled.

"Nicolas, they are talking about passing a law." Suzette looked at him from across the table. When his gaze met hers, she continued. "And when they do, *all* subjects will be taught in English. I just want to make the transition easier on the children."

"Non!" It appeared he'd been right in his assessment. She *was* too good to be true! Beautiful, yes—enchanting, without a doubt. But she also appeared to be stubborn and argumentative!

"Nicolas." Lucia quietly got his attention.

"Yes, Maman?"

"It was your papa who agreed for us to help the children learn. It was what he wanted. I ask you to honor his wishes."

Nicolas sighed. Had he fought a war, been wounded, come home to the death of his father, only to lose his right to speak his own language in his home?

"You may speak the Cajun at the table," his mother continued. "The children can speak the English. It will be a game and help them also. Please, Nicolas?"

Nicolas looked into his mother's eyes. He sighed deeply, knowing he couldn't say no to her. At least *he* could speak his own language at his supper table—but it appeared that he wasn't going to be able to listen to it there. He nodded and gave in to his mother. "All right, Maman."

❧

Suzette did the dishes and cleaned up the kitchen, so that the family could spend Nicolas's first evening at home together. As she washed and dried the dishes, she could hear the murmur of voices coming from the living room. She couldn't be happier for the LeBlanc family—that their Nicolas was finally home.

It must be a bittersweet homecoming, knowing his papa had passed away while he was in Europe. Tears stung the back of Suzette's eyelids just thinking of the joy mixed with sorrow he must be feeling. And because of that she would overlook his irritability over speaking English in his home. She certainly didn't want to bring him more pain, but it was imperative that the young ones learned to speak English well.

Hopefully, she would be able to make him understand the importance of it soon. As it was, she was just thankful that Maman LeBlanc had calmed him down and gotten him to agree to both languages being spoken at home. Still, he must have been longing to hear his Cajun spoken after being gone so long. What horrors he must have seen. . . .

Suzette shook her head. She didn't want to even think about those. She smiled as she heard a burst of laughter coming from the front room. It was good to hear. Maybe now that Nicolas was back, there would be more of it. He looked little like she remembered at her brother's wedding. Although more handsome to her, he also looked older, but she was sure that was from all he'd experienced overseas and the deep sorrow he felt over his papa's death.

She sighed deeply as she dried the last dish and put it away. Turning, she found Nicolas standing in the kitchen doorway, watching her. Suzette caught her breath and held a hand to her rapidly beating heart.

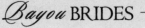

"*Sa me fait de la pain*—I mean. . .I'm sorry. I did not mean to startle you," he said. "I was just wondering if there was any *café* left?"

She let out the breath she'd been holding. "There is. I'll get you a cup."

"Non. I can get it. You've worked long enough tonight. Thank you for helping Maman."

Suzette waved his thank-you away with her hand and took a cup from the cabinet. "It is the least I can do for your mother. She is a wonderful woman."

Nicolas grinned at her. "Ah. Something we can agree on."

She poured the coffee and asked, "Café au lait?"

"Non." Refusing the addition of milk, he took the cup from her. "Thank you."

She smiled and answered in his Cajun, "*Il y a pas de quoi*. I feel bad about taking your room. I will be glad to move out to the cabin, Nicolas—"

"Non. It is fine. I have my things there already, and you are fine here."

"But I don't mind."

He nodded. "I can see that. But it will be better for me to sleep out there. I sometimes have nightmares, and I don't want to frighten the children."

Suzette's heart melted at his admission and his concern for his siblings. She nodded. "All right. But should you change your mind—"

"I will let you know." He took a sip of his coffee. "Maman has sent the young ones to bed. I'm going to join her on the front porch. Would you like to join us?"

Suzette poured the last cup of coffee and added a large dollop of milk and sugar to it. "Thank you, but I think I'll turn in. Besides, your Maman has missed you terribly. It will do her good to have you to herself for a while." She picked up the cup of café au lait and turned to face Nicolas. "I'll take this out to her for you. She likes a cup of café au lait before she turns in."

"Thank you for reminding me. If you put it on a tray, I can take it to her."

Obviously, he wanted no pity for his wounded arm. Suzette put the cup on a small tray, and he added his own to it before taking it from her.

"Thank you. Good night, then."

"Good night, Nicolas. Tell Maman LeBlanc I'll see her in the morning, please."

❧

Nicolas kicked the screen door open and held his foot in place when it closed, easing it out slowly so as not to slam the door loudly and wake the children. He handed his mother the tray Suzette had fixed for them before joining Maman in the swing his papa had hung there when Nicolas was only a child.

"Suzette was retiring for the night." Nicolas took his cup from the tray. "She said to tell you she'd see you in the morning."

His mother nodded as she took her cup of coffee and set the tray on a side table. She took a sip. "She has been such a blessing to this family. I don't know what I would have done without her to help with the children after your papa passed away."

"I'm so sorry I wasn't here, Maman."

"You were where you were needed most, my son. I understood that. Your papa did, too."

Nicolas was glad it was dark out so that his mother couldn't see the sudden tears that formed in his eyes. "I know. I am glad to be home."

And he was. But things seemed so different now. So much had changed since he'd been gone. . .or maybe it was that he had changed. Right now Nicolas wasn't sure which it was.

"Suzette offered to move back out to the cabin, but I told her no."

His mother pulled her shawl closer around her. "It will take some time to get used to being back home, I think," she said, as if she could read his mind. "Your papa said you would probably prefer to be out in the cabin for a while when you came home. So it is a good thing that Suzette had already moved out."

They swung in silence for a while, enjoying the night sounds from the Bayou Teche. It was music to Nicolas's heart. He wondered if Suzette liked the sounds and then wondered why he was thinking of her. She'd been very sweet tonight when he'd lost his temper about speaking the English at the dinner table. And it was obvious that his family liked her. "Is she a good teacher?"

"Suzette? Oui. She is very good. The children love her. She is only trying to help them, Nicolas. Before long it will be against the law to speak French or our Cajun on the school grounds. There has been talk of it everywhere. She is only trying to make it easier for them."

"Maman, I agreed to your terms. But I don't have to like them."

"Non. You do not have to like them. But I thank you for agreeing." She drained her cup and put it back on the tray before getting to her feet. "I am so glad you are home, Nicolas. I'll have breakfast ready for you in the morning. I hope you sleep well."

He stood and bent down to kiss her on the cheek. "I am glad, too, Maman. I'll see you in the morning. Good night."

"Good night." She took his cup from him and added it to the tray before going inside.

Nicolas stretched. It was getting late, and he had much to do tomorrow. He headed down to the cabin along the bayou's edge. The cabin had its own small porch facing the water, and he looked out on the moonlit bayou. Home. He was finally home.

But his heart hurt from both joy and sadness, for it wasn't the homecoming he'd envisioned. Nicolas fought the tears that gathered behind his eyes and shook his head. He'd missed so much in the time he'd been so far away. His papa was gone and there was no bringing him back. His precious maman had aged in her sorrow. His siblings had grown by leaps and bounds, and he barely recognized them now. Amy had turned into a blossoming *memselle*, while Julien was on the verge of becoming a *jeune homme*. Only Jacques seemed similar to the child he'd been when Nicolas left. He wished he could say the same about Rose, but he couldn't. She'd lost her babyish ways and was in school now. Nicolas shook his head.

Changes. . .there were so very many to get used to. One of the biggest was the petite school teacher ensconced in his room in the big house. . .that somehow no longer seemed so large or familiar to him. . .and the news she brought that his beloved language was in danger of being outlawed.

His heart ached with all the changes around him, and yet deep down there was a joy that he was finally back with his family. He let the night sounds wrap around him—the water lapping gently at the bank, the quiet broken by the loud slap of a beaver tail on the bayou, or the hoot owls calling out across the way. The familiar sounds gave him some comfort in knowing that some things *did* stay the same. He only wished everything had.

❧

Suzette was still awake when Maman LeBlanc came back inside. She heard her steps on each of the stairs and heard her check in on the girls in their room and the boys in theirs before she went to her own.

Tired as she was, Suzette hadn't been able to drift off to sleep. She couldn't get Nicolas out of her mind. When she'd turned to find him in the kitchen entryway, there was an expression in his dark eyes that had her pulse racing and her heartbeat loud to her ears.

But the look in his eyes had changed as he glanced around the kitchen, and it had her wanting to tell him everything would be all right, and she didn't even know what was wrong.

He'd just looked so. . .*uncomfortable* was the only word that came to mind. As if he didn't quite feel at home yet. At the same time there was a hint of the joy he must feel at being home. She sent up a prayer that he would adjust to being back home quickly and that he would soon feel more joy than sadness.

Chapter 3

The nightmares he'd experienced in the last few months did not give Nicolas a break on his first night at home, and he was awake long before daybreak. But he wrapped himself in a blanket and went out to the porch to watch the morning mist rise and then disappear over the bayou, leaving behind a beautifully clear blue sky. How he'd longed for the sight of dawn here in Breaux Bridge. He tried to soak it all in—the beauty, the sounds, and even the smells he grew up with—before realizing that if he wanted to join the children for breakfast, he needed to hurry. Dressing quickly, he headed to the main house, and his stomach rumbled with hunger as the smell of pork sausage, eggs, and grits wafted out to greet him.

When he entered the kitchen, the happiness on his mother's face as she greeted him was something he knew he'd never forget. He thought she even looked a little younger this morning.

"Good morning, Nicolas!"

He crossed the room to give her soft cheek a kiss. "Good morning, Maman."

"Did you sleep well? Sit, I will have your breakfast before you in a moment."

He didn't want to tell her he'd been awakened by the nightmare of war. "I woke to the sounds of the bayou. I missed them while I was gone. Where are the children?"

"They've already eaten and are now getting ready for school. Julien wanted to go wake you for breakfast, but I thought you might need your sleep after the long trip home."

"I should have come over earlier. I forgot about the children going to school."

"There will be plenty of time to have breakfast with them. It will take you awhile to get used to the change in time, I would imagine."

"Yes, I guess that's what it is." Tomorrow he wouldn't dawdle. He'd hoped to have breakfast with the whole family this first morning, but instead Suzette was trying to hurry them along and from what he could see, she was doing a good job of it. In only minutes they'd each kissed Maman and him, also, before heading out the door.

"Good morning, Nicolas," Suzette said with a smile.

"Miss Suzette, hurry, hurry," Rose said with a giggle.

"And good-bye!" Suzette told him with a chuckle as Rose pulled her along and out the door.

Before he could take a sip of the coffee his mother set before him, Rose had run back in and climbed up into his lap. She planted a big kiss on his cheek and said, in his beloved Cajun,

"I love you, Nicolas! I'm glad you are home."

"I'm glad too, Rosy. Have a good day." His heart swelled with love for the child as he followed her to the door and saw that Suzette was waiting for Rose as the others had run on ahead. Rose skipped to meet her, and something about the way the young schoolteacher smiled and bent her head to hear what Rose was saying to her touched Nicolas. It was as if Suzette had nothing else to do but listen to what the child was saying.

His mother touched him on the shoulder. "Your breakfast is ready, son. Come eat."

Nicolas turned back to the table. "I'd better hurry, I see Adam coming down the road."

"Non. No need to hurry. Your sister gets sick at the smell of breakfast cooking. I'm sure he'll be glad to join you."

His mother was right. Adam was more than happy to take time for breakfast before they set out to check on the small herd of cattle that provided both families with much of the meat they ate.

Suzette was a little taken back by how eager she was to arrive at the LeBlanc home that afternoon. She told herself it was because the children were so excited about Nicolas's return that some of their enthusiasm had rubbed off on her. But she knew it was more than that: She wanted to know how his day went and see if some of the sorrow had left his eyes.

It had been difficult to concentrate on the lessons she

taught that day, as she couldn't get thoughts of Nicolas out of her mind. She'd been trying to avoid thinking of him, but it wasn't working. She wondered how he would react to the English lessons at the dinner table tonight. Would he find out that she'd been speaking English so long that her French was a little rusty? And that she was much more familiar with the Creole French spoken in New Orleans than with his Cajun French—the French that had come from the Acadians. She could actually use his help in understanding what the children said at times, but how to tell him that without sounding as if she only wanted them to speak English for her sake?

It truly was only a matter of time before speaking French of any kind in the classrooms and even on the school grounds would be a thing of the past. She didn't like it any more than he seemed to. Her ancestors had spoken French, too. But in New Orleans, it was more common to hear English than here in Bayou country. And she'd learned very quickly that the Cajuns clung tightly to their traditions. Giving in to the new rules would be hard on every family she knew in Breaux Bridge. She wanted to make it as easy on them as she could.

She loved this part of Louisiana. Her brother had been telling her for years how much she would like it, but it hadn't been until this past summer when she came for a visit that she decided she wanted to stay. Her decision probably had as much to do with the LeBlanc family as with life along the bayou. She'd fallen in love with them all, and she'd immediately felt at home there. No wonder her brother had never gone back to New Orleans for more than a few days at a time.

Now as the LeBlanc home came into sight and the children ran ahead, Suzette wondered if Nicolas was there or out getting familiar with the land and the bayou again. When he came out onto the porch, a cup of coffee in his hand, and waved, she was surprised by the way her heartbeat skittered in her chest. She waved back and watched as he greeted first one child and then the next.

But once they'd all gone to greet their mother, Nicolas stayed outside, watching her approach. What was it about this man that made her pulse race at just the sight of him?

"Good afternoon, Suzette. How was your day? The children all behaved themselves?"

She couldn't tell Nicolas that her day had been filled with thoughts of him, so she answered the latter question only. "Good afternoon, Nicolas. The children all behaved very well today. How did your day pass?"

"It was a good day. Adam and I took stock of what needs to be done this winter before spring planting gets underway. Several fences need repairing, and we want to enlarge the barns on both our properties. Your brother is a hard worker and because of it, we are well supplied from the fall harvest. My sister did well in her choice of a husband."

"My brother made a good choice, as well, seeing what a wonderful wife he has in Felicia." Suzette climbed the steps to the porch. As she came abreast of Nicolas, he seemed even taller than the day before. "Together, they make each other stronger, and I think they are going to be wonderful parents."

"Oui. I'm looking forward to being an uncle, and it will be

good for Maman to have a baby around again."

"It will be good for us all. I'd better go help your maman with supper."

"The girls will help. You've been working all day."

"Yes. But I love being in the kitchen with your maman. I've learned much from helping her."

"Ah." Nicolas smiled and nodded. "She is a wonderful cook. If you want to help, I'm sure they would be glad for an extra pair of hands."

Suzette opened the screen door, but Nicolas stopped her from going inside by his touch on her shoulder.

"Wait."

She turned to him.

"Maman has told me how much having you here has meant to her. I thank you for being here for her, especially after Papa died."

"You are welcome. I would not have wanted to be anywhere else." She hurried inside before the tears in the corners of her eyes spilled over.

❧

Nicolas went to check the livestock and met up with Adam and Felicia on the way back to the house. When they entered the house, they found it full of the delicious smells that seemed to always come out of his maman's kitchen—and the sweet sounds of women talking and laughing as they got supper ready. Felicia hurried to join in, and he and Adam just grinned and shook their heads. How those women managed to keep up with what each other was saying was beyond them, but they did.

He and Adam played *faire la statue* with the younger children, moving about the living room freely until the leader said stop. Then each one froze in position, and the leader picked the funniest posed person to be the next leader. Soon the laughter in the living room drowned out the giggling in the kitchen.

It was music to Nicolas's heart. They were sounds he'd longed to hear for so long, and he was sure his papa would be glad that the family could finally laugh once more.

By the time the whole group was seated at the table, Nicolas's stomach was rumbling with hunger. The meal of roast pork, potatoes, and gravy, along with his maman's homemade bread, satisfied him in more ways than one.

It was only as the children began to speak the English with Suzette that his mood was dampened. But he'd made an agreement with his mother, and he meant to keep it, no matter how he longed to hear only the Cajun spoken in his home.

But as he listened, Nicolas had to admit that Suzette had a way of making learning the language a game.

She pointed to the platter of roast, and Rose rushed to say, *"Daube de cochon!"*

"Pork roast," Suzette prompted.

Rose grinned and repeated, "Pork roast."

Then Rose pointed to the fresh loaf of bread, *"Pain."*

"Bread," Suzette said. Then she pointed to the bowl of gravy.

Jacques jumped up. *"Sauce rouge!"*

Suzette grinned and said, "Gravy."

"Gravy," Jacques agreed.

And on it went until nearly everything on the table had been named. Even Maman, Felicia, and Adam joined in the game.

When Maman got up and brought back a chocolate *gateau*, everyone except him yelled, "Chocolate cake!"

Obviously they'd learned a prior lesson very well. Nicolas hadn't participated in the game, but he couldn't keep from joining in the laughter.

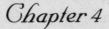

Chapter 4

With each day that passed, Nicolas began to feel a little more at home. He still half-expected to see his papa each morning when he entered the main house, and he wasn't sure his heart would ever stop aching for that sight. But his mother's smile helped ease the pain, and he was glad to see that the corners of her mouth seemed to turn up a little bit more each day.

It wasn't until the end of the next week that he was reminded that Christmas was nearly upon them. No one had mentioned it, and it was only when he overheard the children talking about their upcoming school break as they came home from school on Friday that he realized he needed to talk to Maman about it.

He waited until after the children had been put to bed before bringing up the subject, knowing now that his mother and Suzette usually had a cup of café au lait together before retiring for the night.

He joined them in the kitchen and asked for a cup for

himself. As they sat around the small kitchen table that was also used as a worktable, he took a sip of the fragrant liquid and thought about how to bring up the subject. Perhaps the easiest way would be through Suzette.

He looked over at her. "The children are on break next week?"

"Yes. They are out for Christmas and New Year's."

"Christmas! It is so soon?" Maman asked, on the verge of tears. "I knew it was coming, but I put it out of my mind. I can't imagine it without Papa."

"It's all right, Maman. I'd almost forgotten, too."

"It is understandable," Suzette tried to assure them.

"But the children—" Maman began to cry. "We must try for their sake."

Nicolas and Suzette were both up and at her side. Nicolas gave her a hug and kissed her on the top of the head. Suzette refilled her cup of coffee and patted her on the back.

"Don't cry, Maman. The children do not need to know we nearly forgot."

"And it is not too late to prepare for Christmas. I will help and so will Felicia."

"But your parents are expecting you home for Christmas."

Suzette shook her head vigorously. "Non. I told them in a letter that I wanted to stay here. They mentioned that they might come to stay with Adam and Felicia, but I don't think they've told them yet."

"Oh, I am glad you will be here, Suzette." Maman sniffed and blew her nose with the handkerchief she pulled from her pocket. "And Papa would want us to do our best to carry on without him." She fought more tears. "It will be hard, but the children have been through so much sorrow already. I don't want them thinking they can't get excited about Christmas."

"You are right, Maman. It is what Papa would want. Adam and I will go look for a tree to put up tomorrow."

"And we can have the children help decorate it. They can help make candy and cookies, too."

"Maman, if you think of what you would like to get each one, I can take you into Breaux Bridge and buy the presents for them."

"Oh, I don't know if I can go without Papa, Nicolas. Not this year. Maybe Suzette can go with you?" She looked expectantly from one to the other.

Nicolas wasn't sure how he felt about spending a day in town with Suzette, but he couldn't say no to his mother. "Of course, Suzette can help me, if she doesn't mind."

"I'll be glad to go help Nicolas, if that's what you want, Maman LeBlanc."

"Thank you both. That puts my mind at ease."

That settled it. Nicolas couldn't tell how Suzette felt about the shopping trip, but it seemed neither of them was willing to upset his mother by telling her no. "I'm glad. Just make up a list, and we'll take care of the rest, Maman."

Nicolas drained his cup and stood. "I'll see you in the morning."

"Good night, dear," Maman said as he kissed her forehead. "I am so very glad you are home."

"I'm glad to be here, Maman. Good night to you both."

Suzette smiled at him as she gathered the cups and took them to the sink. "Sleep well, Nicolas."

He went out the back door and headed for the cottage, glad that he'd talked to the two women and relieved that Suzette would be staying for Christmas. With Papa gone, they would need all the help they could get to make it through the holidays.

As Nicolas walked down the path to the cabin, he suddenly stopped in his tracks. He was actually looking forward to spending a day with Suzette. He frowned. He wasn't sure this eager anticipation to their outing was a good thing. She was lovely and sweet, and he'd be lying if he said he wasn't attracted to her, but she was part of the system that was trying to do away with his beloved Cajun and he couldn't let himself forget that fact.

He couldn't seem to quit thinking about her—that she cared about his family was totally obvious, but it was just as clear that she didn't seem to understand the way of life in this part of the country. Not yet.

❧

Suzette washed up the cups and cleaned the kitchen while Maman LeBlanc started on her Christmas list. She found herself looking forward to the shopping trip with Nicolas in spite of herself. The last thing she needed was to fall for a man who resented her for wanting to teach English. He just didn't seem to understand that it wasn't that she wanted his language to be extinct anymore than she wanted the Creole French she'd grown up speaking to be a thing of the past. But neither of them could ignore the changes that were occurring in this part of the country. . .no matter how much they might want to.

The state of Louisiana was leaning heavily in the direction of wanting all of its citizens to speak and learn the same language. Laws were going to be passed. It was inevitable. And all Suzette wanted was to make the transition easier on her students. One day maybe Nicolas would understand what she was trying to do, but she had a feeling that he didn't even want to try right now. And she could understand. He had more than enough to adjust to, just by becoming the head of his family now, responsible for his mother and his siblings, and trying to help them all through this time of year when his own heart must be breaking.

That was one reason she'd told her parents that she was staying here for the Christmas break. After all the LeBlanc family had done for her, she couldn't bear the thought of leaving them to get through this first Christmas without Papa LeBlanc.

Maman LeBlanc broke into her thoughts, "Suzette, are you sure it is all right with your maman and papa for you to stay with us over your break?"

"I'm sure." At least she prayed they were all right with it. Suzette was hoping her parents would come to see Adam and Felicia and spend the holiday with them all. They might then finally begin to understand what it was about these people that had a hold on her heart. Their love of family and spending time together was one of the things she loved most about them. "If they don't come for Christmas, I'm sure they will come when the baby is born. I think they are excited about becoming grand-parents."

"Oui, I'm sure they are. I can't wait to hold that baby in my arms. I just can't believe my Felicia is old enough to be a parent. Time passes much too quickly."

❧

Julien and Jacques were thrilled the next afternoon when Nicolas and Adam let the two boys go with them to find a Christmas tree. There was a stand of young pines on the property, and Adam was sure they would find one that would work.

The girls were equally happy to be included in the candy making. Felicia had come to help, and Suzette thoroughly enjoyed the day. It was fun to watch Maman LeBlanc try to find out what the girls wanted for Christmas. They really asked for very little—and Suzette had a feeling they were trying to make things as easy on their mother as they could. By the time the men were back with a tree for both homes, there was a fresh batch of pralines cooling on the kitchen table and several trays of cookies in the oven. Maman LeBlanc had put on a pot of bean soup, and after supper the children begged to put up the tree early instead of waiting until Christmas Eve.

"Please, Maman. Can we put it up tonight?" Rose asked.

"Yes, please, Maman," Amy added. "We almost had Papa talked into putting it up early last year. Please let us."

"Oh yes, please do, Maman," Jacques begged.

"You are right, Amy. Papa was for it. I was the one who said no. So. . .yes! We will put it up early as Papa nearly agreed to last year. Nicolas, would you bring the decorations down from the attic, please?"

"Of course, Maman," Nicolas quickly agreed.

Suzette had a feeling he thought it would be easier to start a new tradition of putting the tree up a few days early than to continue with the old. She thought so, too. He and Adam brought the boxes down to the living room, and Suzette and Felicia carefully unwrapped each ornament. Then they handed them out to the children to put on the tree while Maman made hot chocolate and brought in a plate of the cookies they'd baked earlier.

Suzette's heart went out to them all as they each seemed to try to hide the sorrow they felt that Papa LeBlanc wasn't there. She had a feeling that tears would be shed when they turned out the lights that night, but for the moment they all seemed to want to make the evening easier on their mother. She tried to help by playing the language game, pointing first to the tree.

Jacques shouted, *"Arbre de Noël!"*

"Christmas tree!" Nicolas answered back. The mood in the room lightened as he joined in the game, and Suzette's heart expanded with joy to see Maman join in the laugher that ensued.

❧

Nicolas brought his papa's 1916 Ford around to the front of the house to pick up his family for church the next morning.

Rose sat on Maman's lap, up front with him, and Amy and Suzette sat in the back. Adam and Felicia had already picked up Julien and Jacques.

Nicolas's first instinct had been to miss church, but he knew his mother wouldn't allow it, so he'd dressed in his one and only suit, which thankfully still fit, and done what he knew was expected of him.

The whole time he'd been overseas, even after he'd been wounded and his buddy killed, he'd felt close to the Lord. But ever since the day he received word about his papa, Nicolas had been filled with more questions than answers, and he'd found it increasingly hard to pray, hard to take everything to Him. At home now, he questioned why his language might soon be extinct. It seemed all he had for the Lord were questions of *why*.

Still, he was a little surprised by how good it felt be back in church with his family again. To sit on the same pew they'd sat on for years. . .and to be sitting beside Suzette. He needed to thank her for helping make last night much easier than he thought it would be. Her silly language game had helped more than he liked to admit, and the least he could do was thank her for being there for them all.

Maybe now it was time to pray, to thank the Lord for getting him back home safely and for keeping the rest of his family safe, for bringing Suzette into his family's lives to help them when he couldn't. And for him to accept God's will. Nicolas bowed his head and silently did just that.

Chapter 5

With Christmas falling on Wednesday, Nicolas and Suzette had little time to spare in getting to town to shop. He was glad that Monday was sunny and not too cool. They had made plans to go into Breaux Bridge right after breakfast, and he was glad to see Suzette ready and waiting for him when he pulled the Ford around.

Maman waved them off with a smile on her face, and for that Nicolas was extremely grateful. He knew everything was an effort for her with Papa gone, and he loved her all the more for trying to carry on so gallantly without him.

"Ready?" He turned to Suzette as she took her seat beside him.

"I am. I have your mother's list with me. I hope we will be able to find everything."

"I hope so, too. We'll do the best we can. So, what is it we are looking for?"

Suzette pulled the list from her coat pocket. "Let's see. For Amy, she would like us to find a scarf and gloves to match in red or purple. It seems Rose has hinted for a new baby doll and Jacques would like a toy boat. Julien would like a new sling-shot. I don't think those will be too hard to find, do you?"

"I don't think so," Nicolas swerved the automobile to avoid a rut in the road, and that sent Suzette sliding across the seat and into his arm that was still in a sling. It didn't hurt, but he was surprised by the electric charge that shot up his arm. He'd been trying to do the exercises the doctor had given him before he was discharged and sent home, but this was the first time he'd felt anything from his fingertips to his shoulder. Perhaps he'd get full use of it soon.

"I'm sorry," he apologized as she tried to right herself. "These roads have gotten worse since I've been gone. Are you all right?"

"I'm fine. But are *you* all right? Did I hurt your arm?"

"No, you didn't. It's fine."

"Good." Suzette straightened the knitted cap she had on and continued with their conversation as if nothing had happened. "She also has a few things down for us to try to find for Adam and Felicia. I hope we haven't waited so long that the stores are sold out of what we need to find."

"There are several different stores in town that we can try. Breaux Bridge has grown even since I've been gone." He did hope they could find it all. The only problem he could see was that his mother had asked him to pick up a gift for Suzette also, and he didn't know for sure how he was going to get that done. If he couldn't manage it today, he'd just have to run back into town tomorrow.

"I do like Breaux Bridge," Suzette said as they entered the town. "It's such a pretty town, sitting here on both sides of Bayou Teche with the bridge connecting it. It's not so big that you don't know anyone, and yet it is large enough to find what you need."

"Well, we hope so," Nicolas said as he parked the car. "Let's go to the Main Street Mercantile. It's really more of a department store than it used to be, and it should have most of what is on Maman's list."

"All right, if we can't find it all there, Maman LeBlanc said there was a ladies store we could try."

"A ladies store?" Horrified with the idea of going into a store for women, Nicolas must have looked as appalled as he felt because Suzette giggled.

"I'll go in, Nicolas. You won't have to. But Maman seemed to think the others might be sold out of scarves and gloves."

His sigh of relief brought another chuckle from her. "I'm relieved to hear that, Suzette. But let's see what we can find in the department stores first."

The Main Street Mercantile did indeed have most of what they were looking for. They found Rose's doll right away. It had brown hair and blue eyes that opened and closed, and they both agreed that Rose was sure to love it. They also found a red and blue toy boat for Jacques and the slingshot Julien was hoping for. But Amy's present was another matter. Both department stores in town had sold out of the items they were looking for.

"Don't worry, Nicolas. I'll run over to Goodwin's and look.

I'm sure they will have scarves and gloves to match."

"Are you sure you don't mind?"

"I'm sure. I can meet you back here—"

"No. Let's meet at the Acadian Café for lunch. Then we can see where we are in our shopping. I want to find something for Maman." He thought for a moment. He'd been through a world war—surely he could manage a ladies shop. "But perhaps I should just come with you and see what I can find there for her. Do you think they would have a cape for Maman? I'd like to find her a nice one."

"I'm sure they will. I've seen one in the display window in the past. But I'll be glad to look for you and let you know if they have any I think she'd like when we meet for lunch."

"No. I'll come with you." He might get an idea of what Suzette liked if he went along. And he'd much rather go in with her to look for Maman's gift now than to go by himself later.

Actually, he rather enjoyed accompanying Suzette to Goodwin's. And once inside, there was nothing terribly frightening about being in the store. The displays were tastefully laid out and since it was two days before Christmas, he found he wasn't the only man in the store.

The salesclerk showed them several styles of capes, and he chose a black silk-lined wool one for his mother. It was simple but elegant, and he hoped she would like it. The store had a nice selection of scarves and gloves, and they picked out a royal purple set for Amy. They both left Goodwin's happy that they'd found most of what was on Maman's list. But Nicolas still didn't know what to get the children from him.

"Actually, Amy likes to read. She loved reading the *Anne of Green Gables* series. The newest book in that series was written last year. It's *Anne's House of Dreams*. I think maybe she'd like a copy of her own. Maybe we could visit the bookstore?"

"That is a wonderful idea, Suzette. Thank you."

"You're welcome. I think Rose might like some paper dolls to play with. Maybe we can find those there, too."

"Oh, I think she would like that. Let's go get something to eat, and then we can finish up our shopping." He had a feeling he would be happy with his purchases for the children if he just listened to Suzette. He'd been gone a long time, and she seemed to know their likes and dislikes much better than he did now.

❧

They'd met up with several friends and extended family of the LeBlanc's as they'd gone around town, and it was obvious that Nicolas was well respected by them all. Now, sitting in the café across from him as they were served steaming bowls of red beans and rice, Suzette wondered how she could ever have thought him gruff.

This shopping trip showed just how much he cared about his family. Her respect for him soared as he'd entered the dress shop with her. There was no way her papa would have entered that shop, yet Nicolas had put away his natural reluctance to go in so that he could get his mother a wonderful present. The salesclerk had almost ignored the fact that Suzette was with Nicolas in her eagerness to help him. But she couldn't blame the young woman. Nicolas was a handsome man, and Suzette had to admit that she was quite pleased to be escorted by him.

"I'm still not real sure about what to get the boys," Nicolas said before blowing on the spoon of beans and rice to cool it down.

"Maybe we'll spot something while we are looking for the girls," she suggested.

As they talked about where to go next and what to get the boys, she felt encouraged to bring up a subject she wasn't sure he would welcome. But he *was* the head of the LeBlanc household now, and she needed his help.

"Nicolas, I must to speak to you about the children's English lessons." She could tell from the way his left eyebrow raised that she was right. He didn't welcome the subject.

"Yes? What about them?"

Well, at least he was willing to listen to what she had to say.

"I've noticed that until the night we put the tree up, you hadn't joined in our word games. You haven't been speaking your Cajun at the table, either." In fact he usually didn't speak at all when they were playing the game.

"I thought the idea was to speak the English only," he said gruffly.

"No. The idea is to teach them the differences in the two."

"You seem to be doing a very good job of that."

Suzette sighed. He wasn't making this easy on her. "I'm sure you've noticed that I don't always get things right."

His tone softened a bit. "I have noticed that sometimes you don't quite seem to recognize the Cajun word, but I thought you were doing it wrong for the children's sake."

She smiled and shook her head. "Non. It is that sometimes the Creole French I grew up speaking and the Cajun spoken here are a little different. It's not too bad with my students, but when their parents. . .or even when you and your Maman and Felicia get to talking so fast, I can't always keep up."

"Oh, I didn't realize—"

"I could use your help, Nicolas." There. She'd said it.

"Mine? In what way?"

Suzette hesitated only a minute. "To help me translate sometimes when I don't quite understand what is being said."

Nicolas bent his head to the side and sighed before saying, "I will think about it."

That was more than she'd hoped for. In that moment, Suzette knew she was beginning to care for Nicolas LeBlanc. "Merci."

"Pas de quoi." He smiled at her.

Oh yes, she cared. Deeply.

꧁꧂

Nicolas wasn't sure just how Suzette had gotten him to agree to even *think* about interpreting the Cajun she didn't quite understand yet. Maybe it was the sweet expression in her eyes when she smiled at him, but he had a feeling it had something to do with the fact that she'd trusted him enough to admit she needed help.

After they left the café and went to the bookstore, they found exactly what they were wanting for the girls, and Suzette even found a couple of books that she thought the boys would like. Then they went back to the department stores to find the things Maman had asked them to pick up for Adam and Felicia.

They split up after that, saying they had a few things to pick up on their own, but Nicolas had a feeling they were both doing his mother's shopping for each other.

He'd been able to ask the salesclerk at Goodwin's to add a blue scarf and gloves that his mother had requested for Suzette to his purchases without Suzette knowing what he was doing, and he went to pick those up first. Then he went to do his own shopping. He picked up several boxes of chocolates and a few things for stocking stuffers, but he didn't know what to get the woman who'd helped his maman so very much.

By the time they got home that evening, Nicolas realized he'd enjoyed the day with Suzette more than he'd enjoyed anything since he'd been home, and he hated to see it come to an end.

Maman had a pot of jambalaya simmering when they entered the kitchen, and the girls had the table set already. Nicolas and Suzette quickly hid their purchases until they could get them wrapped, and then they joined the others for supper. The children knew they'd been shopping for Christmas, and their excitement was contagious. By the end of the evening he was sure that he wasn't the only adult thankful to have children around this first Christmas without Papa.

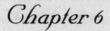

Chapter 6

The next day was filled with delicious smells, whispered secrets, and visits by family and friends. A telegram early that morning brought good news for the family. Maman's sisters were coming from Lafayette for Christmas.

Nicolas drove into Breaux Bridge to pick them up, and he'd never been happier to see his aunts. *Tante* Julia and Tante Louise were both older than his mother and widowed, so he knew their attentions to his maman would be especially tender and go a long way in helping her get through the next few days without Papa.

"My, how handsome you've become, Nicolas," Tante Julia said on the way back home. "I'm sure you have the young ladies lined up for your attentions."

Nicolas laughed. "Tante Julia, I haven't been home long enough to even pay attention to the ladies." That wasn't entirely true. He hadn't been able to get one in particular out of his mind.

"Well, it is about time you do. You aren't getting any younger, you know," Tante Louise said bluntly.

"Oh, Louise, you talk as if he is an old man! He has time. And now that he's back home, I'm sure it won't take him long to find the right one."

That started an in-depth conversation about what kind of woman they thought would make him a good wife.

"Of course she should be a good Christian woman," Tante Julia said, matter-of-factly.

"Well, of course! There is no question about that," Tante Louise agreed. "And after that, she should love your family."

"That just goes without saying, Louise," Julia said with a shake of her head. "Nicolas would not consider anyone who did not fit in with the family."

Nicolas rushed to assure them both, "No, I wou—"

"Of course you wouldn't pick someone who didn't like your family," Tante Julia interrupted. "And she must be able to cook, of course."

"Oh, Julia, of course he will pick a woman who can cook. No self-respecting Cajun would choose a woman who couldn't cook!"

"Well, you'd be surprised, Louise! A pretty face can some-times sway a man."

"A woman can be nice looking and be all of the things Nicolas would want in a wife."

Tante Louise sighed with what sounded to Nicolas as exasperation. "Well, of course she can be, Julia! I didn't mean that he shouldn't marry a pretty girl—just that she shouldn't be *only* pretty!"

"Oh! Well why didn't you say so in the first place?" Tante Julia asked.

By the time Nicolas pulled the automobile up at home, he was extremely thankful that the trip from the train station was a fairly short one. He wasn't sure how much longer he could listen to their suggestions for the perfect wife.

He carried in the aunts' bags while they were pulled into his mother's welcoming arms. Talking over one another as they had in the car, he couldn't help but smile. His mother had their full attention now, and he was a little relieved that she would be on the receiving end of their coddling, and their concentration would be on her and not on what kind of wife he should choose—should he ever get to that point in his life.

He interrupted their welcome only to ask where he needed to put their cases.

"They go up in your old room, Nicolas," Suzette said from behind him.

He turned to find her smiling sweetly at him. "But what about you? Where will you be sleeping?"

"I've already moved my things into Amy's room, and Rose is going to sleep with Maman," Suzette said.

"Oh." He nodded. The arrangement made sense to him. "All right, I'll take them upstairs, then."

His appreciation for Suzette soared that she'd happily given up her room to the aunts and moved in with Amy for the duration of their stay. She didn't seem the least bit put out about it, either.

"I'll help," Suzette said, taking one of the smaller cases and following him up the stairs. As they made their way up the stairs, then down the hallway, Suzette said in a low voice, "I came up because I wanted to tell you that Maman and I got all of the presents wrapped this morning. I hope it was all right that I wrapped what you bought, too. You might just want to put tags on them."

"Thank you, Suzette! I was wondering when I was going to get around to doing that." He'd given the presents for Suzette to Maman the day before, so he wasn't worried that she saw anything bought for her. "Where are they?"

"They are in Maman's room. I'll go get them." She put the small case on the dresser in the room she'd been staying in and then ran across the hall to his mother's room.

Nicolas set the cases on the bed that used to be his and looked around. It had a feminine feel to it now and smelled lightly sweet, like Suzette. It didn't seem like his old room at all and, feeling as if he was invading her space, he hurried out of the room and met her in the hall.

She handed him an armful of prettily wrapped packages. "I've put the names in pencil on the bottom of each one. All you need to do is sign the tags and tie them to the bows."

"Thank you, Suzette. These are lovely and much better wrapped than if I had done them."

"You are welcome." She handed him several blank tags.

"Are you sure you don't mind giving up your room for the aunts?"

"Of course I'm sure. It's the least I could do. After all, you gave it up for me, didn't you?"

Somehow, he didn't think he'd done it as graciously as she had.

❧

Suzette fell in love with the aunts. They talked constantly, argued a lot, but under it all, she could see that they both had hearts of gold. What they wanted most was to ease some of their sister's pain.

So they kept Maman LeBlanc busy talking, cooking, and laughing all afternoon and into the evening. The house filled to the brim with family and friends who stopped by. Suzette and Felicia helped cook, but it seemed their main job was to keep the dishes washed up for the next meal. But there was so much cooking, baking, and tasting going on, one didn't know when one meal stopped and another began.

At one time there must have been five different conversations going on, and even though Suzette had a hard time keeping up with it all, she loved being in the middle of it.

It wasn't until after the last visitor left, the latest dirty pot washed and put away, that the aunts turned their attention to Suzette.

"So, you are the new schoolteacher in town?" Tante Louise asked.

"Yes, ma'am, I am."

"And do you like teaching school?" Tante Julia quizzed.

"I love it."

"But you would like to marry one day?"

Suzette could feel herself blush. "Of course I would, one day."

"Our sister says you have been a blessing to her and the family," Louise said. "Thank you for being here for her."

"She is a blessing to me—they all are."

"Hmm," Louise said, nudging Julia.

"Ah. You like this family?" Julia took a sip from her coffee cup.

"I love this family, Tante Julia. I think they are the primary reason I decided to move here."

"Ah. And do you cook?"

"I love to cook. I've learned much from Maman LeBlanc."

"Hmm," was all Julia said before Nicolas and Adam entered the kitchen.

"I think the children are asleep," Nicolas said. "Is it time for us to put the presents under the tree and fill the stockings?"

"It's time," Tante Louise said before anyone else had a chance to reply.

❧

Christmas Eve was the first night in months that Nicolas didn't waken from a nightmare. He'd dreamed, but all he could remember was that his aunts were in it, his tante Julia smiling and saying, "We told you so." And Suzette seemed to be wandering in and out of it—why he didn't know—but it was a wonderful change from the horrors of war he'd been fighting for months.

He looked out over the Bayou and found himself thanking the Lord.

"Dear Lord, I know I haven't been talking to You much

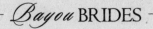

lately. I still have so many questions about why Papa died, and my friend David. . .and so many changes that are occurring here at home. But I know that You have blessed my family and You have given me a respite in the nightmares that have plagued me. I thank You for both those things and ask that my nightmares continue to stay away. Please help me to help Maman and the children through this day without Papa. And thank you for sending the aunts. . .and Suzette to help us all. In Jesus' name I pray, amen."

As Nicolas saw a light in the kitchen window, he dressed, gathered the presents he'd wrapped in the cabin, and hurried over to the main house. Dawn was just breaking, and Christmas day promised to be bright and beautiful.

The children were still sleeping, but Maman and the aunts were in the kitchen, along with Suzette, making a breakfast of *beignets* and sausages to tide them all over until the big meal they would have midafternoon. Nicolas couldn't wait to taste the fried puffed pastry, dusted with sugar and cinnamon.

"Maman, please, may I have one now?" he asked with a grin. "I haven't tasted a beignet since I left home."

"Oh, the poor boy," Tante Julia said. "Lucia, give him that beignet you are taking out of the oil."

Tante Louise handed his mother a saucer. "Here, put it on this," she said. "Suzette, get him a cup of café to go with it. Add a dollop of milk to it."

"Non, Tante Louise. No milk this morning."

"No café au lait?"

"No, ma'am. I got used to drinking it without milk overseas.

It was hard to come by. The coffee wasn't great either, come to think of it. But it served its purpose and kept me awake many a night when I needed it to."

"*Tsk-tsk,*" Louise said. "I'm so glad that war is over."

"We all are," Maman said, giving Nicolas a hug.

The smell of cooking must have wakened the children because Nicolas barely got his beignet down before they heard the clamor of feet on the staircase. The women hurried to meet them in the living room, Louise with a platter of beignets and Maman with a plate piled high with sausages. Julia made sure the adults' coffee cups were full, and Suzette followed behind with glasses of milk for the children.

Presents and stockings were distributed, and paper was torn as packages were unwrapped. The children seemed thrilled with their gifts, and Maman seemed to really like her cape. Suzette was quite pleased with the scarf and gloves Maman had him pick up for her. She thanked him for the box of chocolates he'd bought for her. But the biggest smile he saw was when she pulled out the note he'd written and stuffed into her stocking. He'd merely written, "Yes, I will translate for you."

"Thank you, Nicolas!"

"Just let me know when."

As his mother and aunts were curious to know what Suzette was thanking him for and all started asking questions at once, Suzette laughed and said, "Now! Please!"

Nicolas chuckled and began translating the things she was having a hard time keeping up with and the words she didn't quite get. He actually found it quite fun to be able to interpret for her. He had a feeling that, although she'd picked him up a tie from Maman and added a store-bought box of the pralines he had a weakness for as her own present to him, Suzette's real gift to him was to allow him to teach her something.

Chapter 7

Christmas day went by easier than Nicolas had expected, and he gave much of the credit for that to Suzette and the aunts. Not to mention that it seemed every friend and relative they knew stopped in at some point during the day and evening, keeping them all busy.

Extended family members he hadn't seen since he'd been home came by. Friends of Felicia and Adam stopped by. Families who lived nearby came over. Many came just because it was Christmas and it was their habit to do so. It was a good thing there were extra hands in the kitchen because it seemed food flowed out from it all the day long.

It was a day filled with precious memories of Christmases past when Papa was with them, and there were both tears and laughter. All in all, it was a good day, but emotionally tiring for his whole family because one of them was missing. He was sure that no one was happier to have the day over with than his mother was.

Wanting to make sure Maman was all right, Nicolas stayed

until everyone had gone home and the children were in their beds. His mother and aunts were relaxing around the kitchen table while Suzette made them all a cup of café au lait.

"You want a cup without milk, Nicolas?" Suzette asked.

"Non. I don't think I have room for one more thing. You all outdid yourselves this year. The meal was delicious."

"I don't think I could have done it this year without Julia and Louise and Suzette. I thank you all so much," Maman said.

"It's always better if you have lots of hands preparing. I'm glad we came," Tante Louise said.

"So am I," Nicolas added.

"Did Felicia seem more tired than usual to you, today?" Suzette asked.

"I think she was just missing her papa," Tante Julia said.

"My Felicia is running out of energy, I think," Maman said. "I know she misses her papa, but it is also getting close to her time."

"Do you think Felicia may have the baby early?" Tante Louise asked.

"Wouldn't she be more energetic if she was about to have the baby? I always had a burst of energy when it was time," Tante Julia said.

"I guess it's just a feeling I have," Maman said. "I think it might come early."

"We just may have to stay until that baby is born, Louise," Tante Julia said.

"You'll stay? Really?" Maman seemed to perk up at their words.

"Might as well. With our children visiting their in-laws over the holidays, we have nothing we need to attend to right away," Tante Louise said.

"Oh, I am so glad. So glad you are going to stay with us," Maman said.

And so was Nicolas. His aunts' visit had been good for his mother, and they seemed to help her in a way he couldn't. Somehow he felt it might be easier for her to talk about her sorrow with them.

At any rate, Nicolas decided his maman didn't need him tonight, and he didn't need to hear all this talk about having babies. He pushed away from the counter he'd been leaning against. "I'm going to let you all decide when Felicia's baby will be here. Me, I'm going to bed." He kissed his mother and then his aunts on the cheek. "I'll see you all tomorrow."

He left the women to their talk and went out to the cabin. He'd come to like it quite well, although it was really only large enough for two people. He couldn't help but wonder about his ancestors who'd first lived here, who'd raised their families here long before the main house was built. They had to have been strong in all kinds of ways to have settled here and carved out a place for generations to call home.

The cabin had been built back in the 1700s and had been in his family ever since. It had held up well and been taken care of through the generations, and it was only now that he was living in it that Nicolas had given much thought to the men and women who'd called it home.

Ever since he'd been back home and living in the cabin,

it had become a place to reflect upon all manner of things for him. Tonight it was a place to reflect on the day and the people who meant so much to him. When he'd left to fight in the war, he thought it would be an adventure to see other parts of the world. But what he'd found was that he longed for home and this corner of the world every minute of the day. Now he never wanted to leave it again. His aunts were right in that when it came time to marry, he needed to choose a woman who would love his family and their way of life.

As she did more often than not when he was in the cabin alone, Suzette came to mind, and he let his thoughts rest there. She was everything his aunts said he needed. She loved the Lord; she loved his family. That had been obvious to him from the moment they'd met. And she was a wonderful cook. Not to mention that she was lovely.

She was caring and kind to everyone she met, and Nicolas could no longer deny that he cared for her more and more with each passing day. But she did not understand the Cajun way of life, and he wasn't sure she ever would. If she did, she would be trying to preserve their language instead of trying to help do away with it.

❧

Once the aunts heard that Felicia had indeed had a burst of energy the day after Christmas and cleaned her house from top to bottom, they agreed with Maman that Felicia's time was near. And because Maman was worried about Felicia being by herself while Adam went for the doctor, she went to stay with the couple so that Felicia would not be alone, leaving the aunts and Suzette in charge at home. Amy and Julien were to take turns running to Adam and Felicia's every hour to bring back news. So as not to be left out, Jacques and Rose accompanied them.

But the waiting wasn't easy, and the aunts and Suzette decided to clean the house to ease their nerves. Nicolas wished he could find something to do to ease his. He went out to check on the livestock, stopped by to see how Felicia was doing, and found that she and Maman were in high spirits as she was indeed in labor. Adam, however, seemed to be feeling the strain of waiting, as Maman told him it wasn't yet time to go for the doctor. Knowing that he didn't dare pull Adam away at this time, Nicolas decided he was better off helping the tantes and Suzette than pacing the floor with Adam.

It wasn't long before his tantes decided that Nicolas's cabin needed a through cleaning, too.

"Non. It is fine," he said.

"I don't think it can be very dirty," Suzette said. "Maman LeBlanc and I cleaned it before Nicolas came home."

"Still, he's been here awhile. We will clean for him," Tante Louise said.

"We won't bother anything," Tante Julia said.

"There truly isn't much there to bother. . .or to clean." Nicolas looked in Suzette's direction, hoping she would help convince them that his cabin did not need their attention.

"I think they just need more to do," she said in their defense. "We're all very nervous, waiting for news."

In the end, Nicolas led the aunts to his cabin and let them at it. He moved the furniture—the bed, table, and two chairs—so that they could clean under it. They scrubbed the iron stove in the corner, and then their attention was given to the small loft above the kitchen.

"What is up there, Nicolas?" Tante Louise asked.

"I don't know."

"You've never looked?"

He shrugged "Non. I had no reason to. I think it's just things that have been left here through the years."

"Well, it probably needs a good cleaning up there."

"Maybe, but you two are not climbing up there. I'll go take a look."

"We aren't so old we can't climb a ladder, Nicolas," Tante Julia said.

"No, but if you fell and broke a bone, Maman would never let me hear the last of it. I don't want her angry with me for letting you climb an old ladder. Besides, once Felicia has the baby, you'll be needed even more."

"You're right," Tante Louise said. "Lucia would not be happy if we fell. But you should see if it needs cleaning up there."

"I'll go take a look." He took a lantern up with him but was surprised by how neat things were up there. "Maman and Suzette must have cleaned here, too!" he called back down. "Everything looks orderly. There are some boxes and an old trunk or two."

"Don't you want to see what is in them?" Tante Julia asked.

He was curious. Maybe it was because he'd been thinking

about his ancestors lately, but he did wonder if there was anything up here that would tell him more about them. Besides, Nicolas had a feeling that it would do no good to argue with the two women when they were so determined to keep their hands and minds busy. He just wished Felicia would have the baby so they could give their attentions to her.

Lifting the lantern over the trunks, he saw several books and what looked like a Bible in one. He pushed the lantern to the edge of the loft and looked in another. There were all kinds of old paraphernalia that he would like to go through some day, but Nicolas didn't want to hoist everything down right now. In the boxes were some old clothes.

"Here, Tante Louise, would you take the lantern? There's only this trunk I'd like to bring down right now."

After getting rid of the lamp, he slowly eased the trunk down the rungs of the ladder and put it on the small eating table. "I think this may have some personal family items. Let's see what's here."

"Ah, Nicolas, look. . .a family Bible from long ago," Tante Julia said, pulling the worn leather-bound book out of the trunk. "It's dated in the early 1800s. And what are these? It looks like they're handwritten journals."

Nicolas picked up one of the books and found that it was indeed a journal of some kind. And it was handwritten in his beloved language. He pulled out another, but before he could take a closer look at it, Suzette burst into the cabin.

"Amy and Julien say the baby is on the way! Adam has gone to get the doctor."

Nicolas took the bundle that was his nephew from Suzette. He was small but solid. "Ah, he is a handsome one, isn't he?"

"He is. I see some of your papa in him," Tante Julia said.

"And Adam, too, of course," Suzette added.

"Oui," Tante Louise said. "He does look like his papa."

Nicolas didn't know who he looked like, and it didn't matter. His nephew had a place in his heart already, his tiny finger wrapped around Nicolas's thumb.

"He's adorable," Suzette said, looking over Nicolas's shoulder at the baby.

Just then André Devereux scrunched up his little face and let out a tiny wail. Nicolas jiggled him as he had Rose when she was tiny, but the baby cried only louder. "I think he might be hungry."

"No. He's just been fed," Tante Julia said.

The baby began to exercise his vocal cords in earnest. "Well, something is bothering him. Does he need to be changed?"

"I changed him right before I brought him out," Tante Louise assured him.

"Let me see him." Suzette reached for André. She cuddled him close and began to hum a tune. Soon the crying had stopped, and he was fast asleep in her arms.

"He was just tired of all the commotion, I think," she said.

Nicolas couldn't help but notice how beautiful she looked gazing down at his nephew. She seemed meant to have a baby in her arms, and he'd never seen her look lovelier.

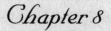

Chapter 8

The next week sped by with everyone's attentions on the new baby in the family. Friends and family flowed between both households, with Nicolas's aunts and Suzette providing the meals for all.

On Sunday, it was announced in the small congregation they attended that André Devereux had arrived. Over the next few days there were even more visits to see the baby and bring gifts. Nicolas was a little surprised that Adam and Suzette's parents couldn't see their way clear to come see their new grandbaby, but he didn't want to upset either one by mentioning it.

That didn't stop the tantes from doing so, however. The day after the baby was born, they were in the kitchen putting together a meal when Tante Louise asked, "Your maman and papa aren't coming to see baby André, Suzette?"

After one look at Suzette's face and seeing that she was upset about it, Nicolas wanted to shush his tante. After all, it really wasn't their business, but he kept silent as he was curious to hear the answer as well.

Suzette shrugged and shook her head. "Non. I went into town with Adam when he telephoned them to let them know little André was here. They just said they couldn't come right now." Her voice filled with tears. "I think he is very disappointed. I wish they could have seen his expression when they said they would come later."

"I'm sure they will pay a visit soon," Tante Julia tried to assure her.

"I hope so. They don't know what they're missing. They're sending a layette from New Orleans, as if that—" Suzette broke off the sentence and sighed deeply. It was clear that she didn't want to talk ill of her parents even though she was not happy with them.

Tante Julia hurried to give her a hug. "They will come, and they will fall in love. Then you won't be able to keep them away."

"Maybe," Suzette said. But she didn't sound as if she believed it. She busied herself with kneading the bread she was making.

Nicolas couldn't help but see the look his aunts exchanged with each other. He could almost hear the silent *tsk-tsk* that surely passed between them. They didn't ask any more questions about the Devereuxes and instead seemed to go out of their way to let Suzette know they didn't blame her for her unfeeling parents.

Nicolas didn't know what to say to her, but he began to see why she was so taken with his family. . .and at the same time how she didn't quite understand the Cajun way of life.

Nicolas did enjoy seeing his aunts interact with his mother, with Suzette, and the rest of the family. They had strong opinions and weren't afraid to voice them. By New Year's Eve, it was apparent that his aunts had taken quite a liking to Suzette, and they were quite vocal in suggesting that he would do well to court her. At every turn they let him know what they thought. Thankfully, they did not say so in her hearing.

"Nicolas, Suzette is so good to your maman," Tante Julia said one morning after Suzette had gone to help at Felicia's. "She couldn't be better to her if she were her very own mother."

"Yes, she's good to us all."

"She loves our family," Tante Louise added her opinion. "And, poor dear, I can see why. At least we show her we care. I wonder what kind of parents the Devereuxes are. That they haven't even come to see their first grandchild is unthinkable to me!"

"I know," Tante Julia agreed with her sister. "I do not know how they can stay away. Why, we have to practically make your maman come home."

"I know." Nicolas didn't feel he had to give long responses to his aunts' comments. He knew them well enough by now to know that they didn't expect—or want—anything more than his agreement with them.

"Well, I must wonder if they realize what wonderful children they have in Suzette and Adam. I am so glad Felicia married Adam, and it will be a lucky man who wins Suzette's heart," Tante Louise said.

"A lucky man, indeed," Tante Julia added.

Nicolas silently agreed—but was very relieved when Amy and Julien came in just then to ask him to take them all to see the baby. It put an end to the conversation for the moment. He didn't want to hear any more about some lucky man wining Suzette's heart.

❦

Suzette was going to miss the aunts. They had been so kind and loving to her since they'd been there. And their visit had helped Maman LeBlanc get through Christmas. Now, maybe the new baby in the family would help ease some more of her sorrow.

"We're leaving tomorrow, dear," Tante Julia said the day after New Year's. "You'll be back teaching school next week. Lucia will be spending most of her days with Felicia, even though she is doing very well. We know our sister is going to be all right with all the love and care she receives from you and Nicolas and the others."

"She will hate to see you two go, though. I know she has loved having you here."

"We'll be back. Hopefully soon," Tante Louise said. "But we can't thank you enough for helping Lucia through such a hard time. We are all blessed you are here."

At hearing those words, Suzette blinked quickly to keep her forming tears at bay. She hugged the older women. "I am going to miss you both."

And she would miss them. She loved hearing the loving banter between the two women. To some it seemed as if they argued all the time, but she'd seen them look at each other with a teasing glint in their eyes and realized it was just the way they related to each other.

They'd both hinted that she and Nicolas would make a good couple, but Suzette had tried to ignore their subtle suggestions. It wasn't that she didn't like him, for she did. The longer she knew Nicolas, the more she realized she was falling in love with him. But she had no idea how he felt about her, and in fact thought that maybe, with the way he felt about her teaching English, she was probably the last woman he'd let himself become attracted to. But at night, in her dreams, there was no ignoring the fact that she would like nothing more than to become a real member of the LeBlanc family, by way of becoming Nicolas's wife.

Nicolas hated to see his aunts leave. He'd enjoyed their visit more each day and had grown to enjoy their verbal sparring. But it was time to take them to the train station, and he loaded their cases into the car while they said their good-byes to Maman, Suzette, and the children.

The sisters were close, and their tears flowed freely as they left, waving at his maman and the others until he drove the automobile around the bend in the road. Then there was much sniffing and dabbing at their eyes before his tante Julia addressed him. "Nicolas dear, Louise and I can't go back home without speaking to you straight."

"What is wrong, Tantes?"

"We are afraid you are a blind man, and we cannot leave without making sure that you are aware that you have the right woman for you sitting right here beneath your very nose," Tante Louise said bluntly.

"You are speaking of Suzette?"

"You know we are," Louise said. "She loves the Lord with all her heart, and she loves your family, Nicolas."

"Yes, she does." And his family loved her.

"She is a wonderful cook."

"She is that." And she was getting better each and every day.

"She is the *right* woman for you."

"Non. She does not understand the Cajun way of life."

"How can you say that, Nicolas?" Tante Julia asked. "Suzette loves it here in Breaux Bridge. She loves the life we Cajuns live. The closeness—everything!"

"If she loved it so much, and understood, she would not be trying to take away our language!"

"Nicolas, she is not trying to take it away. She is only trying to make things easier on the children," Tante Louise insisted.

"You could try to explain to her what is important to you, Nicolas," Tante Julia implored him.

Nicolas only shook his head. It saddened him that they did not understand, either.

"You need to open your eyes and your heart—not to mention your ears, dear Nicolas. You will find your heart's desire, if you only do," Tante Julia urged.

Chapter 9

The house felt lonesome after the aunts left, and Suzette was glad school was back in session. But when she was called into the principal's office that first day back, she was apprehensive about why he wanted to see her.

"Miss Devereux, please. . .take a seat," Mr. Fortier said, motioning to the chair across from his desk.

Suzette sat down and folded her hands in her lap, trying not to show how nervous she felt as she waited to hear why she'd been called to his office.

He looked over his glasses at her and smiled. "Relax, Miss Devereux. You are not a student in trouble."

Suzette released a big sigh and said, "Now I know what my students must feel like when I send them to see you."

They both chuckled before the principal informed her of why he wanted to talk to her.

"Actually, the school board asked me to present a proposal to you. As you are well aware, the state is planning to take away our right to speak French of any kind at schools. It may be a year or so from now, but there is more than a distinct possibility that it *is* going to happen."

"Yes, I am aware. I've been trying to prepare my students for that eventuality."

"That has come to our attention. The children are enjoying the word games you play with them, and it has greatly strengthened their use of English. What the school board is proposing to do is to start an adult evening class where those parents who wish to help their children can learn to speak English, too."

"Oh, that's wonderful. . .but do you think there will be many who will actually want to attend? I know some in the community are upset at the prospect of losing the right to speak their own language at school."

"Yes, well, so am I. But these people love their children and want what is best for them. Most do want them to speak English even though they want them to be able to keep Cajun as their first language. I feel the same way. But we must be prepared for the future and make the transition as easy on our students as we can."

"I agree."

"I know you do. That's why we want *you* to teach the class."

"Oh. I—I don't know if I am good enough. . . ."

"Miss Devereux, you are the most qualified teacher we have for this."

"But for the parents—I am afraid I am not familiar enough with the Cajun dialect to—"

"Knowing you come from New Orleans and are more

familiar with the Creole French, we have thought of that. You may have an assistant. It can be anyone in the area whom you feel comfortable enough to work with, who can translate for you and help the parents at the same time."

"That would be a great help."

"Just consider it and think about whom you might ask to be your assistant. I know you can do this and make it fun for the parents at the same time. With having to work around the planting seasons and again at harvest time for some of the families, we'd like to start this at the beginning of next month or even sooner, if possible. Please think about it, and let us know as soon as you make up your mind." Mr. Fortier stood, letting her know that the meeting was over.

"I–it sounds like a wonderful opportunity. I will let you know soon," Suzette agreed. "Thank you and the school board for your confidence in me, Mr. Fortier."

She left the office and went back to her classroom feeling elated. This was something she would really like to do. It would make things easier on the children and their parents in the long run. But there was only one person who came to mind as an assistant, and Suzette didn't hold out much hope that he would agree.

They hadn't played the language game in several weeks, and she was almost afraid to start it again. But it might be the only way to find out if she even dare let Nicolas know about the school board's proposal.

But apprehensive as she might be about beginning the game again, the family wasn't. Felicia and Adam came to the main house for supper for the first time with the baby, and that gave them an opportunity to start the game again. In fact it was Maman who started it. She pointed to André and said, *"Enfant."*

"Baby!" Rose shouted. Then she pointed to the tiny thumb in his mouth.

Jacques yelled, *"Pouce!"*

To which Suzette corrected, "Thumb."

She then pointed to his nose and said, *"Nez."*

"Nose," Felicia said, turning baby André to her and kissing him on the tip of his tiny nose. "It is a beautiful one, isn't it?"

The baby gurgled and kicked, and from then on the game was forgotten as they all oohed and ahhed over every move and sound he made.

Suzette tried to discern what Nicolas thought of taking up the game again, but he was unreadable tonight. She found his eyes on her more than once, but he'd only smile or look to someone else for the moment, and she couldn't tell what he was thinking. She would just have to gather her courage and ask him for his help. The worst he could do would be to say no.

Before approaching Nicolas, she waited until Felicia and Adam took the baby home, and Maman went up to get her younger ones in bed.

"Would you like a cup of café before you leave, Nicolas? I'd like to talk to you about something."

"Oh? Oui, pour me a cup and tell me what you sound so serious about."

She sat a cup down in front of him and joined him at the table. "I was called into the principal's office today."

"Oh? For what reason?"

"The school board would like to start an adult class for parents."

Nicolas leaned back in his chair and raised an eyebrow. "What kind of class?"

Suzette took a deep breath before letting the words rush out of her mouth. "They want to start an English class for them so that it will make it easier for them to help their children to learn, and they want me to teach it." She watched as Nicolas sat up straighter in his chair, and she could tell he didn't like what he was hearing. But there was no point in stopping now. She hurried to finish. "They also said I could have someone to assist me. Will you help me, Nicolas?"

He pushed his coffee cup to one side and rested his forearms on the table. "Let me understand. You want me to help you teach your adult students English by teaching you Cajun?"

"Well, yes and no. I do need your help with the Cajun. But I want you to help me teach the parents, by translating for us—them and me—when we don't understand each other, or when we talk too fast."

Nicolas pushed his chair away from the table and stood. "Suzette, you are trying to get whole families to quit speaking the Cajun even at home, now? You really are trying to do away with my language!"

"Nicolas, you must know that is not what I want. It isn't that I want anyone to stop speaking Cajun. I just want it to be easier on the whole family when the children can't speak it at school any longer."

"And you are positive that is going to happen?"

"From what the school board and the newspapers are saying, yes, I think it is."

"But it hasn't happened yet."

"No. It hasn't."

"Maybe I should run for office and try to stop it."

Suzette smiled at him. "You could do that. The state could use men like you to help run it."

"Do you have any idea how much I looked forward to hearing Cajun all the time I was away, Suzette?"

Her heart went out to him. "I'm sure you did. It must have been very difficult to be away from everything familiar."

"I had no idea how hard it would be not to be able to speak my natural language. But I do realize it was a good thing I'd been taught the English. Otherwise I wouldn't have been able to communicate at all. I have no problem with the children learning the English. I just don't want them having to give up their own language to do it. And if we teach the parents. . .one day our language will disappear."

"Nicolas, it doesn't have to be that way."

But he didn't seem to hear her as he paced the floor. "Did I fight for this country only to come home to help my people lose their freedom to speak the language they love? Non! I will not help you!"

Suzette was speechless as she watched Nicolas charge out the back door. When the screen door banged behind him, she flinched and began to cry. How could he be so unyielding and stubborn? Anyone but him could see that she only wanted to help. Her dreams of a future with him seemed to shatter with each tear she shed. Maybe it was time she went back to New Orleans.

Chapter 10

Nicolas slammed out the back door and headed for his cabin. His chest burned with frustration. How could Suzette think he would help do away with his language! His aunts were wrong. She did not understand at all, and he didn't think she ever would.

He entered the cabin and flung himself on the bed, angry that she'd even thought he might be willing to help. And yet, as he remembered the look on Suzette's face as he told her no, his heart twisted in his chest at the thought that his words had hurt her. That he loved her was no longer a question within him. He knew that he did, but she was not the woman for him. She could not be if she did not know what it meant to be Cajun. And without that knowledge, they could never have a good marriage. He was foolish to have listened to his aunts and to begin to think they might be right. They were wrong, and it deeply pained him that Suzette did not understand the ways of his people—his ancestors.

Nicolas sat up on the bed and lit the lantern. He picked up

one of the journals stacked up on the table, left there from the day he and his aunts had cleaned. Opening it, he found it was written by Capucine, the wife of Michel LeBlanc who built the cabin and was the first of his ancestors to settle here. The next journal was written by Josée LeBlanc, married to Capucine's and Michel's grandson, Edouard. One after another he read the journals, long into the night. By the time he was finished, Nicolas had much to think about.

Through each and every journal there seemed to be a deep longing for his relations to be a part of this country, to belong. Many of his ancestors had strived to learn the English and to teach their children to speak it. They spoke their beloved Cajun language, to be sure, and wanted to preserve it, just as he did. But they wanted to be able to speak and understand *both* equally. One of his great-great-grandmothers had even taught the neighbors to speak the English from this very cabin. How had he not known that?

Maybe it was because he never bothered to find out. Maman had said it was Papa's wish that they help the children learn. He wanted to support Suzette's efforts to make things easier on them. And tonight it'd been obvious that Felicia and Adam wanted their baby to know both.

Was it possible that Suzette knew the hearts of his family better than he did? All he'd been thinking about since he'd been home was how unfair life was. . .especially to him. Yes, he'd endured much in the last year, losing his papa and his best friend, and being wounded. But others had lost even more. And even if they had loved ones, their relationships weren't always what they could be. Look at how Adam and Suzette's parents treated them. They didn't even seem to care that they had a new grandson—nor did they seem to want to know anything about the family their daughter was living with.

And yet, Suzette and Adam were loving and kind people. Suzette had helped his maman and siblings when he couldn't be here to do so. She'd only been kind to him, in spite of the rudeness he'd shown her at times. He'd be lucky if she even spoke to him again after tonight.

He'd been blaming God for his losses while she'd been holding his loved ones up in prayer and showing Christian love to them. All he'd been doing was feeling sorry for himself. God had been there for him all along. He'd brought him home safe, and his arm was healing and getting stronger each day. He'd brought a woman into his life who was right for him, just as the aunts had told him. And now he might have lost her because of his own stubbornness.

If he'd ruined things with Suzette, he wondered if his heart would ever heal. If not, there would be no blaming God for that. Nicolas knew full well that he'd have no one to blame for that heartache but himself.

❧

After tossing and turning for the rest of the night, Nicolas was a little late getting to the main house the next morning. Suzette and the children had already left.

"Suzette promised the children that if they hurried, they would stop by and see if baby André was awake. That's all it took for them to rush out the door," Maman said.

Nicolas poured himself a cup of coffee and sat down at the table. "I think maybe she didn't want to see me this morning." If he thought his mother would be sympathetic to him, he was wrong.

"I heard you storm out of here last night, son. I was not proud of you—especially when I came into the kitchen to find Suzette crying and talking about going back to New Orleans."

Nicolas's heart plummeted in his chest. For a moment the pain that she might leave took his voice away, and he shook his head. "She cannot leave, Maman! I was wrong. She is good for this family and the community needs her right now."

"It's about time you figured that out, Nicolas. But I'm not the one you need to tell it to. You are going to lose her if you don't do it soon. She was talking about turning in her resignation last night."

Nicolas was on his feet in a flash. "I'll try to catch up with her at Felicia's. If they aren't there, I'll go on to the school."

His mother waved him out the door. "Go. Hurry!"

Nicolas rushed out the door and took off in a run. He could only pray that he hadn't waited too long. *Dear Lord, please let me convince Suzette to stay and do the work You've called her to do. Please let me prove to her that I love her and believe in what she is trying to do. And please forgive me for blaming You for my sorrows. Please help me to be the man You would have me be. In Jesus' name I pray. Amen.*

Suzette and the children weren't at his sister's. And no one was on the school grounds when he got there. He didn't know which room was Suzette's, but he'd come this far and he wasn't turning back now.

He entered the school building and headed toward the principal's office. Thankfully, there was a receptionist there. "Could you tell me where Miss Suzette Devereux's room is?"

"You are the parent of one of her students?"

"No. I am the brother of several of her students. I am Nicolas LeBlanc."

The name must have been familiar to her because she nodded and smiled. "Mr. LeBlanc, her room is number 7, right down the hall to your left."

"Thank you." With that, Nicolas was on his way. Adam was right. The school was modern, much more modern than the one he and Felicia had attended. The wood floors gleamed, and the corridor was so quiet you could hear the tick of the large clock at the end of the hall.

Suzette's classroom door was shut, but light shone through the frosted-glass window in the door. He knocked.

When Suzette opened the door to see him, soft color flooded her cheeks, and for a moment, Nicolas thought she was going to tell him to go away.

"Nicolas! What is wrong? Maman? Felicia—"

"Nothing is wrong with them. I just need to talk to you."

"But school is in session, I can't—"

"It's school business I need to discuss with you."

"Oh?" She looked back into the classroom. "Children, please study your spelling words. There will be a quiz when I return. I'll be just outside the door, so behave yourselves."

There was a bench just outside her room, and she led Nicolas over to it. "What school business do you wish to talk about?"

Nicolas wasn't going to waste time. "I wanted to know if the position of your assistant is still open?"

"My—I'm not even sure I'm going to need an assistant. I may be going back to New Orleans soon."

"Non! Suzette, you cannot do that. This community needs you, and I'm sorry I did not see how much until now. You must take the position. I've been wrong. I've seen the world and know times are changing. I realize that the children will be better off knowing and speaking both languages—and being able to make the choice on which one to use the most. I realize now that you've been trying to help in the best way."

"What brought about this change of heart, Nicolas?"

"Last night I read some journals that were left in the cabin and found that you knew the heart of my people better than I did. I would like to become your assistant, and help you teach the parents, if you can forgive me for my words last night."

The corners of Suzette's mouth turned into the most beautiful smile Nicolas had ever seen. "Oh Nicolas, of course I forgive you! I'm so happy you're willing to help me!"

"There is one more condition. . . ."

"Oh? I'm not sure—"

"I love you, Suzette. I'll be the happiest man on earth if you'll agree to be my wife and help me to teach our children *both* languages. Will you marry me?"

His heart almost stopped as he waited for her answer. But Suzette didn't make him wait long.

"Oh, Nicolas, Je t'aime! And oui, I will marry you."

Nicolas pulled her into his arms and bent his head. Their lips met and clung as they sealed their promise to each other in the language of love.

JANET LEE BARTON

Born in New Mexico, Janet Lee Barton has lived all over the South—Arkansas, Florida, Louisiana, Oklahoma, and Texas— but with her husband's recent retirement, she and Dan, along with a daughter and her family, have recently moved back to Oklahoma to be closer to family. Janet loves being a wife, mother, grandmother, sister, and aunt, and she feels blessed to be able to share her faith through her writing. Happily married to the man she knows the Lord brought into her life, she wants to write stories that show that the love between a man and a woman is at its best when the relationship is built with God at the center.

Dreams of Home

by Kathleen Miller

Dedication

To "Mayor Jan" and in memory of Frank Dyer

LORD, *thou hast been our dwelling place in all generations.*
PSALM 90:1

After much sorrow, much joy.
My dear Michel has built me a home.
My long-lost mère is nearby.
Comforte sleeps on my shoulder as I hold the pen.
Life is full.
FROM THE JOURNAL OF CAPUCINE LEBLANC

Chapter 1

"You may kiss the bride—again."

Justin LeBlanc watched the photographer zoom in for the close-up, and tried to muster a little enthusiasm. After all, it had to be close to a hundred degrees in the shade and, as always, the mosquitoes had crashed the party.

On top of that, he'd done this four times in the past two years.

It seemed as though he'd just finished praying over and paying for one wedding when another LeBlanc girl would be whisked off into matrimonial bliss. With Amanda, his youngest sister, it all ended, and so did the responsibility he'd taken on with the loss of his parents nearly six years ago.

Justin reached for the handkerchief in his jacket pocket and mopped his brow, then stuffed it back in place. This parade of weddings was nothing compared to the hardships his ancestors endured in this land, and Justin knew he had no right to complain. Still, with each wedding the excuses for not fulfilling his dream grew thinner.

Today they would evaporate completely.

He adjusted the awful tourniquet the tux rental place called a *bow tie* and upped the wattage on his smile. As the pretty photographer snapped away, oblivious to the stifling heat, Justin let his mind wander.

No longer could he claim he had too many sisters and too little time to dream his own dreams. Now what would he do with his life?

The sales of the last in a series of six textbooks on Acadian language and culture had assured him a comfortable living, and he'd always wanted to write something more creative than scholarly tomes. Maybe he'd hit the road and write the great American novel.

The idea began to have an appeal, and soon he imagined the wind in his hair and the bugs in his teeth as he sped down the open road. Just a guy, a book, and a dream.

Oh yeah, he'd buy one of those snazzy little laptops and sleep in cheesy motels. Breakfast would be bologna sandwiches, and no one would tell him that was disgusting.

As his mind rolled over the possibilities, he pictured himself following old Route 66 in his father's vintage '60s Mustang convertible, driving along the open road until the story in his head began to gel and. . .

"You, brother of the beautiful bride. Snap out of it!"

The photographer again, and Justin gave her his most baffled look. His baby sister's sharp elbow jabbed his side. "What was that for?" Justin whispered, feigning irritation.

"You're doing it again, aren't you, Justin? You're daydreaming, you odd duck," his sister Amanda said as she reached to straighten his tie. "You know I love you, but just for today can you remain in the present?"

He looked at the bride. She looked cool as can be. What was it about women? They never seemed to perspire.

"Justin, hello?" she said while he stared. "Can't you put the absentminded professor act on hold for another hour or two? It *is* my wedding day."

"I have no idea what you're talking about, sweetheart." Again Justin spoke in a whisper. "The photographer's right, you know. You are beautiful today. Mom and Dad would have been so proud."

A smile was his answer, and Justin committed it to memory before tucking it into a corner of his heart. None of his sisters had been easy to give away to their grooms, but his little Mandy-girl was the hardest of all.

Beside Amanda was the man who'd won her heart. He knew from experience that no man met all the qualifications for joining the family. If he had to choose, though, this one— Miles Simms—came closest.

Still, it seemed like yesterday that Amanda cheered on the sidelines and her new husband threw touchdown passes. Where had the time gone?

"Smile!" the lady photographer demanded. "Just one more family shot and then you can all go have your cake and punch. Try and look happy, please, brother of the bride. Remember, this is a wedding, not a funeral. Show some happiness if you can."

Happiness: state of joy achieved by good circumstances or great contentment.

Yes, he knew the definition, but then there were few words from the big ten-pound dictionary in his father's study that he didn't know. If only figuring out women were as simple.

"Hello?" Amanda this time. He looked down at his sister, then back at the photographer.

Everything in Justin ached to complain, to tell the pushy camera-wielding woman to cease and desist with the negativity, but he stifled his comments in deference to his sister. Amanda had always been the peacemaker in the family; no way would he ruin her wedding day by speaking his mind. Still, he wondered why Amanda had hired someone so. . .

Description evaded him.

A grip of steel wrapped around his upper arm, and he looked down into the big brown eyes of the object of his thoughts as she moved him an inch closer to Amanda. "One more minute, big guy," she said, "and then you can get back to your daydreams, okay?"

Big guy? Justin opened his mouth to reply with some sarcastic comment, then felt Amanda's elbow return to his side. "Yes, ma'am," he said instead.

An eternity—and fifteen minutes on the clock—later, the wedding party filed inside the grand old home to continue the celebration with a reception, then a sit-down supper for half the town. Although he longed for the air-conditioned comfort of the home's interior, Justin hung back to watch them go.

Today marked the end of an era for this generation of

LeBlancs. The big house would be empty now, an abomination for a family so prolific in its offspring and so close in its ties.

The meaning of family had changed in the generations since the LeBlancs fled Nova Scotia with little more than the clothes on their backs. In this modern world, where e-mail had replaced visiting, and volumes were written on the demise of the family unit, only the bayou seemed to move at the same speed.

And in the midst of it all, like a man looking through a window at the world, Justin stood watching it all happen. But what could he do except become a part of the exodus? Certainly no one other than Bandit, the springer spaniel, and Tip and Mitten, the pair of mousers now living in the empty barn, would miss him should he take to the road.

His sister Sarah, closest to him in age, hadn't been back to the old home place since she married last spring and moved to Indiana. Bonnie, the eldest of the twins, divided her time between the West Coast and Dallas, having entered graduate school at Southern Methodist University just months after marrying an airline pilot.

Only Becky, Bonnie's junior by three and a half minutes, had driven the hour from Baton Rouge on any sort of regular basis, and she would soon be moving north now that her politician husband had been elected to the House of Representatives. Amanda's marriage and subsequent move to New York to become a fashion designer would complete the emptying of Justin's nest.

Justin swiped at a mosquito and missed. Inside, the music swelled until the somber violinist switched from a discreet Brahms concerto to an upbeat Zydeco number. A peal of laughter that could only belong to Amanda accompanied the abrupt change. A second later, the other three joined her, sending a chorus of joy—that mixed perfectly with fine Acadian music—rolling toward him.

Amanda's white-clad form passed the largest of the three windows on the back of the house, in her hand the bouquet of white roses she'd carried down the aisle. She lifted those roses in mock salute to him, then stuck out her tongue. Cheeky female. Justin leaned against the gazebo's painted post and returned the gesture before folding his arms across his chest to cover the emptiness there.

As Amanda linked arms with the twins and retreated into the throng of family and friends, the scene shifted and blurred. *Thou tellest my wanderings: put thou my tears into thy bottle: are they not in thy book?*

Words from the Psalms his mother had used to comfort him as a child; words he had spoken to his sisters over the years. Why now did they reappear?

"You're awfully somber for such a festive occasion."

Justin whirled around to see the photographer watching him from the corner of the porch. Had she guessed the depth of his despair? He swiped a cuff discreetly across his cheek in case some evidence of the shameful tear remained.

Preoccupied with staring across the wide expanse of lawn toward the little cabin and the black waters of the bayou beyond, the woman seemed not to notice. Justin took advantage of the moment to study her.

The photographer he knew only as Lucy, owner of Lucy's Lens, was a study in contrasts. A wild riot of copper-colored curls teased high cheekbones and danced across dark-clad shoulders that were just a bit too broad for a woman so tiny.

Two cameras slung around her neck and a third in her hand, Lucy stood in a beam of sunlight that made the cross at her neck gleam. With a pale hand, she pushed an auburn curl off her forehead and actually smiled.

Her nails were red, he noticed. Not a shy, just-a-touch-of-crimson red but rather the deep cherry of his father's convertible when it was new.

The comparison struck him. Yet again, he found it odd. But then nothing about this woman seemed the least bit comfortable or familiar.

As he watched her fingers toy with one of the camera straps around her neck, Justin realized he hadn't responded to her comment. Or had she asked him a question? Something about her made him feel as though he should say something brilliant, something that would cause her to hold him in a higher regard than she obviously did.

That something, whatever it was, refused to budge from his throat. He sent up a quick prayer to his Savior to get him out of this mess—and out of this gazebo—with some measure of dignity.

She turned to stare in his direction. "Looks like you're going to miss her," she said, mercifully ending his torment.

"Yeah," he said, stifling the complaint rising in his throat. "It will be quiet with them all gone."

The photographer nodded toward the house. "I would suspect so."

A warm breeze blew between them, lifting a strand of her hair, then settling it once more against the ebony of her sweater as she directed her gaze toward him. In quick sequence, she lifted the camera to her eye and began to adjust the long lens toward the open doors of the house.

Three clicks later, she lowered the camera and smiled—her first of the day. "You've got a beautiful place here."

Her tone was almost wistful; as if she longed for something the old home could give her. Roots? Maybe a sense of place? Permanency, perhaps.

Yes, permanent: abiding and constant with a sense of durability.

Justin shook his head. Enough with the mental dictionary. Amanda was right; he was an odd duck.

What else accounted for the strange assumptions he made and the way definitions to words popped into his head without warning? It must be lack of sleep or the pinch of the starched collar around his neck that caused his mind to wander in such strange directions.

"Yes," he said, as much to respond to her comment as to rid his mind of his foolish imaginings. "LeBlanc sweat and blood built this house and that cabin over by the bayou. It's a grand home, but I must admit I prefer the cabin."

She nodded as if to agree. Justin drew a step nearer so as to better view the solid wooden structure off in the distance. Nearly as old as the trees surrounding it, the cabin had been the first home to the LeBlanc family. Kept as if the original settlers would be returning on the morrow, the cabin had been meticulously preserved as an excellent example of early Acadian architecture.

Justin thought to devote an entire book, possibly the seventh volume in his series, to the structure. Every piece had been catalogued and documented, every moss-filled mattress and cypress-hewn chair repaired or replaced until the modest cabin stood as a monument to the past. Only a severe case of wanderlust and a deep need to write from something other than the facts kept him from pursuing the idea.

"I sleep there most nights when the weather and the mosquitoes allow," he said as he took another step forward. "There's a peace there that the big house doesn't have."

With a roll of her shoulders, the photographer repositioned the wider of the two camera straps around her neck. "I can see that."

"Maybe it's the lack of company, or maybe it's because God seems to always meet me when I'm there. I don't know."

The confession, spoken to a perfect stranger, horrified him. Why hadn't he chosen to be a solid, reliable farmer like the men in generations before him rather than an eccentric wordsmith, underpaid educator, and avid preserver of the past? Now she would truly think him an idiot rather than the esteemed author and professor of Acadian studies his colleagues and readers knew him to be.

"We all need a place where God meets us, don't we?" Their gazes met. "You're fortunate to have found that place."

"Fortunate," Justin repeated. *Favored by circumstances.* "Why, yes, I suppose so." Actually he'd never given it much thought. It seemed as though God and the LeBlancs had walked this bayou together for centuries, each keeping an easy relationship with the other.

" 'Ye are blessed of the Lord which made heaven and earth,' " she whispered as she raised the camera and aimed her lens toward the cabin to fire off a rapid series of shots.

"Blessed." *Favored by God.* He spoke the word as he entertained the thought. "Yes," he decided upon quick reflection, "we LeBlancs are blessed indeed."

But as he allowed the statement to settle between them, Justin LeBlanc began to feel more belligerent than blessed. Perhaps it was the importance of the day, or the copious amount of strong chicory coffee he'd consumed prior to the ceremony, or maybe it all centered on one auburn-haired, brown-eyed photographer who quoted the Psalms and strummed the strings of his mind with cherry red nails.

Chapter 2

I'm sorry. We haven't been properly introduced. I'm Justin. Justin LeBlanc. Brother of the bride." His halting words stood in stark contrast to his firm handshake and easy smile. "But then I guess you know that."

"Yes, I figured that out right away."

She stared at him and tried to get a handle on what he might be like had he not been forced to fight with an uncomfortable tuxedo and a baby sister flying the coop. This was a man who was comfortable in his skin, she decided, even as he was uncomfortable in his tux. That easy air of assurance probably was a result of the decades he obviously spent in this one beautiful place.

I wouldn't know what that was like.

Lucy's fingers itched to photograph him at that moment, an image of perfect lighting and interesting bone structure. Instead, she decided to mind her manners.

"I'm Lucy Webber." Lucy looked past him to the grand Acadian home where the reception was going strong. "Lovely home you have."

Justin followed her gaze and the expression on his face softened. "It is, isn't it?"

"You sound surprised."

He seemed to study the structure for a moment before nodding. "I suppose when you look at something every day, you don't really notice."

"I wouldn't know what that's like." As soon as the words were out, Lucy cringed. Thus far, she'd managed to keep silent on her rootless past.

Thankfully, the brother of the bride seemed absorbed with something going on inside the house. The door opened and laughter danced toward them on the grass.

"Justin, where you at, boy?" An older man stepped outside, clad in an odd combination of some sort of military uniform, a bowler hat, and a white sash with what looked like writing on it.

"Out here." Justin gestured over his shoulder toward the strangely clothed gentleman. "Hezekiah LeBlanc. My dad's eldest brother and the former mayor of our fair city." He winked. "He likes to remind us all at family gatherings of his glorious political past."

"Well, come on back once you finish showing the pretty lady the LeBlanc charm, eh? I wouldn't want you to be last in line for the gumbo and end up with nothing but the roux."

"Will do, Uncle Hez." Justin chuckled. "Trust me. My uncle got all the LeBlanc charm. You're in no danger. Unless you're a history buff, that is."

She watched the man in question straighten his hat and

adjust his sash before returning to the celebration. Then Justin's words registered, and she turned her attention to the brother of the bride. "What was that? Did you say you're a history buff?"

He nodded. "More than a buff, actually. It's how I make my living." At her confused look, he added, "I'm a professor of Acadian studies at the university."

Oh my. Brains and a photogenic face. "Wow."

"No, really, not wow." The wind lifted a strand of his hair and set it back in place again. "It's kind of like telling your family story over and over, then flunking anyone who doesn't remember it properly."

What an odd way to describe his profession.

"I don't know you, Justin, but I'm going to guess that you don't find the history of the Acadians as fascinating as I do. I just have to wonder why that is."

At this his interest seemed to pique. "Do you really?"

"Yes, well. . ." She'd said too much—again. Too late to retreat to her familiar disinterested facade. Rather, she squared her shoulders and took a deep breath. "Okay, this is what I don't understand. Generations of your family have grown up in that house, and you've lived here all your life, right?"

An amused look crossed his face. "Right."

"And during that lifetime of, what, thirty-five years?"

He shifted positions to lean against the tree and cross his arms over his chest. "Thirty-one years."

"Okay, thirty-one years." She cut him a sideways glance. "Sorry. And in those thirty-one years, have you ever thought about the fact that there are people who don't have the privilege of roots? And what about the fact you're shedding light on the history of a people who have the most interesting stories to tell?"

Too much said. Lucy ducked her head and played with the f-stop on her camera while she waited for his answer. What was it about this stranger that made her want to talk about things she generally kept private?

"Look, never mind. I should let you get back to the party. It was nice meeting you, Justin." She turned to head down the brick path leading to the road.

"Wait." Justin jogged up beside her, then slowed his steps to match hers. "I'm sorry."

"You're sorry?" Lucy stopped short and cradled the camera. "For what?"

"Well, actually, I'm not sure why I'm sorry, but evidently I've said something that offended you." He paused. "And for that, I am truly sorry."

Lucy smiled. *What do you know? A gentleman.*

"Honestly, you don't owe me an apology. I just said more than I'd intended, that's all." She gestured toward the house where the celebration had begun to spill out into the yard. "You've got people waiting on you, and I've kept you far too long. Just let Amanda know her proofs will be ready on Thursday, would you?"

"No."

Again she stopped to turn around. This time, Justin LeBlanc had stood his ground. Like two gunslingers poised for battle, they faced one another on the path.

"No?"

He gave his tie another tug. "No."

Lucy lifted the digital and aimed it his direction. With the light filtering through the cypress trees, Justin looked like a man from another century. A man transported from modern Louisiana to a place and time far removed from here.

She lifted the digital to her eye and focused. Perfection. Her finger hovered just above the button. "Give her the message or I'll shoot, Justin."

"My sisters say I would forget my head if it weren't attached. So. . ." He paused and struck a pose. "I'm going to have to stick with that no."

Lucy smiled despite the trickle of perspiration forging a path down her spine. "Good thing your head's attached. I don't take crime-scene photos."

Justin burst into laughter, and she captured the image. "Hey," he said. "Stop that."

"It's my job," she said with a giggle. "Now go back to your party. I'll call Amanda myself."

Lucy made it all the way to the car before Justin caught up with her. When she reached for her keys and clicked off the security system, Justin opened the door for her.

"Thanks." She reached for her camera cases, but Justin beat her to them. Before she could protest, he'd taken the digital out of her hand and deposited it into the case marked with the brand name.

"I used to have one like this," he said as he handed the

digital back to her. "Lost it in the bayou last summer."

"Ouch," she said.

"Yeah, I forgot I left it out here, and a tropical storm came up." His strained expression made her groan. "See, I forget things."

"I don't know what I would do without mine."

"It's not a big deal. I take lousy pictures." He shrugged. "Becky gave me another one for Christmas. One of those fancy ones like that." He pointed to the newer of the cameras still slung around her neck. "These are great for people who know what they're doing, but I didn't have a clue. I liked the auto focus feature the digital had."

"Funny, I've never used it. Hazard of the profession, I guess, but I like to tinker with things."

"Me, too, but mine usually have internal combustion engines and a fancy paint job." At her confused look, he explained. "Cars. Right now I'm restoring my dad's 1968 Mustang."

As she loaded the items into her trunk, she watched Amanda's brother out of the corner of her eye. He leaned against her car with an air of authority. As if he ruled the roost in this corner of the world.

Slamming the trunk, Lucy reached over to shake Justin's hand. "You're a nice guy, Justin. I appreciate your help with the cameras."

A fresh wind dashed past, bringing with it the earthy scent of wet leaves and damp skies. Rain tonight. The weatherman had already predicted it. Thankfully the Lord had ignored the meteorologist and created a breathtaking sunset to draw a close to a beautifully sunny afternoon.

With the right lens, she could capture an image of God's handiwork that would be absolutely stunning. But what lens?

"Nice meeting you, Lucy."

She jumped at the reminder that she was not alone. "Sorry, I was daydreaming."

His smile softened to become a look of what seemed to be surprise. "Really? You do that, too?"

Great. Another person to make fun of her penchant for wandering down the rabbit trail of musings in the middle of a conversation.

"I've been known to." She paused to gauge his reaction and found no trace of amusement, only interest. "Well, it's been a pleasure, Justin."

Justin offered a nod. "Same here."

She climbed into her car and allowed Justin to shut the door for her. As she cranked the engine, she had a thought. "Say, would you mind if I took a few pictures here someday when the light's right?"

He glanced in her direction, then turned his focus back to her. "Sure. Why not?"

Lucy shielded her eyes with the back of her hand. "I'll call first. I wouldn't want anyone to set the dogs on me."

Justin laughed and shook his head. "You obviously haven't met Bandit. Show up any time. The gate's never locked, and I guarantee the only trouble you'll get from my mutt will be in the form of too much attention. Besides, he's an air-conditioner dog."

Driving away from the LeBlanc house gave Lucy the oddest sensation. It was like catching a glimpse of home, then blinking to find that it had disappeared.

Chapter 3

L ucy took Justin at his word and brought her favorite camera out to the LeBlanc property a few days later. The rain, a real gully washer as her grandpa would have said, wiped away any traces of dust the old cabin may have worn and turned the cypress boards a deep earthy color.

Leaning against an oak tree for balance, she took a few test shots, then moved her position and tried a few more. Satisfied this was the spot for the best angle, Lucy set up her tripod and shot three rolls of the facade of the old cabin.

Then came the real fun.

Removing the camera from the tripod, she wandered around the perimeter of the old structure, snapping odd angles and focusing on the unique details that made the hand-hewn cypress cabin so interesting. She rounded the building a second time and aimed her camera at the eaves of the roof over the porch and the outside stairs that disappeared into the interior's attic above.

On a whim, Lucy followed the outside steps that led into

the cabin's attic and took a half-dozen pictures looking down at the porch. The patterns of sunlight dancing off the window on the south side caught her photographer's attention, and she sized them up for a shot. No, she would have to come closer to get the proper angle.

She would have to step up into the attic. Lucy looked back toward the house and saw no one. "Guess I can't ask to go in if no one's home. I'm going to have to believe Justin won't mind. After all, he did give me permission." Once inside, she stood and reached for the low ceiling's center beam to steady herself.

She sneezed as her eyes adjusted to the dim light. Lucy looked around and realized what she had expected to be an empty space was actually populated with boxes and canvas-covered furniture of some sort. Filled with the scent of age and dust, the room wrapped around her like a glove. History was stored here, many generations of it.

Lucy took a step backward and hit something solid.

A trunk.

Kneeling, she ran her hand over the well-worn wood, then tried the metal latch. It swung open on noisy hinges. Inside was a collection of items that looked as if they had not seen daylight since the turn of the last century. Atop the folded linens and a woman's pink frock was a book that looked to be some sort of journal.

Lucy lifted it gingerly from its resting place and opened it. In a feminine handwriting, someone had written the date. She gasped. "This was written in the seventeen hundreds."

Turning to the inside cover, she noted the name written in

the topmost corner: *Capucine LeBlanc. Must be a relative.*

She flipped over to the journal entry beneath the date and began to read aloud, " 'After much sorrow, much joy. My dear Michel has built me a home. My long-lost mère is nearby. Comforte sleeps on my shoulder as I hold the pen. Life is full.' "

Life is full.

What must it feel like to utter those words? To be able to write them on paper for generations to read? Oh, she'd felt the peace of the Lord, experienced the fullness of His presence. But this woman wrote about the fullness that came from home and family. That sort of statement Lucy couldn't make.

Lucy's curiosity begged her to turn the page, but her heart stopped her. The book was not hers to read. She closed the lid and stood, dusting off her hands before retracing her steps down the stairs and onto the porch.

The clouds had shifted, causing the cabin to sit in a whole new light. This change called for more pictures, and Lucy ended up filling two more rolls with shots of the cabin and its scenery before loading her car to head home.

As she drove past the old cabin, then the newer LeBlanc home nearby, she wondered what it would be like to be a part of something so old, so certain. Something other than a life spent following a father more concerned with his army career by making any move asked of him rather than putting down roots.

The longest she'd lived in one place had been college. Four years of staying in the same city had been pure bliss.

Well, maybe not bliss. She'd had her share of roommate

troubles and cranky professors, but knowing there would be no surprise moves in the middle of the semester had been the closest thing to bliss she'd ever known.

Amanda's car approached on the gravel driveway, and Lucy pulled over to roll down her window. "Welcome back. How was the honeymoon?" She felt a blush start as soon as the question was out. "What I mean is, how was the cruise?"

The gorgeous brunette removed her designer sunglasses, and the sparks of sunlight glinting off her enormous engagement ring nearly blinded Lucy. "Heavenly, of course, but not nearly long enough. With the big move just two weeks away, we couldn't spare more than a three-day trip."

Lucy drummed her fingers on the steering wheel while she contemplated the appropriate response. "It's going to be hard to leave here, I know."

Amanda giggled. "You're kidding, right? I am so ready to exchange the prying eyes of this precious town for the anonymity of New York City."

"Really?" She blew a strand of hair from her eyes. "Personally I think anonymity is highly overrated."

"Maybe, but no matter what, I will always have a home here to bring my children back to. We grew up having our pictures taken on that porch over there, and I want to keep that tradition alive with my own family."

Lucy glanced over in the direction of the house and pictured taking her daughter or son to a family home like that. Imagined taking her photograph beside the home generations of their family had inhabited. Imagined leaving a journal hidden away in the attic of that place for her grandchildren's grandchildren to read.

Too bad such a place never existed.

Oh, Lucy knew by tracing her mother's family tree that she had roots here in the muddy Louisiana soil. Someday, perhaps. . .

"So, did you come out here to see my brother?" Amanda upped the wattage on her smile. "I mean, a girl would have to be blind not to have noticed the sparks flying between the two of you at my wedding. I felt I was watching two kindred spirits meeting for the first time."

Stunned, Lucy found it hard to respond. When she could manage a few words, she said, "I think you have me confused with someone else."

Amanda's eyes narrowed and her brow creased. "No, I think you're the only person he held a conversation with, period. At least one that lasted longer than three minutes. My brother is adorable, but he is a bit of a loner and an old soul. A hazard of taking on too much responsibility at a young age. I think the conversations in Justin LeBlanc's head last much longer than any he's ever actually had."

"Oh?"

"His other job, besides being a professor, is writing books." She leaned further out the window. "I probably shouldn't be telling you this, but my brother has a tendency to daydream. See, he's got the great American novel rolling around inside that goofy head of his, but all he writes are textbooks. A classic case of arrested creativity if ever I have seen it."

"There's nothing wrong with daydreaming," Lucy blurted

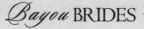

out. "I've been accused of doing that myself. Personally I like to call it *thinking*, although it did frustrate my family when I disappeared into self-induced fogs."

Amanda gave her a knowing look. "As I said, kindred spirits."

To Lucy's relief, the conversation headed toward safer topics like what day the proofs would be ready or when Amanda was leaving for New York. As she bid her client good-bye, Lucy once again wondered what it would be like to be a part of this place, this family.

What it would be like to have a porch to pose a family on year after year.

"Stop daydreaming," she whispered as she turned onto the main road. "Dreaming doesn't make it so."

Nearly an hour later back at the shop, Lucy emerged from the darkroom tired and full of excitement. The photographs from the LeBlanc wedding turned out incredibly well. It didn't hurt that the entire clan was extremely photogenic.

Especially Justin LeBlanc.

Her favorite photograph of the bunch was the last one she'd taken before leaving on Amanda's wedding day. In it, a grinning Justin stood twenty paces away. His posture spoke confidence while his eyes. . .well, his eyes spoke to her through the lens and made her heart flutter.

"Idiot," she muttered as she closed the darkroom door. "There's nothing special about Justin LeBlanc. He just photographs well."

But as she kicked off her sneakers and padded to the

kitchen to scramble some eggs for dinner, she failed to convince herself of that statement.

Justin pushed aside the rest of his bologna sandwich and stared at the pile of papers cluttering his desk. Half of them were assignments from his students that needed grading and the rest were bits and pieces of a book that begged to be written.

Rarely did he pass off essay tests to his teaching assistant, but tonight he made the executive decision to do just that in favor of assembling the collection of facts and memories into a viable proposal for a book on Acadian architecture.

The centerpiece of the book would be the LeBlanc cabin. With centuries of history having taken place inside its sturdy cypress walls, there was more than ample information there.

Funny, he'd procrastinated all through the spring semester, putting off his agent and his publisher rather than work on the seventh book in his Acadian history textbook series. Part of the problem was the sheer volume of data he'd collected over the years on all things Acadian. The other issue, which cut closer to the heart, was the fact that when this text was completed, he would no longer owe a book to his publishing house.

Justin reached for his father's silver pen and balanced it on the tip of his finger. The scratches and imperfections, evidence of a well-used past, reminded him of his heart. He never used his father's pen for fear of losing it.

Funny, I've done the same thing with my heart.

Where did that come from?

He straightened in his chair and pushed away from the desk. The sun had begun to set over the tree line, dancing off the black waters of the bayou and giving them a rare orange tint. To the south, the little cabin sat in the long shadows.

Justin never looked at the little place without thinking of all the people who'd crossed its doorstep. Names that were nothing but words written in the dusty journal in the attic became real when he applied his imagination. Odd duck. Perhaps there was some truth in that.

Crossing his arms over his chest, he gave the cabin one last look before turning his back on the window. Perhaps it was time to give those people he'd imagined a voice. Time to give the cabin beside the bayou a written history.

Something more permanent than the ink-stained pages of the ancient journals that resided in its attic.

Chapter 4

T he shop's bell jangled as the door opened and closed. "Be right there, Amanda." Lucy wiped her palms on her apron and rounded the corner to reach for the envelope marked LeBlanc-Simms. "You're right on time. I put the ones we talked about in front and some others I thought you might like behind them. The rest are just—"

"Actually, Amanda's running late."

The masculine voice stopped Lucy in her tracks. There, leaning against her counter, was Justin LeBlanc. He wore denim and boots and looked as if he'd just stepped out of an ad for some expensive aftershave. Despite the near-record heat out-side, he looked cool and collected.

An odd ripple of surprise mixed with the sudden need to smile assaulted her. Lucy ignored it. Amanda's kindred-spirits statement floated across her mind, then disappeared into the haze. She realized she was staring and looked away.

"She said something about a long line at the buy-two-get-one-free sale over at Shoe Palace." He shrugged. "I assume this is something only a woman would understand."

Lucy giggled, then tried not to cringe. *What an idiot. So the man is handsome. Professional photographers meet attractive people all the time. He's just another brother of the bride.*

She forced her mind back on the situation at hand. "Yes, I understand. I should probably close up and join her. Just kidding." Lucy set the package of proofs on the counter between them, then pushed them toward the dark-haired man. "There's a proof sheet with numbers beneath each picture and a page with a numbered proof list. Tell her to check off the pictures she likes."

"Will do." Justin traced the edge of the envelope with his finger but made no move to pick it up. "Amanda told me you took some pictures of the old cabin."

"Yes, I hope you didn't mind."

"No, I'm really glad you took me up on my offer to come and photograph it." He glanced up at her, and her stomach did a little flip-flop. "So I was wondering something."

Lucy forced a serious look. After all, she was a trained professional, and trained professionals do not go goofy over handsome men.

"What's that?" *Good job, Lucy. You barely sounded interested.*

"Well, I—"

"I'm here." Amanda LeBlanc-Simms breezed in with an apologetic look. "Did Justin tell you about my shoe emergency?"

She crossed the shop to link arms with her brother. Identical smiles aimed Lucy's direction.

"Shoe emergency?" Justin shook his head. "Is there really such a thing?"

Amanda's perfectly plucked brows rose. "Help me out here, Lucy. Tell the man that some things are worth the wait."

When Justin swung his gaze to collide with Lucy's stare, she blinked hard. "Yes, that's right. Some things are worth the wait." Lucy swallowed back the ridiculous butterflies in her stomach. Her attention turned to Amanda. "So what did you get?"

Justin held up both hands and took a step backward. "Oh, no. This is where I bail. I've got a class in an hour, and I know from experience that it's going to take my sister much longer than that to answer your question."

"Hey, I resemble that remark." Amanda gave her brother a playful tap on the shoulder. "And for the record, I'm no worse than you, big brother." She turned to Lucy. "Ask him anything pertaining to Acadian studies and see how long it takes him to answer that question."

Justin gave Lucy an innocent look. "I have no idea what she's talking about, but I'm getting out while I can. Good to see you again, Lucy." He winked at Amanda. "As for you, well. . ."

"Well, nothing. How about you stick around, and we talk about that book you need to be writing? The one about the cabin?"

Justin gave his sister an astonished look, then quickly recovered to turn his attention to Lucy. "Amanda is my biggest cheerleader when it comes to my books."

"I read them all, even the boring ones."

"Hey." Justin frowned. "I don't write boring books. Textbooks can be fascinating."

"Yeah, sure, fascinating." Amanda tugged on his sleeve. "Why

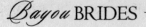

don't you tell Lucy the idea you have about writing a book on the old cabin? Now that's fascinating. You wouldn't believe all the things that have happened there. Justin's an expert on the place. Practically lives there. I know he's read the old journals out there a hundred times. Ask him anything. I'm sure he knows the answer."

Lucy cut a sideways glance toward Justin who looked extremely uncomfortable.

"On that note, I really must go." Justin gave his sister a kiss on the cheek, then reached to shake Lucy's hand. "It's been memorable, ladies," he said as he made tracks for the door.

"Arrested creativity," Amanda said. "There goes the poster boy." She leaned against the counter as the door closed and the bells jangled. "I give Justin a hard time, but he's a rock, you know? He was only twenty-five when Mom and Dad died. He never really had a life outside of my sisters and me. It's no wonder he's so boring."

Boring? Lucy watched the denim-clad professor cross the street and reach to take the helmet off the handlebars of a black motorcycle.

"Don't let the bike fool you, Lucy. He probably rides it because it saves on gas. I'm telling you, he's the most boring man I know."

One long leg stretched over the motorcycle as Justin settled onto the seat and buckled the chinstrap on his helmet. Was it her imagination or did he glance over toward the shop before cranking the engine and rumbling away?

"So I was wondering. Are you interested in helping my

brother to see what he's missing?"

"Missing?" Lucy frowned as the motorcycle and its rider disappeared around the corner. "I have no clue what you're talking about, Amanda."

"I'm talking about kindred spirits, Lucy. Don't think I missed the sizzle going on between you two. Why, it was practically lighting up the room."

"Again," Lucy said as she shifted positions, "I have no idea what you're talking about."

For a moment, Amanda seemed to be considering her words. "So you don't find my brother interesting?"

"Interesting? Sure."

The new bride studied her nails, then looked up, eyes sparkling. "Funny, he said the same thing about you."

Lucy's heart jolted. "Justin thinks I'm interesting?" She realized she'd said the words out loud when Amanda grinned. "What I mean is, well, never mind. Let me know about the proofs, okay?"

"Okay," she said, but it was obvious to Lucy that Amanda was not thinking about her wedding pictures. "About this thing with you and my brother, I was thinking—" Thankfully, her cell phone rang. After a two-minute conversation with her "honey love," she hung up and shook her head. "I'm sorry, Lucy, where were we?"

"We were talking about your proofs." She tapped the envelope. "If you can get them back to me by Monday, I should have them finished before you leave. If you need more time, I can always ship them when they're done."

Amanda lifted a dark brow. "Or I could have Justin come

and pick them up."

Lucy pressed her palms against the counter and regarded Amanda with what she hoped would be a neutral stare. "Amanda, I'm not sure why you've decided to play matchmaker for your brother, but please, don't include me in whatever plans you have for him. I'm far too busy trying to get Lucy's Lens off the ground without complicating my life any further."

"I understand. It's not easy to admit when you've met the man God intends for you. I know it took Miles months to get me to realize that." Amanda held up her hands to silence Lucy's protest, then tucked the envelope into her shopping bag and adjusted the shoulder strap on her purse. "That's all I'm going to say on the matter, Lucy. Just don't forget to call me and let me know when the Lord proves me right."

"Yeah, sure," Lucy said.

But as she watched the door close behind her client, Lucy had to wonder if Amanda wasn't on to something. Not that she believed in the whole kindred-spirits thing.

She did know a thing or two about arrested creativity, however.

Until she opened this place five months ago, she'd worked in a family law office. How she spent seven years of her life drafting warranty deeds and property settlements, she would never know.

"Maybe that's how Justin feels."

❧

Justin handed the graded essays to his teaching assistant before dismissing the class. When the last of the students were gone, he bid his assistant good-bye and began to load his briefcase. Amanda's challenge still rang in his ear. *"How about you stick around and we talk about that book you need to be writing? The one about the cabin?"*

Swallowing hard, Justin pulled out his cell phone and dialed his agent. With the pleasantries out of the way, he dove into the subject of his call.

"So, Bob," Justin said, "I had this idea for the final book in the series. It would be of a narrower scope than the others, so I don't know if it's worth pursuing."

His agent chuckled. "I don't know when I've heard an author less enthused about his own ideas. What's the topic?"

"Well, remember when I had you out for Fourth of July last year and you stayed in the cabin?"

"Oh, yes, I loved that place. As I recall, I said it would make a great setting for a novel."

Justin gulped. "Yes, well, I was thinking that given the fact the history of that place is fascinating, it might make a good topic for a textbook. I would make it much broader in scope, of course. Something along the lines of the history of Acadian architecture. The novel would come later—much later. What do you think?"

The long pause that ensued had Justin ready to jump out of his boots. Finally, his agent cleared his throat.

"I think that would be great, Justin. Would you like me to negotiate an option for two or three more? In my opinion, this series could go on indefinitely."

"No!" He realized he'd not only spoken quickly but loudly when the dean of the department stuck his head in.

"Everything all right, Justin?"

He covered the phone and nodded. "Fine, Dean Mills. I'm just talking to my agent about the next textbook."

"Well that's wonderful, son. I love it when my faculty is prolific. The myth of publish or perish is alive and well around here." His shoulders rocked up and down as he disappeared out the door.

"Sorry," Justin said. "So when do you need the proposal?"

"You know you don't have to do a full proposal, kid. Just give me a general outline and a couple of pictures."

Justin picked at a piece of lint on his sleeve. "Pictures? I never had to do that before. Are they really necessary?"

"No, but it would help." His agent paused. "Look, this is a departure from the standard textbook. Unless I misunderstand, you're wanting to tell a story and give the reader a history lesson, right?"

"Right."

"Then I want the editorial staff to see what you see. This is your vision. I want marketing to understand what your concept is so that when this goes to committee it doesn't get shot down or, worse, changed into something neither of us is happy with."

"Okay." He exhaled slowly. "I can probably come up with something. How many do you need?"

"One or two is fine, or you can send a sheet of slides if you have them. If at all possible, keep them as near to what will appear in the book as possible. I don't want family photos with a cabin behind it, okay? This needs to be professionally done if I'm going to put your name on it."

"Okay, but it might take some time." Then it dawned on him. "Wait, I think I know of a photographer who has some recent shots. I'll get back to you soon."

"While you're at it, why don't you put together a proposal for that novel, too? Knowing you, it wouldn't take more than a day or two."

Justin gripped the phone and let out a long breath. "One thing at a time, Bob. Let me deal with the textbook first; then we'll talk."

Chapter 5

oward: one lacking courage. Okay, so maybe he *was* a coward.

Justin tugged at the stubborn bolt holding the Mustang's radiator fan in place. Not only had he failed to contact the proprietor of Lucy's Lens to inquire about pictures of the cabin, he'd passed on several opportunities to stop in and speak to the owner herself. He'd even considered having one of his sisters approach her on his behalf.

His agent had accepted the proposal with no small amount of hesitancy, stating that without pictures it was still a toss-up whether the book would get through committee. At that moment, he knew he was supposed to write that book, to tell that story.

Once he finished that book, he had the feeling God had another writing assignment for him, one that was way out of his comfort zone. That's when he knew he needed to turn to the Lord.

He did his best praying while working on his dad's Mustang.

So, when he could reason out his problem no longer, Justin turned to the garage and the classic sports car that was all he had left of his earthly father.

"Well, Lord," he said as he swiped at his brow, "I've got some trouble brewing this time. See, I walked into the dean's office today and asked for next semester off. Turns out it wasn't a problem. Dumb idea, I know, but I figured to hit the road in this sweet ride."

One more yank and the bolt gave way.

"I'm not doubting You're in control." The bolt pinged as it hit the pan. "It's just that I don't have a clue what You want me to do."

Write the book, Justin.

The wrench nearly hit his boot as he let it fall from his hand. "Is that You, Lord? I don't believe I've ever actually heard You speak before. You want me to write the book. Trouble is, I don't know if You mean that book on the cabin or the novel I've been thinking of writing from the road."

Both.

"Well now, I wasn't expecting that answer."

And yet it set well with him as he pondered it. Yes, he could write a textbook on Acadian architecture in no time flat—definitely before the first summer session ended. He had everything he needed in his head, his library, and the journals in the trunk at the cabin.

That novel, well, he might have to think on it a bit more. He certainly couldn't write a story worth reading in the short time allotted before the fall semester began, but maybe he could put together an outline and start working on some chapters.

Just start it. I will do the rest.

"I can't argue with that, God. Now if I can just get past the fact that there's someone here in town who turns me tongue-tied every time I try to talk to her. The last thing I need is to get interested in a woman when You clearly mean for me to hit the road."

When no answer seemed forthcoming, Justin went back to work. Half an hour later, the old fan had been replaced and the thirty-eight-year-old engine purred to life. The only way to test his work was to take the Mustang for a drive. With the evening closing in around him, Justin put the top down on his father's vintage convertible and aimed it toward town.

At this time of the evening, shopkeepers had long since closed their businesses and gone home. The usual bustle of the town's main street had been reduced to a stray dog and three parked cars, all in front of the only store open: the former mercantile turned video store.

Two doors down, a light glowed in the apartment above Lucy's Lens. Justin wondered what the pretty photographer was doing, then, for the briefest of moments, considered ringing her bell to inquire.

His limited knowledge of the building, information gleaned from a summer working in the former pharmacy as a delivery boy some fifteen years ago, told him the light he saw would be in the kitchen area.

Justin imagined Lucy up there making iced tea and peanut butter sandwiches, then upgraded his musings to include a three-course meal with an apple crisp for dessert. At that point, he knew he was every bit as strange as his sisters claimed. What sort of idiot sat on the corner and tried to guess what a woman he barely knew was making for dinner?

An odd duck, that's who.

The Mustang started to idle rough, and Justin let up on the clutch. Rolling past the photographer's front window, something caught his eye and he pulled to the curb.

Lucy had left a light on in the back of the store behind the counter, illuminating a large black-and-white picture. Justin killed the engine and pocketed the keys, then loped across the street to get a better look.

Shielding his eyes from the glare of the neon light above him, Justin leaned against the glass. There behind the counter was an amazing sight.

Framed in a simple black frame was the most incredible black-and-white picture of the LeBlanc cabin he'd ever seen. Flanked on either side by smaller photographs of what must be pieces of the same whole, the cabin seemed to fairly jump out of the frame.

He'd seen many pictures of the old cabin, from tintypes to more recent photographs. None captured the essence of the historic structure like these.

Hesitating only a moment, Justin reached into his shirt pocket for his cell phone and typed in the code for his agent. "Hey, this is Justin LeBlanc. Write this number down." He took a step backward and read the phone number for Lucy's Lens off the door. "I want this photographer for the book and no one else. Have the folks at the publishing house contact her."

There. Buying a few of Lucy's photographs for the book was just good business.

"Wait. It's not that simple, Justin."

❧

Lucy could stand it no longer. Justin had been outside on the sidewalk for nearly ten minutes. She'd heard him before she actually saw him, mindful of the rumble that preceded the classic Mustang's arrival on her block.

Either she ignored the man and went back to the movie she'd been watching or she took the opportunity to see a classic car—and an interesting man—up close. She opted for the latter, checking her hair and adding a touch of clear gloss to her lips before bounding down the back stairs.

She heard Justin's voice and he sounded irritated. Perhaps this wasn't such a good idea.

"Look maybe we should just forget it. There's no way I can ask her to do that. She's a professional."

Pause.

"Yes, I know the house only works with professionals. What I mean is, I don't see how I can ask Lucy to clear her schedule and produce enough photographs for a full-length book in two weeks. I'm sure she's going to say no."

"Actually, she might say yes, but you'd have to ask her first."

Justin turned around slowly. "I'm going to have to call you back." He shut the phone and deposited it into his shirt pocket. "Hey," he said.

"Hey."

"I was just. . .well. . .it seems as though I have a problem."

Lucy smiled. When had this man become so impossibly gorgeous? Just yesterday she'd thought him merely handsome but now, here in the moonlight. . .

"You see, I have this series of textbooks."

"On Acadian history." Lucy leaned against the side of the building. "Amanda told me."

"Yes, well, anyway, I just got off the phone with my agent, and it seems as though I've just sold the last in the series."

"That's great. Congratulations."

"Thank you."

For a man who'd just sold a book, Justin did not sound enthused. In fact, he sounded just the opposite.

"Something wrong with that? Seems to me I'd be happy."

"Happy, yes, I suppose I am."

He gazed inside Lucy's Lens, and it seemed his attention was focused on the cabin photographs. She walked over to stand beside him.

"You suppose?"

Justin shrugged. "There's a catch."

"Oh?"

He turned to face her. "Those pictures are incredible. You really captured the essence of the old place."

"Thanks." She averted her gaze as heat rose in her cheeks. Odd, she never had trouble receiving compliments on her work before. "So what's the catch?"

Justin stuffed his fists into his jeans and rocked back on his heels. "Oh, that. Well, the catch is they want your pictures to go along with my text." His swung his attention to rest on her. "It looks like you and I are a package deal. Are you interested?"

Lucy nearly forgot to breathe. Interested? Was the moon shining in the night sky?

Before she allowed herself to get caught up in the excitement of the moment, Lucy took a deep breath and let it out slowly. "So, Justin, what exactly does this mean? I've never been part of a 'package deal' before."

Chapter 6

Somehow the explanation of what the publisher wanted from Lucy moved from the sidewalk to the studio. There, Justin got a better idea of the scope of Lucy Webber's talent. Book after book of proofs filled the shelves in her neatly organized office.

"Are these all yours?"

Lucy nodded. "Coffee?"

"Sure." He reached for one of the albums, then thought better of it. "Do you mind if I take a peek?"

"Go right ahead." Lucy paused. "Cream or sugar?"

"Neither, thanks."

While he waited for her to come back from the upstairs apartment with two mugs of coffee, he snagged one of the albums, set it on the counter, and let it fall open.

There, on the middle of the page was a series of pictures that took his breath away. Not only was the vehicle a Mustang, it was a convertible just like Dad's except in color.

Wearing a coat of shiny blue paint, the car's white interior gleamed against the backdrop of a wood-framed garage. Beside the car stood a heavyset gentleman with a rather stern-looking face and a dark-haired beauty who could have passed for Lucy's older sister.

"My parents," Lucy said as she set the mug on the counter beside Justin. She pointed to the car, then gestured to the vehicle parked across the street. "What are the odds?"

"So your dad was into muscle cars, too?"

She nodded and took a sip. "It was about the only thing he and I had in common."

"Interesting."

Lucy looked up sharply. "Why do you say that?"

"I could say the same thing about my dad. Oh, I never doubted that he loved me and everything I know about the Lord started with the lessons he taught me." He paused to contemplate his words. How much to say to this near stranger. "Still, I never really connected with him except when we were both under the hood of the Mustang."

He took a taste of the coffee and found it excellent. "I see you've taken to our chicory coffee, Lucy."

"My mother was Acadian. She compromised on a lot of things, but good coffee was not one of them. Until my grandmother died, she would send cases of the stuff to whatever army base my dad had been assigned."

"So you were an army brat."

She rested her elbow on the counter and lowered her lips to touch the rim of her mug. "Surprised?" she asked as she took another sip.

Surprised: amazed, astonished, or bewildered.

"A lot of things about you surprise me, Lucy Webber. Pleasantly so."

Words he wanted to reel back in as soon as they were spoken. Then he saw it. "Are you blushing?"

"I don't know what you're talking about." She set the mug down and gestured to the Mustang. "Mind if I take a look at her? For old time's sake," she added.

Lucy unlocked the front door, then locked it behind them. Trotting across the street with the prettiest photographer in town on his heels made Justin stand a little straighter. Her interest in his dad's car made him smile.

He pointed out the work he'd just done, as well as the things that were original to the vehicle. To his surprise, she asked intelligent questions and seemed truly knowledgeable about the car.

Slamming down the hood, Justin made a snap decision. "Would you like to go for a drive?"

She thought about it for a second longer than Justin liked. "Sure." Pausing, she grinned. "Guess it wouldn't do any good to ask if I could drive."

Justin put on his broadest smile. "None whatsoever."

Lucy took the news without complaint, smiling when he beat her to the passenger side and opened the door to help her in. "Top down?" he asked as he climbed behind the wheel.

His passenger slid Justin a sideways look. "Is there any other way to ride in one of these?"

That's when Justin knew that even though his book would

have the best photographer in Louisiana, his heart was in serious danger.

※

Riding beneath the summer moon brought back memories for Lucy. Nights when her dad came home before bedtime were usually spent just like this. Sometimes Papa would stop and tinker beneath the hood. Always, Lucy shadowed him. Eventually it was she who did the driving and tinkering until the cost of maintaining the old car became greater than her widowed mother's budget could bear. The car was sold and the money applied to long-standing debts.

Most times when she saw a vehicle that resembled her dad's, she longed to open the hood and tinker. Tonight, however, Lucy was content to sit in the passenger seat, although she wanted to ask a question or two along the way. Justin told her of the work he'd done, elaborating only when he realized she knew her way around a car engine.

"I watched my dad," she said by way of explanation. "It's my favorite memory of him. The only one, actually. He was gone most of the time."

Lucy cringed. What was it about this man that made her blurt out things she normally kept private?

Justin had the decency not to comment. Rather, he changed the subject.

"I learned to drive in this car." He signaled to make a left turn, then headed away from the lights of town. "My dad drove to the other end of the field and gave me two choices. I could either drive home or walk. If I walked, the car would go to my sisters."

Chuckling, Lucy swiveled to face him. "So you drove?"

He joined her in laughter. "Well, sort of. I'm ashamed to say I wasn't a natural at driving a manual transmission car."

Lucy made a face. "Not pretty, eh?"

"To say the least. My dad stood there laughing, which only made me more determined to learn. When I finally got the hang of it, he was so proud he could hardly stand it." Justin braked for a stop sign, then met her gaze. "Years later he told me that he didn't learn to drive stick until he was in college. My mother taught him."

Lucy heard the engine's idle change, and she cocked her ear to listen. "Has it always sounded like that?"

"Like what?" Justin shook his head. "What exactly are you hearing?"

"I'm not sure. I mean, I'm not familiar with this car, so I may be wrong, but it sounds like there's an issue with the idling. Have you had problems with it?"

"Yeah. I had to tinker with it on the way to town." He accelerated, then cast a glance in her direction. "What are you thinking?"

"There's a parking lot up ahead with lights. If you don't mind pulling over, I can show you."

He looked doubtful but did as she asked. Two seconds after he lifted the hood, she saw the problem and pointed it out to him.

"You think so?" He scratched his head and took another

look. A smile dawned. "Hey, you're right," he said as he made the adjustment she suggested. When he finished he handed Lucy the keys. "Start her up, and let's see how she sounds."

It was Lucy's turn to look doubtful. "Oh, I don't know, Justin. I mean, this is your father's car. I wouldn't want to—"

"Women," he said in mock dismay. "Even when they get what they want they're not satisfied."

Lucy grinned. "All right then."

She fitted the key in the ignition and pressed on the brake and clutch. For a moment, she was back in her father's garage, a little girl starting the car so her father could check the engine. Lucy could see her dad, could smell the scent of motor oil that permanently pervaded the old garage on—

"What are you waiting for?"

"Sorry," she said as she turned the key. "Guess I must have been daydreaming."

The engine cranked to life and settled immediately into an even purr. Justin came around to give her a high five.

"You're amazing, Lucy," he said as he slammed the hood shut. "I've been pulling my hair out trying to figure out that idle problem, and you diagnose it in no time. Where have you been all my life?"

"On the road," she said as she set the parking brake and opened the door. Once again she'd said too much. "Keep in mind, that repair is only temporary. You'll need to order a new part or face this problem returning."

Rather than climb into the driver's seat, Justin leaned against the fender and crossed his arms over his chest. Moonlight cut a swath across his face and the streetlight behind him added to the picture. His grin went south and Lucy frowned.

"What's wrong?"

His expression quickly changed, and he returned to his jovial self. "Nothing," he said. "Just daydreaming."

"Ah, a kindred spirit." Lucy walked around the back of the car to settle into the passenger seat. "I used to drive my mom crazy."

Justin remained in place. "Yeah," he said. "My sisters call me an odd duck." Their gazes collided. "I'm afraid they're right."

Handsome.

The word crowded out everything else in her mind.

Odd, but until she met Justin LeBlanc, she'd never been one to look at physical beauty as something to admire except from behind the camera lens. Something about this man, though, made her acutely aware of his gently worn features and his quirky smile.

Kindred spirits.

Amanda's statement came to mind, and she grinned. Perhaps they were kindred spirits.

"Well," she said as she leaned against the car door and looked up at Justin, "I, for one, don't think there is anything wrong with being an odd duck. Who wants to be normal anyway?"

He laughed out loud and she joined him. When he climbed into the driver's seat, he had to wipe his eyes with the backs of his sleeves.

When he placed his hands on the wheel, she assumed they

were about to leave. Instead, he turned to face her.

"Amanda was right."

Justin's statement startled her. "Right about what?"

He opened his mouth to speak, but the siren drowned out his voice.

Chapter 7

A second later a spotlight illuminated the interior of the car and cast Justin in an eerie white light. Lucy covered her face with her hand and tried to look away.

"I'll need to see some ID," a gruff voice called. "Passenger, you first, and don't make any sudden moves."

"Glenn, is that you?"

Lucy peeked from beneath her hand to see Justin climb out of the car and embrace the source of the light. A second later the world went dim as the light disappeared.

"Justin? Justin LeBlanc. What are you doing out here? I thought we had car thieves or teenagers."

Blinking to remove the spots dancing before her eyes did not work, so Lucy groped for the door handle. Failing to find it, she settled for remaining in place.

"Lucy, Officer Glenn Benson. I went to high school with him."

"Pleased to meet you, Officer." A hand grasped hers, and

307

she made out a heavyset policeman through the spotlights still decorating her vision. "Lucy Webber."

"Lucy owns that new photography place in town," Justin said.

"Oh yeah, Lucy's Lens," the officer said. "I know that place. Didn't I see pictures of that cabin of yours in there?"

"That's right." Justin moved into her field of vision and seemed to be smiling in her direction. "She and I are going to be working on a book together."

As Lucy's sight grew sharper, she watched the two men go through the backslapping ritual of saying good-bye. By the time Justin climbed back behind the wheel, she could almost claim perfect vision again.

"Well, that was interesting," she said. "I can't remember the last time a policeman caught me in a parking lot with a man." This time she blushed and didn't bother to deny it. "Don't you say a word," she warned Justin. "What I should have said is that I have never been caught by a policeman while sitting in the parking lot with a man, because the situation never came up. I'm not that kind of girl. Besides I was too much of a geek for guys to notice." Justin gave her an appraising look, and the heat in her face flamed hotter. "What?"

"Nothing." He shook his head. "It's just that I find that hard to believe."

"What? That I wouldn't be caught with a guy in a parking lot?"

"No, it's hard to believe that guys wouldn't notice you." Justin shrugged. "You must have gone to a school for the blind."

"So, about these photographs of the cabin." Justin hoped the change of topic didn't seem too abrupt. He'd spoken his mind about the pretty photographer, then regretted it a moment later. What woman wants to hear cheesy comments about how pretty she is?

Lucy leaned back against the seat and stared up at the moon. The night wind danced around her and tossed her hair into her eyes, but she didn't seem to mind.

"What about them?"

"I've got a short window of time. The book won't take long to write, especially with the added amount of photographs. I've been doing research and taking notes for years. I plan to use those notes as an outline. Fleshing it out shouldn't take more than a month. I can do that from the road."

"The road?"

She sounded surprised. A quick glance told him she'd forsaken her relaxed position to sit rigidly upright, her attention on the gravel road ahead.

"Yes," he said. "I've got the second summer session off, and I'm planning to take full advantage by getting away."

This time when he checked, she'd relaxed visibly. "So you want the photographs done before you take your vacation then?"

"Right."

Out of the corner of his eye, he watched her rest her arm on the door, then nod. "If the light is right, I only need a few hours. I can have proofs ready for you within two days. Will you need slides or negatives?"

"I'm not sure. Can I get back to you on that?"

"Sure."

They drove the rest of the way back into town in silence. When Justin pulled the Mustang to a stop outside Lucy's Lens, he tried to think of something witty to say as a good-bye. Instead, he jogged around and opened the car door for Lucy, then helped her out without comment.

She touched his hand and smiled. "Thank you, Justin. Your sister was right. You're quite the gentleman."

Gentleman: an honorable and well-bred man. Justin smiled.

Words, ever his friend, escaped him further as he followed Lucy to the door and waited while she fumbled with an over-large silver ring of keys. Unwittingly, he turned his attention to her face, to the expression of irritation she made while looking for just the right key and then the smile of victory when the key was found.

"Thanks for the ride. It was fun." She stabbed the key into the lock, then glanced at him over her shoulder.

As he nodded and mumbled something that resembled "You're welcome" or maybe "Me, too," Justin felt the oddest sensation. Not quite the suave impression he wanted to convey, but the best he could do under the circumstances.

"Well, good night, Justin."

Lucy had already walked inside and locked the door before Justin found his voice. She disappeared into the darkness before he managed a feeble, "Wait."

A car rolled past slowly, and Justin turned away from the street. This town was too small. By the time he got home all four sisters would probably know that their brother was loitering on the sidewalk outside Lucy's Lens.

As the car turned at the corner, Justin risked a quick glance to try and discern the identity of its occupants. When he saw there was a teenager behind the wheel, he let out a long breath. The last thing any teenager would notice was an old guy standing on a sidewalk. And he'd taught at the university long enough to know anyone over twenty-five was an old guy.

He took two steps toward the curb, then stopped and thought better of his plan to leave. Rather, he reached for his cell phone and punched in the numbers for Lucy's Lens, the ones that decorated her front window.

Calling the store was a calculated risk. In his experience, most shop owners ignored the phone when it rang outside business hours.

Justin trotted across the street and leaned against the front fender of the Mustang, looking toward the apartment above the store as he pressed the SEND button. He watched a shadow cross the shades as the phone began to ring.

"Hello?" She sounded out of breath.

"Good night, Lucy."

Silence.

Justin watched the shadow cross the shades again. "Lucy?"

"I'm here." She paused. "You called me to say good night?"

"Silly, huh?" It was his turn to pause. "It's just that, well,

I didn't respond when you said good night, and I thought. . . never mind what I thought. I have a proposition for you."

"Oh, I don't know, Justin." Her voice sounded happy, playful. "I'm not used to being propositioned by men I hardly know."

Her giggle was infectious. "Point taken," he said. "What I meant was I would like to meet with you tomorrow and see if we can work out an agreement to collaborate on the Acadian cabin book. Did that sound better?"

"Hey, I'm not complaining about the first statement. I'm just saying I'm not used to it."

Did I just say that? Lucy suppressed a groan. Flirting had never been her strong suit. For that matter, she would be hard-pressed to recall the last time she'd attempted it.

Besides, she barely knew the guy.

"Lucy?"

"Yes, I'm here. What time tomorrow did you have in mind?" There, that sounded much more dignified.

"I'm teaching until one. What about a late lunch? We can discuss the project over red beans and rice at the Crab Shack. After all, it's Monday. You do know what that means, right?"

Lucy grinned. Of all the dishes she'd tasted in her adopted home, red beans and rice topped with a serving of local sausage was by far her favorite.

"I know a thing or two about Louisiana history. Let's see. Monday was washday in Acadiana, and housewives a century ago set red beans on to cook while they washed clothes. Are you impressed?"

"Very." He paused. "So, one o'clock at the Crab Shack?"

"Let me check my calendar." She reached for her day planner and paged over to the coming week. In bold letters at the 1:00 p.m. slot she'd written the name of a potential client. "Wait, I can't meet at one. I've got an appointment, but I should be finished by two thirty."

"I teach from two until three."

"My meeting is over near the university. What if I met you after class?"

"Sure. Are you familiar with the campus?"

"No, but I'm great at following directions. Let me grab a pen."

Lucy finished writing the directions, then closed her planner. "Okay then, I'll meet you in the quad at a quarter past three." A movement outside caught her attention, and she lifted a slat on the blinds. "Justin, is that you down there?"

He waved up at her. "Yeah, it's me."

The embarrassment in his voice made her smile. "Why are you still here?"

Justin paused. "I don't know exactly," he said. "It's such a nice night and, well, I should go."

As much as she longed to argue the point, she said nothing beyond a quick good-bye and a wave out the window. The pretense of peeking out the window long over, she lifted the blinds and leaned against the sash.

Lucy watched the Mustang stop at the light, then disappear

around the corner. "I don't know what just happened, Lord, but if this is from You, I'm all for it." She closed the blinds. "If it's not, then send him away now before I fall for him."

Chapter 8

Lucy stood at the classroom door just out of the line of sight of the man at the podium. The classroom was large, one of those auditorium-like spaces where a hundred students could spread out comfortably. Those assembled today looked anything but comfortable, however, as Justin, clad in jeans and an open-collared white shirt, told the story of heartache and fear as Acadians were driven from their homes and forced to flee south. At several points during Justin's lecture, Lucy noticed female students wiping away tears and males grimacing. Hollywood couldn't have created a more dramatic story than the one surrounding the plight of the displaced Acadians, and Justin told it well.

Forgetting her intention to stay out of sight, Lucy settled into a seat on the back row and listened as Justin wrapped up the tale. At one point in the story, his gaze swept her way and locked with hers. To his credit, Justin didn't miss a beat. He did, however, give her a quick smile and a brief nod.

When the last laptop was closed and the stream of students

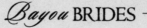

had left the room, Lucy rose. "I'd give you an A+, Professor."

"Thank you. I didn't know you were auditing Intro to Acadian History." His grin turned serious as he checked his watch. "Am I late? I didn't expect to see you here in class."

"No, you're not late." She shrugged. "My meeting ended early. Guess I didn't need the full two hours to convince them I should photograph their wedding. I thought I'd sneak in and listen to your lecture instead of waiting for you outside."

Justin gave her a sideways look. "Had nothing to do with the fact that it's 110 degrees in the shade, did it?"

Lucy pretended offense. "It's only ninety in the shade, Professor."

They shared a chuckle until Justin turned serious once more. "You haven't come here to tell me you changed your mind about taking the photographs, have you?"

"No, why would you think that?"

He seemed pensive for a moment. "I don't know. It's just that this morning I felt like the Lord was trying to tell me something about this project and those pictures." He met her stare. "Don't pay any attention to me. I'm just a little dense. When God speaks, He needs to carry a sledgehammer to hit me over the head or else I'll miss it entirely."

Lucy giggled. "I'm that way, too, sometimes. My mother used to claim that if God ever chose to speak to me, He would find me daydreaming."

Justin gave her a sideways look. "Hey, my sisters say the same thing about me."

"That's because you're an odd duck. You admitted as much

to me last night."

Merriment danced in his eyes. "Well, as long as my secret is safe with you. I have an image to maintain around here."

Lucy rose and gathered her purse. "You do? What sort of image is that?"

"Dignified professor," he said as he feigned a serious look. "Is it working for you?"

Pretending to be impressed, she nodded. "Yes, of course."

"Justin, I was wondering if—" A silver-haired gentleman stuck his head in the door. "Oh, I'm sorry. I thought class was over." He regarded Lucy. "Please forgive me for intruding."

"Lucy, this is my boss, Dean Mills. Dean, this is Lucy Webber. She's the photographer I mentioned."

The dean shook Lucy's hand and offered a broad smile. "Oh yes, I have heard great things about your work. My wife told me she's dying to get her hands on those pictures of the LeBlanc cabin you have in your shop."

Lucy felt the heat begin to rise in her cheeks. "That's very nice of you to mention my work, but those photographs aren't for sale."

"Too bad," Justin said. "I pitched them as a possible front cover to my agent. I was hoping you wouldn't mind?"

"Front cover?"

The dean shook his head. "I better go. High-level literary discussions are better left to the creative geniuses in the group." He turned to Lucy and shook her hand once again. "Young lady, I'm pleased to meet you. I can't wait to see the finished product."

"Thank you, Dean Mills, but I'm sure Justin's work will far outshine any pictures I might take."

"That was nice of you," Justin said when they were alone again.

Lucy shrugged. "I've read your work. You're good."

"You have?" He seemed genuinely surprised. "Really?"

"Really." She allowed him to lead her into the hall. "Remember, I'm a history buff."

"Oh, that's right. A woman after my own heart."

Their gazes met, and Lucy felt the collision down to her toes. With his hand on Lucy's elbow, Justin led her toward the door.

Blinking hard as they emerged into the afternoon sunshine, she forced her mind to remain on the topic at hand. "Do you have anything in particular in mind as far as photographs, or did you just want me to shoot a few rolls as test shots?"

He stopped short and raked his hands through his hair. "I don't know, Lucy. How do you usually do this?"

She chuckled. "Well, this is my first book, but if I were scouting a wedding location, I would take the camera out and do test shots at a few different spots, then go back to the darkroom and see what develops."

It was Justin's turn to laugh. "Pun intended, right?"

"Absolutely."

Rather than accept a ride on the back of his motorcycle, Lucy followed Justin to the Crab Shack for a quick late lunch, then down the country lane leading to the LeBlanc property for the photo shoot. Up ahead, the cabin came into view. Even in the late afternoon summer sun, the rockers on the porch of the old place looked cool and inviting.

Justin slowed and allowed her to drive up beside him. "I'm going to go let Bandit out."

"Bandit?"

He nodded. "My springer spaniel. It's too hot to leave him outside, so he gets the privilege of air-conditioning while I'm teaching."

"Okay. I'll get started."

Justin nodded and sped off toward the main house. After parking her car and grabbing her cameras, Lucy headed for one of the rockers to load her film. Realizing she'd left her cooler in the car, she strolled out to pop the trunk.

From her vantage point, she could see the slow moving water of the bayou. Lucy left the cooler in the shade beside her car and headed toward the bayou with her favorite camera.

Bandit raced ahead of Justin, barking and making circles around Lucy's car. The pretty photographer stood beside the bayou, her camera lifted toward the center of the stream.

The afternoon sun threaded highlights into her fiery hair and burnished her cheeks with gold. Justin stopped in his tracks in order to better appreciate the sight of Lucy at work.

"Lord, something's stirring between us, isn't it? If You don't intend for me to take an interest in this lady, I'd appreciate it if You'd let me know fairly soon. I think I'm already a goner."

The dog yelped as if to hurry Justin along. A moment later,

Bandit put his nose to the ground and made tracks for the bayou. Before Justin could stop him, the hyperactive hound bounded into the photograph Lucy was taking.

Justin prepared an apology. To his surprise, it was unnecessary. Lucy knelt and held out her hand to allow Bandit to sniff a proper greeting.

"Well, hello there," she said. "You must be Bandit."

The spaniel gave her hand one more sniff, then rolled over and presented his belly for scratching. When Lucy obliged, Justin grinned.

"That's amazing." At the sound of Justin's voice, Bandit turned his head toward him. He made no move toward his master, however. "You've thoroughly charmed my dog. No one has managed that feat but me."

She looked up and grinned. "What can I say? Bandit has great taste."

"That he does. Hey, sorry he messed up your shot."

Lucy rose and dusted off the knees of her jeans. "Are you kidding? He made the picture. Do you think I could get him to pose up on the porch?"

"This dog?" Justin shook his head. "Good luck. He's got the attention span of a gnat. The first time a butterfly lands on the honeysuckle, he'll be off and running."

"It's worth a try anyway." Lucy knelt and rubbed the dog's belly. "Let's go see how well you photograph, Bandit."

Justin watched in awe as the traitorous animal jumped up and trotted at Lucy's side. All the way from the bayou to the cabin, the dog remained a step away.

When Justin caught up with the pair, he shook his head. "How'd you do that, Lucy? I can't get that dog to listen to me for anything." Bandit looked up at him with big brown eyes, and Justin frowned. "Yeah, I'm talking about *you*, dog."

"See, there's the trouble, Justin. You're talking to him like he's a dog. You've got to talk to him like he's, well, a person." At his doubtful look she held her hands up to protest. "Never mind. So, do you want the photographs for the book to have Bandit in them?"

"I don't know." He shrugged. "Why not? I can decide whether to use them later, right?"

"Right." She reached into her bag and pulled out a camera, then began adding something to the lens. When she finished, she pushed a few buttons, then held the camera up and looked through the lens. Pointing the camera in his direction, she clicked three times.

"Hey, I'm not supposed to be in the pictures."

She smiled. "Test shots, Justin. Be patient." Checking the screen on the back, she played with a few more settings. "Okay, now it's your turn, Bandit."

Chapter 9

For the next half hour, Justin watched Lucy pose the dog at various places on the sunny side of the porch. Wherever she put the dog, he remained, even when a butterfly landed on the rail mere inches from his oversized paws. He even sat still while Lucy took three steps backward. She actually shot a whole roll of film with the dog and butterfly peacefully coexisting.

"All done," she finally said. "Thank you, Bandit."

As if on cue, the dog scrambled up and raced down the steps, heading out across the lawn toward the house. Justin laughed. "What can I say? He's an air-conditioner dog. I'm guessing he's probably made it through the pet door and is already slobbering at the water bowl."

"Now that's an attractive picture. But I have to agree with him. If given a choice I prefer the air-conditioning, too." Lucy swiped at her forehead. "For now, however, I can't wait to see more of this old cabin. What's next?"

Next? I'm thinking dinner.

Justin cleared his throat and his thoughts. "At this point, I'm more interested in exterior shots than any taken inside. I would like to get a few pictures of the old upstairs sleeping area, though."

She leaned against the stairs and looked up. "The attic?"

"Well, that's what we use it for now, but back before the tax laws changed the boys in the family would sleep up there." At her surprised look, he continued. "Homeowners were taxed based on how many staircases they had inside the house. By putting the staircase on the porch, they could avoid the extra cost and still have the bedroom space for the large families they had back then."

"Justin, has anyone ever told you that you're fascinating?"

Fascinating: possessing the ability to charm or captivate with a pleasing personality and manners.

He leaned against the porch rail and crossed both arms over his chest. "Thank you. Fascinating was exactly what I was going for."

Lucy looked as if she might say something further on the topic of his charm and pleasing personality, so Justin leaned forward.

"Don't move! Oh, Justin, this is amazing."

This is amazing. Not you *are amazing.* Justin tried not to let his disappointment show.

Several camera clicks later, Lucy's moment of amazement seemed to be over. She lowered her camera, then gave him a sheepish look. "I'm sorry. That was really rude of me. It's just that standing there with the light and shadows just right, well, you looked. . ."

"Amazing?"

Her gaze collided with his. "Yes, actually."

Something in his heart cracked, and warmth flooded forth. *Lord, what is happening here?*

"Are you all right?" Lucy rested her hand on his forehead. Her touch felt cool and soft.

As if he had no say in the matter, his fingers reached for hers and entwined with them. Justin brushed Lucy's fingertips against his lips.

"Actually, I'm amazed, Lucy." *Amazed: the state of bewilderment or surprise; stunned.* Justin leaned forward. He might be wrong, but it seemed as if Lucy did the same. "Oh, yes," he said slowly, "I am definitely amazed. . .bewildered. . .surprised. . .stunned. . . ."

And then her phone rang.

"Excuse me," she said after checking the number. "This is the bride I met with this morning. She's supposed to be getting back to me with a date for the ceremony."

Justin nodded and pointed over at the ladder leading up to the attic. He'd been meaning to fetch his favorite old journal before he left, the one filled with wisdom from Capucine LeBlanc, who presided over this Acadian home so long ago.

He'd read all the journals and sifted through hundreds of letters, postcards, and photographs over the years. None of them compared to the simple words of the dignified Acadian woman:

In the year of our Lord, 1769
　　I, Capucine LeBlanc, write this with my own hand.

These are my thoughts in this new land. After much
sorrow, much joy. My dear Michel has built me a home.
My long-lost mère is nearby. Comforte sleeps on my
shoulder as I hold the pen. Life is full.

"Life is full." How he longed to utter those words and
mean them. Until he knew what he was missing, he would
never realize that depth of peace.

Lucy moved toward him, and he turned to watch her
approach. When she smiled and mouthed an "I'm sorry" he
merely shrugged. Truly he didn't mind. Just watching her made
him smile.

What an odd duck he was.

"Okay, give me a couple of hours to finish up and get back
to the office. I'd rather not book the appointment until I take a
look at my calendar," he heard Lucy say. "What if I call around
five?" She met his gaze as she hung up. "I'm sorry."

"It's fine," he said as he led her down the stairs to walk
the perimeter of the old building. Occasionally Justin would
stop to point out something about the cabin, and Lucy would
photograph it.

At the back corner of the property, he pointed out the spot
where the old well used to stand. Lucy strolled over to get a
closer look, then raised her camera and began adjusting the
lens.

Justin followed her, amused. What could she possibly find
to photograph in an old pile of rocks and a rusty bucket and
spoon?

"I'm curious about something," Justin said as he watched Lucy work.

She lowered the camera and eyed him with some measure of suspicion. "What's that?"

"Is everything a potential photograph?"

Lucy surprised him with a wide smile. "My mother used to ask me the same thing."

"And?"

"And I guess the answer would be yes." She glanced past him. "For instance, when you look at the side of the cabin what you see are cypress boards nailed up in straight lines, right?"

"Right," Justin said slowly.

"Well, I like to think of things like that as God's artwork. What I see is a pattern with lines and color." She must have noticed his skeptical look because she held her hand up as if to stop his protest. "What I mean is, the planks on the cabin are incredibly beautiful when viewed through this lens at this distance. Want to see?"

Justin glanced over at the wall, then back at Lucy. Art in old wood? "Yes, I believe I'd like to see that."

Lucy moved over to make room for him, then handed him the camera. "Okay, stand right here and point the lens toward a spot just below the window. What do you see?"

He did as he was told. "A blur?" When he looked her way, Justin noticed she was frowning. "Maybe I'm not doing it right."

Lucy leaned over to look at the back of the camera. She made a few adjustments to the lens in the front, then held the camera up and looked toward the cabin. A second later, she handed it back to Justin.

"Try it now."

With doubt still uppermost in his thoughts, Justin turned the camera in the direction of the old house. A gray pattern appeared, still out of focus but showing distinct possibility. Perhaps that was the effect her art demanded.

"Am I supposed to see it clearly?"

"That's the idea. Maybe it's the difference in our heights. Why don't we try this sitting down?" She settled onto the grass and patted a spot beside her. "Let me adjust the lens."

When he handed her the camera, their fingers brushed. Justin froze. So did Lucy.

Their gazes met. Something passed between them, a spark or maybe just a passing interest. Whatever it was, it threw Justin for a loop.

It was all he could do not to scramble to his feet and run. Something about this woman scared him worse than his grandmother's banty rooster. In the case of that nasty bird, Justin learned to stay out of its way. In the case of Lucy Webber, he couldn't get enough of her.

His hand covered hers. She set the camera on the grass between them, never breaking eye contact.

Justin entwined his fingers with hers and brought them to his lips. She blinked hard as he pressed her knuckles to his lips.

"No red polish today?" he asked.

A pretty shade of pink colored her cheeks. "No."

Lord, if this feeling is not from You, stop me from kissing her.
No such message arrived, however, so Justin kissed her.

Soon as he realized what he'd done, Justin picked up the
camera and snapped Lucy's picture. He wanted to remember
this moment for the rest of his life.

Even without the photograph, he knew he would never
forget.

Chapter 10

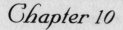

Lucy Webber, the woman her mother repeatedly stated was destined to be alone, had kissed a man. And almost a perfect stranger at that.

Stunned did not begin to cover the feelings swirling around Lucy's addled brain. "You kissed me, Justin."

She blinked hard when she realized she'd said the words aloud. Heat flamed her face and embarrassment caused her to clamp her mouth shut rather than speak further foolishness.

When he swung his attention back to her, Justin seemed as surprised as she about the kiss. He did not, however, look a bit sorry. "Yes, I did kiss you, Lucy," he said softly. "Should I apologize?"

She allowed her eyes to close, then, lest he think her flirting, opened them quickly. "Well, I don't know. It depends."

Justin leaned toward her. "On what?"

His voice was low, soft, and oh, so appealing. Another minute in his presence and she might kiss him again. *Oh, who needs a minute?* Lucy pretended to study the pattern of sunlight

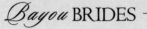

and shadows beneath the nearby magnolia tree. "Justin?"

She felt him set the camera aside and move closer. "Yes?" came out in a rough whisper.

Lucy lifted her gaze to meet his. "Do you make it a practice to kiss women you barely know?"

A horn honked as a brown delivery truck rolled toward them. They scrambled to their feet, and Lucy swiped at the grass decorating her khakis. As the air brakes squealed and the truck stopped, Justin took two steps back and crossed his arms over his chest.

"Hey, Justin, you ole pole cat. *Comment ça va?*" A thin man barely out of his teens appeared in the door, clipboard in hand. "I got somethin' for you. I think it's those car parts you were waitin' on."

"*Ça va bien*, Phil." Justin's expression changed but his gaze never left hers. "Go ahead and drop it off at the garage."

"But this is the stuff you been waitin' for. That package you had to send for twice." The man looked positively perplexed as he stood in the door of the big brown van. He removed his cap, then placed it back on his head. "Somethin' wrong wit you t'day?"

He spared Phil a brief glance, then returned his attention to Lucy. Blinking twice, he shook his head. "No, I'm fine. Hey, meet Lucy Webber."

"Lucy Webber, eh?" Phil bounded across the grass to shake her hand. "You own the camera shop downtown, don't you?"

"Yes, I own Lucy's Lens. It's a photography studio, not a camera shop, but yes, it is downtown." She picked up the camera, then offered Justin a weak smile. "I should go now."

"No," he said a bit too quickly. "Don't leave, Lucy. Not yet."

Surely the delivery driver knew what had transpired between them. It had to be obvious. In a moment he would surely comment.

Rather, Phil merely smiled, then tucked his clipboard under his arm. "I'll run this down to the garage, then."

"Yes, thanks."

Lucy couldn't help but notice the combination of amusement and surprise on the driver's face as he walked back to his truck, shaking his head. Justin captured her hand again, and butterflies danced in the pit of her stomach.

"Are you all right?" he asked.

She looked up at him and attempted a smile. "I think so."

What was it about this man? Did this kind of thing happen to real people?

"I think so, too." He squeezed her hand. "Come with me."

As the delivery truck disappeared around the corner of the cabin, Justin led Lucy to the rockers decorating the porch. He settled in one and patted the other, indicating Lucy should sit.

Rather than sit, she stared at the empty chair and debated her options. A part of her longed to stay and see what direction the conversation might take. The rest of her, the logical part, told her to turn tail and run.

"I really should go," she said after a moment's consideration.

Justin rose and stuffed his fists into his pockets before shrugging. "Look, I want you to know that I didn't bring you up here to kiss you. In fact, that's the last thing I had in mind."

What? Was he apologizing for the kiss? *I hoped he'd decided that wasn't necessary.*

"Okay, so maybe it wasn't the last thing, but it certainly wasn't on the agenda." His gaze pleaded; his expression tugged at her heart. "I really do appreciate your work as a photographer, and I hope this won't make you change your mind about doing the pictures for the book."

"No, of course not." She straightened her shoulders and forced her thoughts on a topic less close to her heart. "So, what's this about car parts? What are you doing to the Mustang now? Fixing that idling issue, dare I ask?"

"Well. . ." Justin launched into a discussion of his intentions for tuning the car's engine and adding more horsepower, a topic that would have held her interest in other circumstances. He paused for a moment, then added, "You could come and take a look if you'd like."

Lucy found herself crossing the lawn at Justin's side. The garage was an overlarge structure sitting some twenty yards from the main house. Constructed of what looked to be cypress timbers, Lucy could imagine the building as some sort of barn in the previous century.

"Grandpa LeBlanc's barn," he said by way of explanation as he opened the latch on the huge wooden door and swung it aside. "He kept his horses on the east side and his Ford on the west. Hold on a second." Justin brushed past her to hit a switch. Florescent lights blazed overhead, illuminating a thoroughly modern garage and three vehicles: the Mustang, a rather nondescript farm truck, and a buggy.

"Wow," she said under her breath as she stepped inside.

❧

Wow is right. Lucy crossed the garage to study Great-great-grandpa LeBlanc's buggy, and all Justin could do was trot behind her like a love-struck puppy.

Even under the harsh glow of the florescent lights Lucy Webber was drop-dead gorgeous. *Gorgeous: magnificent, splendid, beautiful.*

"Beautiful," he whispered. "Oh, yes, indeed."

She turned abruptly, and he stopped short to keep from slamming into her. "What did you say?"

Justin shrugged. "Nothing."

Lucy reached for her camera and began taking pictures of the buggy. A moment later, she walked around to the front and examined the old wooden wheels. "This buggy's been well taken care of."

He joined her. "Well restored, actually. Dad and I worked on it the summer before he. . ." Emotion clogged his throat, and he bit back the rest of the sentence. Better to change the subject now before he gave away too much. "If you'll excuse me a minute, I'll go take a look at those boxes Phil left."

Strolling to the corner of the garage at a forced slow pace, Justin studied the labels on the boxes for a full minute before the words registered. They were the very items he'd struggled to order and receive—twice.

"Is it what you were expecting?"

He turned to look at Lucy. "You could say that." *It was my*

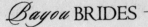

feelings for you that I didn't expect.

The realization made him fall into the car's driver's seat. Feelings? For Lucy Webber? Sure, she made him want to kiss her and yes, of course, he found her attractive. Then there was her obvious talent at photography. He'd even grudgingly give her a greater-than-normal ability to diagnose Mustang ailments.

But feelings? Dare he think in those terms? Could that be where the Lord was leading?

Feelings: the state of having deep emotions; a strong like of or love for another person.

"Whoa. I'm not there—yet."

"Something wrong?"

He looked up in time to see Lucy aiming her camera in his direction.

"Man, Justin, that was very deer-in-the-headlights." She fired off a series of shots before he could gather his wits.

"Deer-in-the-headlights?" He shook his head. "Explain."

She ducked her head to chuckle. "Have you ever been driving down a road and came upon a deer that seemed too shocked to move?"

"Sure."

Lucy lifted the camera. "Same expression." When he laughed, she clicked. "Now that's better. You have a nice smile." A few more shots and she put away her camera. "Okay, enough of that. Show me what's in those boxes."

"Boxes?"

"The car parts, Justin. Show me what you got."

Stunned amazement quickly gave way to action as he leaped from the car and retrieved the packages. An hour later he had the parts installed, with the help of the prettiest photographer in town.

"Okay, start her up, Lucy," he said as he swiped at his brow.

She turned the key and smiled as the car's engine roared to life. That smile quickly went south, and she turned off the ignition. "I don't like what I'm hearing."

"What? It sounds fine." He set his tools aside and reached for the edge of the hood to close it.

"Hold on a sec," she said. "Let me just look at one thing." Bounding from the vehicle, she leaned under the hood and reached for the needle nose pliers. To her credit, she looked up and asked a quick, "Do you mind?" before making a few adjustments. "Okay, now start it and see if it doesn't idle a bit smoother."

Justin gave her an incredulous look as he settled behind the wheel and put his foot on the clutch. Turning the key, he leaned back in the seat and waited to see if he noticed a difference in the sound of the motor.

"Oh, man," he said a second later. "She purrs like a kitten." He swung his gaze to meet Lucy's. "What did you do?" When she told him, he slapped his forehead. "Of course. I should have noticed that."

She shrugged and set the pliers back into the toolbox. "You would have," she said. "It's obvious from the work you've done that you're an excellent mechanic."

He couldn't help but smile as he killed the engine and

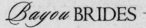

pocketed the keys. When she announced she must leave, Justin fought the urge to convince her to stay longer. Rather, he resolved to keep his distance and let the Lord speak before getting in too deep with Lucy Webber. *Well, before getting in any deeper anyway.*

That decided, Justin walked her to her car and made arrangements to view the proofs from today's photos. As Lucy started her car, Bandit raised his head, then came to nuzzle Justin's hand.

"Looks like I forgot to say good-bye to someone," she said as she began to climb back out of the car.

Justin smiled and stepped forward, his resolution to keep his distance all but forgotten. To his surprise, she dropped to one knee and began to rub Bandit's ears. Soon after, the dog fell over on his side and offered Lucy his belly, which she rubbed with enthusiasm.

When she rose, she gazed into Justin's eyes and, for a moment, he thought she might smile. Instead, she nodded and climbed into her car without comment.

"See you Thursday!" she called as she drove away.

"Thursday," he responded. Suddenly three days seemed like an eternity. Maybe he would call her tomorrow. Just to see how she was progressing on the pictures, of course.

But as he thought it, he knew it was more. He cast a glance skyward. "Lord, You worked overtime on that one, and I sure do appreciate the extra effort. Now if I could just figure out what to do about her."

Lucy's taillights disappeared around a bend in the road,

leaving Justin alone on the porch with only Bandit for company. He leaned forward in the rocker and scratched the springer spaniel behind his floppy ears.

"All that and she can fine-tune a Mustang, too." Justin gave the dog one last pat, then leaned back and sighed. "I think I'm in trouble, old buddy."

Chapter 11

"Oh, boy, am I in trouble." Lucy sank onto the stool at her worktable and looked over the collection of black-and-white photographs spread out before her. Each one sparked a memory; a few caused a smile.

One in particular gave her that funny feeling in the pit of her stomach.

She reached for the photo and waited for the butterflies to subside. Justin LeBlanc sat behind the wheel of his vintage convertible, a study in great bone structure and excellent lighting.

Lucy dropped the picture like a hot potato, and it fluttered back to the table's cluttered surface.

Another caught her attention and she reached for it. Justin had snapped a photograph of her. But when?

She closed her eyes and tried to remember. "Of course. After he kissed me."

That kiss. The feeling of a slow fire being lit rekindled now as she slowed the moment in her mind, then froze it in place. Justin was looking at her like no man had ever looked at her.

Feelings swirled around her, bound together with the knowledge that this was right. Good. And most important, of God.

The phone on her desk rang, and she jumped.

"Good morning, sunshine."

Lucy smiled at the sound of Justin's voice. "Good morning to you."

"I would like to tell you that I'm calling to ask about the pictures, but that wouldn't be the truth at all." He paused. "Actually, as corny as it sounds, I was on my way to the university, and I had the strongest need just to hear your voice."

Her heart did a flip-flop. "Really?"

"Really." The sound of the Mustang shifting gears was quickly followed by Justin's voice. "Look, I don't know what is happening between us, and I'm not good at playing games. I'm just going to say what's on my mind. Is that all right with you?"

Another flip-flop, this time in Lucy's stomach. "Please do."

"I took a picture of you out at the cabin the other day. Have you developed it yet?"

She glanced down at the worktable. "Yes, actually, I have."

"Well, I have that picture in my mind. Can't seem to get rid of it." He paused. "Don't want to, actually. Every time I close my eyes I see you, Lucy. I've never felt like this. Tell me I'm crazy and I'll hang up now, but I sensed that you might have felt the same way."

She paused to debate how much of the truth to tell him. Before she could say a word, she saw the Mustang pull to the curb in front of her shop. Justin turned to look at her, the phone still pressed to his ear.

"I don't have to teach until eleven. Can you close up shop and take a drive with me?"

Lucy glanced at her watch. Ten after nine. Her next appointment wasn't until half past one, and the proofs were complete and ready to be shown.

"I suppose I could forward the phones," she said as she reached for her cell phone.

"No. Don't do that. I'm going to be really selfish and ask for some uninterrupted time so we can talk. Is that okay?"

A moment of indecision passed quickly. "Yes, okay."

Replacing the phone on the counter, she grabbed her keys and headed for the door. When she'd locked up, she climbed into the passenger seat. Without warning, Justin wrapped her in a warm embrace. "I missed you."

"It's only been one day." She caught the disappointment that flitted across his face and amended her statement. "One long day."

When he reached for her hand and squeezed it, she smiled. Before long, they arrived at the road leading to the bayou. Rather than turn toward the house, Justin eased the Mustang down a narrow lane and stopped under a stand of pines just a few feet from the bayou.

The summer morning still held a hint of last night's cool air as Justin turned off the car and swiveled in his seat to face Lucy. "I'll get right to it," he said. "You said something to me the first time we met that has stuck with me."

Lucy turned to lean her back against the car door. "I did?"

He nodded. "You said that everyone needs a place where

God meets them. Do you remember that?"

"Vaguely."

"Well, you had no way of knowing this, but when you told me that, I was in need of hearing it. See, I've been living my life, waiting for things to happen before I began living my life. I don't know how much Amanda has told you about our family, but my parents died when she was still in school. I had to choose between letting the girls go to a foster home and trying to finish raising them while finishing my education. Somehow the Lord allowed me to accomplish that."

Justin paused to study his hands, then clenched his fists. For a moment he seemed far away, his attention seemingly riveted on the black water of the bayou. Suddenly, his focus returned to Lucy.

He reached across the car to grasp Lucy's hand. "How long have we known one another?"

The warmth of his fingers entwined with hers distracted her for a moment. "It's been a little over a month since Amanda's wedding."

"Before that day, all I wanted was to shake the dust of this little town off my boots and hit the road." He chuckled. "I thought that writing the great American novel would somehow get rid of the unsettled feelings."

"Unsettled?"

"Unsettled: restless, seeming to have no firm foundation; the inability to feel at peace." Justin cringed. "Now you know my secret. I'm a closet grammarian."

Lucy grinned and squeezed Justin's hand. "Grammarian:

one who has a talent for words; possessing a vast and expansive knowledge of one's native language."

His smile broadened. "Lucy Webber, that sounded like it came straight from the dictionary."

She nibbled on her lower lip, eyebrows raised. "When I was seven, my dad brought home a dictionary for me from one of his travels. It was so big I could barely carry it around. By the time I was ten I had most of the words memorized. A hazard of always being the new kid in school, I guess."

"Funny, I used to wonder what it would be like to be the new kid. Nothing in my life ever changed." He ducked his head, then swung his gaze in her direction. "Until I met you, that is." Without warning, Justin leaned over and kissed her. "I've been wanting to do that since you got into the car."

A warning bell rang in her heart, and Lucy considered whether to give voice to her concerns. Finally she decided that remaining silent would be wrong.

"Justin, before we talk any further. . ." She cast her eyes downward for a second. "Or kiss again, I need to tell you something."

He released his grip on her hands to touch the tip of her nose with his forefinger. "What's that?"

"I'm not sure about this."

The color drained from his face. "What?"

"You're ready to hit the road in the beautiful car, and I'm just now putting down roots. How can the Lord possibly intend us to. . ."

"To fall in love?"

She nodded.

"Too late for questioning Him about that, Lucy. I think I've already fallen in love with you. There's no place I'd rather be than right here with you, whether this car is parked in front of Lucy's Lens or pointed toward the open road. Love isn't dependent on a place or even on conventional logic. It's about God and who He wants us to be with."

Her heart soared. "I think I've fallen in love with you, too, Justin."

He leaned across the seat to wrap her in an embrace. When they parted, he kissed her. To her surprise, he then opened the door and raced around to the trunk to retrieve something. Returning to his place behind the wheel, he set an ancient journal in her lap—the one she'd opened while in the attic.

"There's something I want to read to you," he said as he opened the journal. "It was written by an ancestor of mine, Capucine LeBlanc. 'I wish I knew then that joy is not based on people, places, and things. Those change. My God does not.'"

"That's beautiful, Justin," Lucy said through a shimmering of tears. "And so true. It really doesn't matter what changes in our lives, as long as we realize our Lord never changes."

Justin closed the book and leveled a serious look in her direction. "Do you believe with time and prayer we will know for sure whether the Lord intends us to be together?"

Lucy let out a long breath. "Yes," she said slowly, "I do."

He nodded and turned the key to start the car. "All right, then. It's settled."

"What's settled?"

Justin threw the car into reverse and looked over his shoulder to begin backing up. "I'm postponing the road trip I planned for next month until I hear from the Lord on when we should get married."

"Married?" She straightened in her seat. "What are you talking about?"

He gave her a grin she hoped to continue seeing for the rest of her life. "Check your calendar, sweetheart. I'll turn over the wedding planning to you, and if you want, my sisters can help. I, on the other hand, will be planning the honeymoon. Suffice it to say we will be taking the old Route 66 and driving with the top down."

Lucy giggled, then affected a serious look. "I have only one request."

"Anything for you, Lucy."

"Can we sleep in cheesy motels and eat bologna sandwiches for breakfast? You'll write the great American novel, and I'll read it and proclaim it brilliant. How's that?"

"Okay, technically that's more than one request but"—Justin let out a whoop that echoed over the purr of the Mustang's engine—"Lord, You are amazing. She's perfect!"

At the stop sign, Lucy leaned over and kissed Justin soundly. "I'm perfect, eh? Then you won't mind letting me drive the Mustang."

He closed his eyes as if in prayer, then glanced heavenward. "Thank you, Lord, for making her *almost* perfect."

KATHLEEN MILLER

In addition to her job as publicist for Glass Road Public Relations, Kathleen is a multi-published, award-winning author of Christian fiction who also writes under the name Kathleen Y'Barbo. A tenth-generation Texan, she holds a marketing degree from Texas A&M University and a certificate in Paralegal Studies. She is the former treasurer of American Christian Fiction Writers Guild, as well as a member of Words for the Journey Christian Writers Guild, Inspirational Writers Alive, Fellowship of Christian Writers, Writers Information Network, the Houston Paralegal Association, and the Writers Guild. The proud mother of a daughter and three sons, she makes her home in Texas (where else?).

A Letter to Our Readers

Dear Readers:

In order that we might better contribute to your reading enjoyment, we would appreciate your taking a few minutes to respond to the following questions. When completed, please return to the following: Fiction Editor, Barbour Publishing, Inc., P.O. Box 719, Uhrichsville, OH 44683.

1. Did you enjoy reading *Bayou Brides*?
   - ❏ Very much—I would like to see more books like this.
   - ❏ Moderately—I would have enjoyed it more if _____
   _____
   _____

2. What influenced your decision to purchase this book?
   (Check those that apply.)
   - ❏ Cover
   - ❏ Back cover copy
   - ❏ Title
   - ❏ Price
   - ❏ Friends
   - ❏ Publicity
   - ❏ Other

3. Which story was your favorite?
   - ❏ *Capucine: Home to My Heart*
   - ❏ *Language of Love*
   - ❏ *Joie de Vivre*
   - ❏ *Dreams of Home*

4. Please check your age range:
   - ❏ Under 18
   - ❏ 18–24
   - ❏ 25–34
   - ❏ 35–45
   - ❏ 46–55
   - ❏ Over 55

5. How many hours per week do you read? _____

Name _____

Occupation _____

Address _____

City_____ State_____ Zip_____

E-mail_____

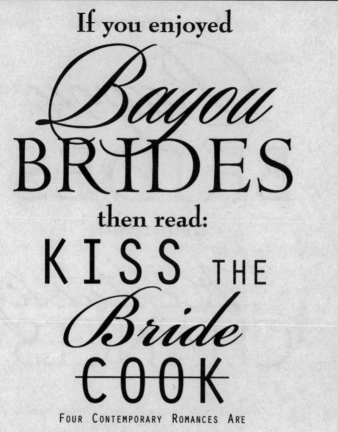